emotional, acutely observed and, written from
a male point of view, particularly refreshing'
Fanny Blake

'At my age I am still amazed when a writer with the gift of the written word can make me care about a character so much that I can be reduced to tears one minute and laughing the next – but this author manages to do just that'
Sun

'Frank, funny and bittersweet, *The Two of Us* is a love story about what happens when a relationship *looks* all wrong but *feels* all right. This is a book with its heart firmly in the right place'
Louise Candlish

'Touching, funny and real, Andy Jones's novel about what happens *after* the love story had me laughing one minute and crying the next. I loved it'
Jane Costello

the TROUBLE with HENRY and ZOE

ANDY JONES

**SIMON &
SCHUSTER**

London · New York · Sydney · Toronto · New Delhi

A CBS COMPANY

First published in Great Britain by Simon & Schuster UK Ltd, 2016
A CBS COMPANY

1 3 5 7 9 10 8 6 4 2

Simon & Schuster UK Ltd
1st Floor
222 Gray's Inn Road
London WC1X 8HB

www.simonandschuster.co.uk

Simon & Schuster Australia, Sydney
Simon & Schuster India, New Delhi

A CIP catalogue record for this book
is available from the British Library

Paperback ISBN: 978-1-4711-4246-8
Australian Trade Paperback: 978-1-4711-5513-0
eBook ISBN: 978-1-4711-4245-1

Typeset in Bembo by M Rules
Printed and bound by CPI Group (UK) Ltd, Croydon, CR0 4YY

Simon & Schuster UK Ltd are committed to sourcing paper
that is made from wood grown in sustainable forests and support the Forest
Stewardship Council, the leading international forest certification organisation.
Our books displaying the FSC logo are printed on FSC certified paper.

To Sarah

For showing me where the good stuff is

the TROUBLE with HENRY and ZOE

PART 1

Henry

The Question Keeping Him Awake

The question keeping him awake is this . . .

Which is worse: marrying the wrong woman, or taking her heart and smashing it to pieces in front of one hundred and twenty-eight guests?

Or maybe it's the answer that is troubling him.

Too late for all that now, though. He checks the time on his phone – 2.48 a.m. – and sees it is a little less than ten hours until he is scheduled to say 'I do'. He'll have bags under his eyes, he thinks, and his mother – the local hairdresser and unqualified beautician – will be furious. Every Sunday for the past six, she has forced Henry to endure a viciously thorough facial routine, but all her work is now undone.

Within months of proposing, Henry quit his job in the UK's fifth largest city and returned to the open fields and

3

narrow lanes of his childhood. He took a job at a local dental practice and moved into his old bedroom above his parents' pub. Last Sunday, his mother subjected him to a final 'calming' facemask.

'It's a wonder he's not bent,' his old man said, standing in the living room doorway like a matinee idol gone to seed – muscular forearms crossed above the landlord's paunch; handsome eyes, still bright in his tired face; his thinning but stubbornly black hair cut in an immaculate rockabilly quiff.

'What you doing up here?' his mother says, applying a layer of cold green gunk to Henry's face.

'Khazi.'

His mother sighs. 'Jesus. Thank you for sharing.'

'You asked.'

'What's wrong with the gents?'

'We've had this before, it's brass monkeys in there.'

'Because you haven't fixed the window's why.'

'I said I'll do it.'

'Yeah. Said but didn't do, story of your life.'

Henry's father unfolds one arm and nags his hand back at his wife. From where he's standing, the former boxer and one-time local celebrity can't see Clark Gable raising his cocktail on the mute TV screen. Henry watches his mother's eyes flick from his father to the TV and back, observes her expression slip from resentment to disappointment.

Propped up on the sagging and threadbare sofa, his face tight under the contracting clay mask, Henry says to his father, 'I'll sort those barrels as soon as I'm done here.'

'Wouldn't want you to chip a nail,' the old man says.

'Leave him alone,' snaps his mother.

'I will if you will.'

His father shakes his head and walks off down the corridor. Henry's mother smooths the clay at the bridge of his nose and sighs. 'Your poor nose,' she says. 'Your poor poor nose.'

Henry (named after the British Heavyweight who briefly floored Muhammad Ali) knows that, after his birth, his mother had twice miscarried before resigning herself to never having a daughter. In place of an unrealized girl – to have been named Priscilla Agatha – Henry sat beside his mother on this same sofa and watched *From Here to Eternity*, *The Apartment*, *His Girl Friday* and dozens more.

'You'll turn him soft,' his father would say.

'I'm teaching him how to be a real man,' Sheila would counter.

And so his father dragged Henry to the boxing gym, and his mother sat him in front of the TV, neither forgiving the other for the damage done to their son – a broken nose, a scarred eyebrow, a sissy's taste in movies. Sometimes these resentments would pass as nothing more than routine bickering, other times (his mother deep in drink, his father tending an empty bar) it would escalate into ugliness.

He's seen the photographs: Clive 'Big Boots' Smith, cocksure and potent, with his arm around his girl's waist. *Made for each other* is what people would have said. And it's true, as if each were designed by the same toymaker – but made rigid and fragile with no moving parts.

They *looked* perfect together.

The way everyone says Henry and April look perfect together. Like the sugarcraft bride and groom atop their three-tier cake. He and April don't fight. They have had their disagreements and spats, of course, but they seldom acquire any heat. Certainly nothing approaching the rancour so easily accessed by his parents.

Still, is not fighting a good enough reason to get married?

The imminent groom shifts in his bed – an uncomfortable single in the rent-a-castle that will very soon host the reception. They live less than five miles down the road, but April wanted a castle and April's father isn't one to deny his princess. The fourteenth-century building (weddings, conferences, corporate events) has two wings: the bridal party in one, the groom's in the other, everything carefully orchestrated to ensure the two don't meet before the big event.

And isn't that a thought.

Again, Henry turns the question over in his mind. Should you marry someone you like? A beautiful girl you've known since you were fourteen, someone who loves you ... should you marry that person when you know in the chambers of your heart and coils of your guts that you don't *love* this girl? Not like they do in the movies, not like Rhett loved Scarlett or Rick loved Ilsa. There is love, yes, but has it peaked? And is love an absolute? Can you love a little or a lot? And how far will a little take you – five years, ten?

Should you marry her anyway, because you have been together (more or less) for twelve years, because your fiancée is the next best thing to the daughter your mother never had, because she cuts hair in your mother's salon, because her father is building a house for you to grow old and die in? Should you smile and say 'for better or worse' when you suspect that of the two options the latter is by far the more likely? Should you lift her veil, kiss your bride on her beautiful lips and whisper (loud enough, of course, for the congregation to hear) 'I love you so much'? Even though you don't – not like Ben loved Elaine, Calvin loved Fran or Walter loved Hildy. Should you do this because you know everyone in this village and they know you and the alternative is unthinkable?

And why now, Henry? The last twelve months have been a blizzard of magazine cuttings, fabric samples and lists of lists. For the last three months April has not worn slippers, instead watching TV and making cups of tea in a pair of ivory-white stilettos, the six-inch heels pockmarking her mother's carpets as she breaks in the shoes ahead of a short walk and a night of dancing. Henry almost laughs at the thought, but there is nothing funny about what he is contemplating.

Which is what, exactly? Knocking on her door after breakfast, asking how she slept and then: 'Listen, I've been thinking . . .'

Unthinkable, he thinks. He can't, he cannot imagine a workable scenario that accommodates him telling his fiancée that actually, having slept on it, he thinks – in the long run – they would both be happier if they called the whole thing off.

It is not the first time this black idea has occurred to him. It has been festering for months. Two weeks ago he was performing a root canal on Mrs Griffiths, and as she lay with her fingers laced beneath her bosom, the overhead light had glinted off the stone in her engagement ring. And in that flash, he had thought, *This is not what I want.* And just as quickly – his brain had run the scenario he was too afraid to consciously acknowledge. April would say *No.* He would tell her he was having second thoughts, and April would reject the idea. She would tell him he was being silly; that it's normal to have doubts; that they were made for each other. Or maybe she would receive his declaration with sobbing hysterical tears, waking her bridesmaids and parents. Waking her father and semi-psychotic brother. And does Henry really think they would let him walk away from all this?

When he was at university, people would ask: *Where are you from?* Henry would sigh inwardly as he answered, and wait for the inevitable shake of the head. They know the area in the broadest sense; have maybe even visited one of the hundreds of towns and villages that make up this stained green rug in the centre of England. But not the village where Henry went to school, had his first fight, his first kiss. A village so small that everyone is, if not known, then known to someone known to you. In a community of fewer than two thousand people, no one gets divorced without everyone else hearing about it. Your daughter sleeps around, your son's into drugs, your dog shits on the pavement – everybody knows. Buy new shoes; someone will mention it to someone else over supper that evening. Leave your fiancée at the altar ...

Unthinkable.

Between eight and nine the bridal party will breakfast in the scullery, then at nine-thirty, and not a minute sooner, the groom and his will do the same. From there he will have two hours to shave, fasten his cufflinks and get me to the church on time – a three-minute drive costing in the region of six hundred pounds in hired vintage automobiles. After the service the wedding party will return to the castle for food, drink, speeches, dancing and happily ever after. *April and I will sleep together in a four-poster bed, make love and wake up as Mr and Mrs Smith.* After breakfast April will sign the guest book with the signature (wide, left-leaning letters, the tail of the 'S' curling back, up and over the crossbar of the 'A') she has been refining for the last three weeks. A few final photographs; hugs, handshakes, tears; 'look after my girl for me' and off to the airport. Two weeks of colourful cocktails and lazy days by the pool, perhaps a sightseeing trip and a night in a big-name club. A final bottle of champagne on the beach at sunset then back to the square brick house built for them by Henry's (now) father-in-law.

As a consequence of dating a landlord's son, perhaps, April has a preference for old songs and classic tunes. When they were still too young to drink in the pub, Big Boots would give them a handful of coins to feed the jukebox. April's favourite song is 'Sweet Home Alabama', and if you sing it at a steady pace, giving due time to the air-guitar solos, then you can get from the opening riff to the closing keys in the time it takes to walk from April's parents' house to the young couple's new home. Five minutes, give or take.

It comes with two bedrooms and a nursery. 'Or a study,' Henry had said. 'Study what?' said April. 'It's a nursery. Don't you want children?' – 'Yes, of course, but not necessarily straight away.' – 'We've been together twelve years. It's a nursery.' See, no argument. The kitchen is brand new and unused, new beds, new tables, new chairs, new television. Everything sitting perfectly still and gathering dust.

April compiled the wedding list: bedding, pans, knives, his and hers dressing gowns. Henry wanted an old-fashioned record player – April chose a wireless speaker. He doesn't mind – he can't pin his doubts on his fiancée's need for domestic control. Nothing unusual in that. April is funny, athletic, beautiful. She visits her grandmother in the nursing home every week, takes flowers, knows all the residents by name and listens to their looped stories without looking away. She paints her mother's toenails every Sunday, and makes her father a thermos full of coffee every weekday morning. She calls Henry's dad by his old boxing handle and throws playful punches at his belly. April also works in Love & Die, his mother's hair salon, and the two women take the train into town together to shop for clothes at the retail park. She works occasional shifts in the pub, and is always first up when they do a karaoke. April walks her next door neighbour's dog. If you need someone to check on the fish while you're on holiday, you ask the prettiest, sweetest, loveliest girl in the village. So who cares if she wants monogrammed cush-ions. As an engagement present, April's father gave them a house brick wrapped in a pink bow. It now sits on the mantelpiece of their two-bedroom, one-nursery house.

Henry's parents bought them crockery, twelve of everything, white with a blue trim.

'He builds them a house, we give them plates,' his mother had said, as if it were her husband's fault.

'What do you expect me to do about it?'

Sheila Smith laughed. 'I don't expect you to do anything.'

The cost of the wedding is common knowledge. Flowers, food, band, dress, cars and everything else besides, the day will cost seventeen thousand, six hundred and forty-six pounds. All paid for by April's father. The house is worth ten times as much.

Henry would have been happy with a toaster. *Happier* with a toaster.

'We can buy our own house,' Henry had said when the idea first came up. 'I am a dentist, after all.'

'And my dad's a builder. Each to his own.'

No shouting, nothing thrown, no cruel words. And three weeks later they are looking at architect's plans.

'We could move out?' Henry says.

April's nose wrinkles when she frowns, as if at a bad smell. 'Out? Where out?'

'I don't know, it doesn't matter. Chester, Liverpool, anywhere.'

'Anywhere? Babes, why would we live *anywhere*? We already live in the nicest place in the world.'

The local mantra. But it strikes Henry that people who insist they live in the best place in the world tend not to have seen very much of it.

'Or Manchester?' he tries. 'You would *love* the shops in Manchester. All on your doorstep.'

'It rains in Manchester.'

'It rains here.'

April kisses him, holds his face in her hands. 'Hey,' she says, 'I thought you'd got all this out of your system.'

'It's just . . .' He trails off, sighs.

'It's normal to be nervous,' April says. 'It's a big step. We'll be a family, have kids and we'll bring them up in *the nicest place in the world*. Dogs, walks, family.' She kisses him again, longer than the first.

She is very beautiful.

'There he is,' says April. 'There's my handsome man.' And she kisses him again.

In the hush of the castle, the clock ticks over to 3.00 a.m., and Henry swings his legs out from under the blanket. It's cold, so he pulls on his socks, his jeans and a t-shirt. Just because it's cold.

He goes over to the window, parting the heavy velvet curtains and looking out onto the castle grounds. The moon is heavy and low-slung tonight, casting enough light to pick out the shapes of trees and the distant peaks. 'Rolling', people say of the hills, but to Henry they appear to shift and fidget, complaining but never moving.

Zoe

An Unexpected Fumble

Zoe thinks maybe she should get out of bed. The kitchen sink is full of dishes, the carpets need a hoover, the bathroom needs cleaning. But she is tired, warm and enjoying the subsiding flush of an unexpected Saturday-morning fumble. Alex is a lark and Zoe an owl, and lately it seems that whenever one is in the mood the other is seven-eighths asleep. Besides this morning, she wonders how long it has been since they last made love. They've been living together for nine months now, and she would be surprised if they had made the bedsprings creak much more than half a dozen times in the last three. He had taken the initiative this morning, though, and when Zoe muttered something about being sleepy, he had kissed her ear and whispered, 'You can keep your eyes closed.' That had made her smile; his breath had tickled her ear and his hand, sliding up inside her t-shirt, had activated her nerve endings a little lower down. It had been nice.

He was a bit quick to the finish line, now that she thinks about it, but it was ... it was nice. He had done that thing – *the grappler*, she called it – where he hooked his arm under her left leg. Normally Zoe wasn't keen on the manoeuvre (aside from feeling a bit silly, she wasn't that flexible and it could get quite painful down her hamstring), but Alex had been gentle this morning, and it felt somehow that ... she's not sure how to put it ... like he *meant it*, she supposes. At least he hadn't attempted *the lockdown*; last time he'd done that she'd had to turn her face into the pillow to smother her laughter. No, this morning was nice, and then – after a respectable interval with cuddling and nuzzling – he'd jumped out of bed and said he was going to the shops to get some 'stuff'. 'Go back to sleep,' he'd said, 'I'll bring you breakfast in bed.' And who is she to argue with that?

Sex, she thinks. Tremendous fun, but it doesn't bear overthinking. Because if you think about it, isn't the whole thing a bit daft? She knows Al's routine almost by heart, the sequence of hands, lips, fingers across her body. *Like a pilot preparing for take-off* ...

A part of her knows that once you start to scrutinize

a thing, *a person*, the tiny flaws can begin to occlude the larger picture. *Just like these walls*, she thinks.

There is enough light in the room that Zoe can just make out the messy patches of darker paint showing through two coats of Dawn Mist. Alex claims he can't see the imperfections; says Zoe is imagining them. He insists on this with such conviction that Zoe wonders if he isn't right. *Focus on the positives*, she says to herself.

And the positives are what? Alex is cool, handsome, has a nice if somewhat softer than when they met body, and he's good (. . . *or is he just okay?*) in bed.

Zoe has slept with eleven men. Six boyfriends and a smattering of flings ranging from one to a few nights. She has never ranked these men and boys in terms of their bedroom prowess, but she knows without hesitation who tops the list: Ken Coleman, a third-year Maths student she dated for two terms in her second year. 'Ken Wood' someone – Vicky, more than likely – had nicknamed him. The worst, too, is a no brainer (Jacob Kentish, Philosophy, small penis, bad breath, funny noises), but the remaining nine are more difficult to order. As her mind begins sorting these men of its own accord, Zoe shies away from the exercise – *what if Alex falls in the wrong half of the group?* If he does, she certainly doesn't want to confirm the fact. They share a mortgage now – the modern equivalent of marriage – so it doesn't do to be making these schoolgirl-ish comparisons. Alex is a good lover: he is considerate most of the time, clean most of the time, and she has a pleasant little orgasm most of the time. Not the bone-marrow boiling, eye-crossing, narcotic wobblers she had at the hands of Ken, granted, but there's only so much of that a girl can take.

Although – and this is a new thing – about a week before her period is due, she has found herself . . . *craving* is the best word she can think of . . . *craving* sex. Not lovemaking, but primal, vigorous sex. Zoe wonders if her body clock is sending out its stalk on a spring. She won't be thirty for another eleven months, so it seems early. Maybe it's because she and Alex have bought a house, set up a nest. *Who told my bloody ovaries*, she thinks.

Zoe realizes she is holding her breath – a habit she seems to have developed some time in the last year. She catches herself doing it several times a day – sitting at her desk or lying in bed with her chest hitched and her lungs tight with held air. It's comforting almost, but at the same time a little odd – having to remind yourself to . . . *breaaathe*. Stress, she imagines.

Is the idea of being a mother really that stressful? Or is it the idea of having a baby with Alex? Zoe shakes herself mentally. Exhales . . . breathes.

In the bright October sunlight, Zoe thinks again about how tender Alex had been this morning, and reminds herself to live in the now. She slides open her bedside drawer and fishes out the strip of contraceptive pills. She pops one into the palm of her hand and swallows it dry.

When she wakes again Zoe needs to pee. The house is cold and she has lost the afterglow of the unexpected fumble. The bathroom tiles will feel like the surface of a frozen lake on her bare feet, and she pulls the duvet close to preserve any residual warmth. Christmas is only two months away, and she thinks maybe she and Alex should buy each other slippers – cheap, practical and . . .

'Good God almighty,' she says out loud, 'I'm turning into my mother.'

Still, slippers would be nice.

If she concentrates on something besides her bladder, Zoe thinks, maybe she can get ten more minutes in bed. Five at least. The boiler has obviously decided to go on strike again. It needs replacing, but there is little cash and less flow; so they'll just have to cross their cold blue fingers that it has one more winter in its pipes before dying quietly or exploding.

Bad word choice, Zoe thinks, feeling a twinge in her bladder. She looks at the clock – 10.15 – and wonders how long she has been dozing. Ten minutes? An hour? She listens to the house and it is silent – no sounds of cooking, no boiling kettle. She calls Alex but he doesn't answer, leading Zoe to believe she can't have been sleeping for long. She throws back the duvet and tiptoes to the loo.

Looking at her dancing feet as she relieves herself, Zoe notices a constellation of dried splash marks on the tiles. Why is it, she wonders, men seem incapable of weeing *inside* the bowl? Or is she generalizing? Alex is the first man she's lived with, so she has nothing to compare him to. Well, except for her father, but her parents have their own en suite and a cleaner who comes twice a week. Maybe Alex is just a splasher. It's not as if the bowl isn't big enough; surely an elephant could manage to pee in that thing without getting it all over the rim and on the tiles. She smiles at the image of an elephant taking a pee in her bathroom and thinks it might make a good premise for a kids' picture book. Maybe she'll tell her boss on Monday, see if one of their authors can do something with it. Or maybe she'll do it herself – after all, how hard can it be to write eight hundred words about the bathroom antics of animals? She'll call it *The Loo at the Zoo*; maybe spend an hour or two kicking it about this weekend.

Zoe wipes the splash marks with some damp tissue, which she drops into the bowl before flushing. When she sees her reflection in the bathroom mirror (tooth-paste spatters like freeze-framed snow) she catches herself scowling, her brow pulled into ugly furrows that might become permanent if she isn't careful.

'So what's it to be?' she says to her reflection.

She has three choices: clean the bathroom mirror, get in the shower, or go back to bed.

Zoe's reflection pulls a face that says, *Are you mad?*

'Well, I'm talking to you, aren't I?'

Get back into bed and let the boy make your breakfast. God knows he's not going to help you clean the house.

'Fair point,' says Zoe.

Her reflection nods: *I know.*

Walking back to the bedroom Zoe steps on the creaky floorboard in the hallway and experiences a twang of annoyance. Two weeks ago, she had stepped on a proud nail, ripping a hole in a new pair of twelve-quid tights. It was the second time this had happened, so Zoe had attempted to pry the nail out of the floorboard with a pair of scissors, which she knew was the wrong tool for the job, but the right tool was somewhere in their small and cluttered shed and it was raining. But instead of laughing at Zoe for her endearing, feminine ways, Alex had barked at her for breaking the scissors and told her to ask him if something needed fixing. He had apologized quickly enough, but she was nettled by this flash of temper. And despite it all, he still hasn't got around to fixing the fucking thing. And it's not just this one board; there is another creaker in the spare room and a third under the table in the living room. Zoe is tempted to fetch the hammer and take care of it herself, but she is worried it will cause an argument. And this – this apprehension in her own hallway – annoys her more than the floorboard.

Too alert now to sleep, Zoe opens the bedroom curtains and looks out of the window into the rows of back gardens all squashed together on their terraced street. It's a beautiful day and Zoe thinks they should go for a ride down to the Thames where they can drink a bottle of wine and watch the rowers glide past. The bicycles are wedged into the cobweb-strewn shed, snuggled together under a pile of collapsed cardboard boxes on top of which are balanced several paint cans. It's almost too much effort, but Zoe thinks the ride will be good for them in more ways than one.

When they moved into this house everything needed fixing: from carpets to wallpaper and bathroom to kitchen. All of it. But the deposit, stamp duty, legal fees, appliances and basic Ikea furniture have emptied both of their bank accounts. They must have received five hundred pounds' worth of flowers and champagne as moving-in presents, but, churlish as it sounds, Zoe would rather have had John Lewis vouchers. At least that way they could have bought some nice glasses and a new doorknocker.

Last month, Zoe had suggested doing at least some of the improvements on a credit card, but Alex refused. Refused, ultimately, even to discuss the matter. 'Forget it, Zo,' and there was a sharpness to his voice – an assumption of control – that made Zoe's stomach knot.

'The repayments aren't that bad,' Zoe had said, keeping her tone neutral.

'They're a damn sight worse than nothing, Zo. That's exactly how people end up financially fucked. It's a fucking trap.' She hadn't liked that – the 'fucked', the 'fucking' – but she forced herself to remain reasonable. 'Our salaries are only going to go up, Alex.'

'Mine is, you mean,' staring at Zoe, defying her to contradict him. A low blow, Zoe thought, holding his eyes with equal defiance, breathing through her nose because her teeth were so tightly clamped. Worse than that, it was a betrayal. After all, wasn't it him who encouraged her to quit her high-paying job?

'Fine,' she had said, 'I'll do it. I'll get a card.'

'No,' Alex had shot back. 'No, you will not. We're in this together, Zo.'

'So let's discuss it together.'

'There's nothing to discuss. I'm already late.'

And that was that. Alex went out to play football, and the minute the front door closed – not a slam, but harder than necessary – Zoe had taken hold of a loose corner of wallpaper and pulled. The first strip had come away easily, but the next was stuck to the bedroom wall as firmly as a bad idea sticks to an angry mind. After she chipped her second nail, Zoe went downstairs and gathered up the fish slice, a sharp knife, a sponge and a bowl full of soapy water. Three hours later the floorboards were as slick as the deck of a ship at high sea, Zoe had two more broken nails, a painful blister on her hand and it was apparent that whoever had decorated this room had made up for their poor taste in wallpaper with unrivalled skill at hanging the stuff. Zoe had so far removed four strips of tatty paisley. There were eight strips remaining, and for the first time since they moved in, Zoe was glad the bedroom was as small as it was. Estimating that it was going to take another six hours to complete the job, Zoe jumped in the shower and then headed into town to spend some of the money they didn't have.

It was dark when Zoe returned, and she slid her key into the front door with a sense of guilty trepidation. She had transferred all her purchases (two hundred pounds she didn't have on shoes and jeans she didn't need) into a single bag from the least exclusive store, but even so, she could do without the inquisition. Creeping into the living room, she was relieved to find Alex asleep on the sofa; an old war movie on the TV, a bottle of half-drunk beer precariously close to his feet. Avoiding the creaky steps, Zoe tiptoed upstairs, and quickly unpacked her shopping into the wardrobe, folding and hiding the bag beneath a pile of shoes.

It wasn't until she closed her wardrobe door that she noticed the walls. All four were bare plaster; not a scrap of paisley wallpaper or welded-on backing paper. The debris had been cleared away, the floor cleaned and mopped, even the bed had been made with pillows on top of the duvet the way Zoe liked them.

'Surprise,' said a quiet voice close behind her left shoulder.

Remembering this now, Zoe feels petty for letting the bad eclipse the good. She places her hand on the wall and slides it over the places where Alex claims the paint underneath doesn't show through.

The day after Alex had stripped the walls they drove to B&Q and bought paintbrushes and a half dozen sample-sized pots of paint. When Alex had suggested Fresh Sage, Aubergine Dream and – to Zoe's eye – *Suffocating Blue*, her instinct was to ask was he joking, but he clearly wasn't and she didn't want to ruin his fun after he had made such a gallant and romantic gesture the day before. So Zoe let him pick various shades of bruise, while she selected samplers of Cold Pebble, Dawn Mist and Quite White.

Wearing unloved jeans and forgotten t-shirts, they had applied the samples to the walls. While Zoe painted neat swatches in the corner, below eye level, Alex daubed the wall with a conspicuous aubergine love heart. He was trying to make this fun, she knew – wacky, romantic, anecdotal – but all he was making was a mess.

'Try something more discreet,' she suggested. 'In case we go for something lighter.'

'Chill out, Goblin,' Alex said, pulling the stupid face he invariably made to go with the stupid epithet.

'Sure,' she said. 'Just ... you know ... in case.'

Alex came for her then with the paintbrush. 'Maybe you could use a bit of retouching.'

Zoe had watched this set-piece in numerous films and sit-coms. Funny once, perhaps, it was clichéd now; and instead of being amused, she was simply irritated.

'Don't you dare,' she said to Alex.

'A bit of purple would suit you,' he said, raising his brush.

'Seriously, don't.'

'Bring out the colour of your eyes,' he said, flicking the brush at Zoe.

Zoe felt the cool gobs of Aubergine Dream hit her forehead, cheek and chin. 'Jesus, Alex!'

'What?'

'I've just washed my hair!'

'Christ, someone really is a goblin today.'

And he looked so hurt.

'I'm sorry,' Zoe said. 'Tired.'

'I'm sorry, too,' Alex said. 'But, well, it does kind of suit you.'

The laughter had salvaged the moment, and also given Zoe an easy segue into their paint selection.

'Maybe so, mister, but I don't think it suits the wall.'

'I know, something more discreet, right?'

They made a second trip to the DIY superstore, this time coming back with litres of paint, rollers, trays and all the other decorating paraphernalia. Zoe had attempted to clean the walls before they began painting in earnest, managing to remove most of the aubergine love heart, but enough had remained to show through three coats of Dawn Mist. When they ran out of paint (and Alex was running out of patience) Zoe had suggested driving back to the store to buy a few pots of something darker.

'I thought you wanted Dawn Fucking Fog.'

'Mist. And do you have to? There's no need to swear at me.'

Alex took a deep breath. As if the effort of being reasonable required it. 'Zo, I stripped the walls, we went with your choice of colour and' – laughing – 'my arm is hanging off.'

'But—'

'Zo, you're imagining it. I can't see shit.'

'That's because it's getting dark.'

'It's a f—' Another calming breath. 'It's a bedroom, Zo. It's going to be dark pretty much every minute we spend in it.'

Zoe backed off before they ended up turning full circle into another argument.

Standing in the bedroom three weeks later, it isn't dark and Zoe thinks that if she stares at the wall a moment longer she might punch it. So she walks out of the room and runs a bath.

Applying shampoo, Zoe twists a long hank of hair into a tight rope-like coil and begins to pull. As the flesh of her scalp is stretched into hundreds of hot peaks, the old familiar pain is worryingly enjoyable ... *How long has it been?*

Not since she changed careers from law to publishing, so almost three years now.

Maybe I should buy myself a badge, she thinks.

She remembers sitting in the bath on a Sunday evening, heavy with depression and anxiety at another week in a job she hated. Pulling handfuls of hair until it felt like her skin would tear if her hair didn't come loose. Twice, in fact, Zoe had pulled too hard and found herself holding a fistful of long black strands. An online search told Zoe that this compulsion was called trichotillomania; the fast alliterative syllables made her scalp itch, and the accompanying images of plucked shame-faced women, staring out of the screen like abandoned doll-heads, proved to be fast and effective therapy. *Went cold turkey, before I ended up looking like a plucked chicken*, Zoe thinks, relaxing her grip on her hair and reaching for the conditioner.

As the conditioner soaks in, Zoe shaves her legs with Alex's razor. He hates her using it on her legs, but she hates him leaving it out on the sink, so that makes them even. When he'd hooked his hands under her leg this morning, Zoe cringed, knowing he would have felt the wild stubble scratching against his soft hands. She inspects her shins for patches of eczema and sees none.

And why would she? Life is good: she's working on a new book – not a 'baby-book', thank you very much, but a story for emerging readers. Sure, it features a rhyming cat and a gnomic cheetah, but it's a book with an important message for the little ones: be happy with who you are. *An important message for the big ones, too.*

Zoe taps the razor on the side of the bath, her and Alex's intermingled stubble floating off together in a clag of green-tinted soap. Almost romantic in a gross kind of way. And Alex is romantic when the mood takes him. Yes, he's a bit blokey sometimes – a bit forgetful, maybe, a bit messy, a bit . . . whatever, blokey. But it goes with the strong footballer's legs, the hairy chest, brown voice and dimpled chin. She knows she's biased, but of all her friends' men Alex is easily the best looking. And besides, isn't he her knight in shining armour? If she's enjoying her new career, then she should thank Alex for giving her the courage and support to leave the last one.

The bathwater has turned cool and the surface is speck-led with black dashes of Alex's beard and Zoe's leg hair. She holds her breath and sinks under the surface, pinching her nose closed with one hand and fanning out her hair with the other. She'll have to shower before she towels off now.

When she gets out of the bath, she calls down the stairs to Alex but he still hasn't returned from the shops. Unless he's playing his decks or some Xbox game with his headphones on. He can be incredibly thoughtful like that, after all. He knows how much she likes her sleep and has learned where all the creaky floorboards are so he can move about the house 'like a ninja'. It would be easier, of course, if he would just fix the floorboards, but less cute, perhaps. If he is downstairs, Zoe hopes he's playing records and not shooting zombies. She likes seeing him behind his decks, pouting a little as he nods to the beat; some men look silly when they head-nod, particularly when they pout, but Alex is handsome enough to pull it off. Plus, he always gives the impression that he's not taking himself entirely seriously — a glimmer in his eye that says: *I know.* He can slide his head side to side like Indian ladies do when they're dancing — but rather than thinking it makes him look cool, it always seems to amuse him. Whenever she went to watch him play a set, when he did his head-wobble thing, he'd seek her out, dancing in the crowd, and wink: *I know.* She fell in love with that look, with the man behind it. He did it the first time they met.

It was Zoe's fourth summer party at the law firm, and after making an exhibition of herself at the second and third, she was drinking slowly and selectively. As such, she was relatively sober when the handsome DJ had appeared beside her at the bar.

'Buy you a drink?'

'It's a free bar,' Zoe had said, returning his smile.

The DJ lowered his voice. 'Shh . . .' he said, winking. 'Let's pretend.'

Zoe nodded. Whispered back: 'Okay.'

'Hey,' he said, as if just noticing Zoe. 'Buy you a drink?'

'Sure, I'll have a glass of champagne, please.'

Affecting surprise, panic, anxiety at this lady's expensive tastes. 'Champagne? I . . .'

Zoe played along with the improvisation. 'Is that a problem?'

After a moment's hesitation. 'No, God no, it's just' – the DJ patted his pockets – 'I think I've left my wallet in my Ferrari.'

'We've all been there,' Zoe said. 'Let me get these, you can buy them next time.'

The DJ raised his thick eyebrows (*If we had children, they would be born with thick black hair*, Zoe thought). 'Next time?'

Zoe wasn't given to acts of bold flirtation, but having stumbled into this one she allowed herself to be carried along. 'Is this a routine?'

'Not yet,' he said, laughing.

The role-play over – but at the right time, before the charade became forced and clunky – Zoe turned to the bar and ordered two glasses of champagne.

'So what do I call you?' Zoe asked.

'DJ Lexx' – the head wobble and self-deprecating smile – 'if you want to book me for a set. Alex if you want to meet me for a drink next week.'

Zoe clinked her glass against his. 'Cheers, Alex.'

Henry

Locally Sourced

In the castle it is now only nine hours until Henry slides a ring onto April's finger. His room comes with a small kettle, mugs, teabags, cartons of everlasting milk and sachets of cheap coffee. Henry fills the kettle in the en suite bathroom and brings it back into the room to boil. The small appliance sounds like a steam train in the pre-dawn hush and, afraid of waking his best man, Henry unplugs it before the water is fully boiled.

Brian mutters something in his sleep. They have been best friends since the day Henry relieved Brian of a tooth, and Brian helped Henry acquire a new nickname. In their early teens they made birdhouses to sell to the tourists, perfecting a simple design made from a single plank of wood. Recycled slats from builders' pallets were fine, but needed sanding to remove the splinters. The boys' preferred material was 'reclaimed perimeter panels', and for several years there wasn't an intact fence in the village. Fortunately for the enterprising vandals, no one connected the mysterious phenomenon with the boys' booming trade in birdhouses – 'Handmade with locally sourced materials'.

Is Brian happy? Henry wonders. He left school at sixteen with four GCSEs, took an apprenticeship changing tyres and oil in a small garage, still works there now, drives a nice enough car, lives in a nice enough house and shags a nice enough girl whenever the opportunity presents itself. He gets pissed on Fridays, plays rugby on Saturdays and – Henry has no doubt – sleeps as soundly as a child seven nights a week. Yeah, why wouldn't he be happy?

Locally sourced, Henry muses.

He remembers filling in university applications. He and April had been dating for less than six months, but neither one doubted that this was the real thing. April had no plans to stay in school a moment longer than necessary, and Henry had promised to apply only to 'local' universities. They would see each other every weekend, and throughout the holidays. And after all, they said, everyone knows that absence makes the heart grow fonder. And so, while his mother braided April's hair in front of

Pretty Woman, Henry completed forms for Manchester, Liverpool, Sheffield, Leeds. London held a greater allure, but while April had said it was his decision, her tone had made the consequences clear. And he loved her; if it was a choice between April and London he would take April, and gladly.

'Why dentistry, anyway?' April had asked.

Henry had thought about this, of course, and had his theories, but they sounded insincere, mercenary or – infinitely worse to a seventeen-year-old boy – silly.

Henry's family moved to the village just in time for Henry to complete the last two years of primary school. He had thought that being a boxer's son would make him popular, or at the very least deter anyone with designs on his lunch money. So the new boy made sure to introduce the fact as quickly and often as possible. Within a day he had been in two fights (losing both) and acquired the nickname Little Boots. One of the earliest domestic arguments Henry remembers is the one about his pugilistic education. Big Boots had wanted to get Henry in a pair of gloves as soon as the boy could walk, but his mother – under threat of divorce – had insisted he go nowhere near a boxing gym until he turned eleven. So while his father taught him to throw a stiff jab and a reasonable right cross, Henry was in no way a fighter. And as this fact (the black eyes and split lips) became increasingly apparent, there was no shortage of boys eager to take their turn dumping the boxer's son on his backside. Henry lost these playground bouts more often than he won, but invariably came a good second, making up in heart what he lacked in talent. In all likelihood, Henry would still be known as Little Boots today, had he not punched out Brian's tooth and earned himself a new alias. Stunned at this rare success, Henry had picked up the dislodged tooth, wiped it on the front of his shirt and handed it back to his bleeding and bewildered assailant.

'Thinks he's a flippin' dentist,' someone had said from the circle of surrounding boys.

And that's all it took.

Of course, he hadn't chosen a degree based on his primary school nickname; but neither could he entirely dismiss the notion that a seed had been sewn the day he went home with tooth marks in his knuckles.

'Dunno,' said Henry in response to April's question. 'So long as people have teeth they'll need dentists, I suppose.'

'Talking of,' said his mother, indicating a laughing Julia Roberts, 'you wouldn't want her taking a bite out of your apple.'

And his girlfriend returned her attention to the movie.

*

With few exceptions, Henry climbed on a train every term-time Friday night for his first three and a half years at university. He knew the timetable, how many paces the platform was from one end to the other, the pattern of the stonework on the station's outer arches, the shape of its iron skeleton. He lost count of the parties, stunts and trysts he heard about on Monday mornings. The circle he had associated with in the crucial first term remained friendly, but, inevitably, they stopped asking what he was doing on a Friday night, stopped the cajoling charade of imploring him to stick around for the weekend. Henry sensed their frustration at having to clarify (and consequently diminish) the in-jokes that had blossomed at parties he had missed, and so he stopped asking for explanations, instead grinning through the laughter in mute isolation. He stopped rugby training in the week because he couldn't play matches at the weekend; he stopped going to the cinema because he felt like a gatecrasher in a gang and a creep on his own. He attended all his lectures, studied hard and scored high eighties in all his exams.

During the summer between his third and fourth years, April had begun talking about engagement. Two of her friends had children now, another was engaged, another married; at nineteen years old April was talking about life passing her by. The conversations they had in bed on Friday nights were frequently melodramatic and often tearful; accusations thrown and demands made. His mother harangued him for taking 'that sweet beautiful girl' for granted. 'Don't you dare turn into your father,' she had said. And inside his head, Henry shot back: *Just so long as she doesn't turn into you.*

After an entire summer together – squabbling not infrequently – it seemed the couple could quite easily bear to be parted. Henry had suggested it might be better if he came back once fortnightly from now on, citing the old line about absence and its effect on the human heart. April had immediately and unsmilingly accepted the idea, and Henry discovered that skipping one weekend made it easy to skip two. He made new friendships, went to fancy dress parties, seventies discos and indie gigs. He and April talked on the phone, sent texts and emails. They missed each other, they said, but Henry suspected April's declarations were as hollow as his own.

So while it was fundamentally sad, it was neither a surprise nor an intestinal wrench when, halfway through the final term of his fourth year, April told Henry it was over.

It had been Theresa Johnston's birthday that weekend, and in the evening a gang of them had followed the girls into town to celebrate in a new American-themed bar with bric-a-brac décor and a small illuminated dancefloor.

They drank sweet cocktails, ate chicken wings, sticky ribs and nachos, and – in the diluting presence of a dozen other bodies – enjoyed themselves tremendously. Henry spent more time that evening talking to April's friend Bobbi than to April. After close to a year travelling around Asia, Australia and New Zealand, Bobbi was departing for Edinburgh University in the autumn. Like many of her friends, April had left school at sixteen, and Henry was somewhat in awe of Bobbi's almost defiant intrepidity. They sat at the bar sipping Long Island iced-teas, while Bobbi told about hidden coves, island spiders and full-moon parties, intercutting her anecdotes with questions about the more proximal mysteries of campus life, student cuisine and mixed-sex housing, her eyebrows arching suggestively at this last. She asked how Henry was coping with a 'long-distance' relationship, her expression turning sincere and solicitous. 'Is everything okay?' she asked, placing her hand on top of Henry's.

Bobbi wasn't pretty in the way that April was; in the way of footballers' wives, girl-band members and minor blonde celebrities. Ask ten men in this bar to choose between them, and ten would pick April. At Edinburgh University, though, the ratio might not be so overwhelming. Freckled, gap-toothed and with messy, shoulder-length ringlets, Bobbi had something more appealing than a conventional aesthetic. She was interesting. Henry looked into her eyes as she told him about the modules – child development, behavioural economics, personality and cognition – she would be studying in her first year. He watched the way she tucked her hair behind her small but slightly prominent ears and saw that she would never 'scrub up'; she would not one day pull a clip from her hair, ditch a pair of spectacles and transform into an ideal of beauty – no, this was it, gawky, asymmetrical, wide-nosed and still . . . not beautiful, but confident and honest and sexy. And Bobbi knew it, which only added to the effect.

'How far is Edinburgh from Sheffield, do you think?' Bobbi asked after a long pause, during which Henry had failed to answer her question about long-term relationships. Henry looked up from the table (Bobbi's hand still lying unselfconsciously on top of his) and smiled. 'Only a few hours on the train,' he said. 'Maybe half a bottle of wine and a few chapters on child economics, or whatever.'

Bobbi had burst out laughing. 'Sounds like my kind of ticket,' she said, inclining her head to the side as if inspecting a painting for some revealing detail. She looked at Henry that way for a moment before abruptly clapping her hands together and jumping down from her barstool. 'Right,' she said. 'Got dancing to do. See you around, okay.'

Henry spent the remainder of the night talking to Brian, reminiscing about old times and drinking too much cheap lager. He watched a succession of men dancing in amongst the girls, bumping deliberately up against them, then cupping their hand against an ear and nodding towards the bar. By far the most popular target was April, and Henry watched with neither pride nor jealousy as his girlfriend laughed flirtatiously, frowned in mock reproval, smiled at some compliment and, ultimately, shook her head. He wondered how this scenario would play out in his absence, and found himself wondering if April wouldn't be happier with someone else.

In their taxi home at the end of the night, April had snuggled up close to Henry, linking her arm through his and nestling her head against the side of his neck. But Henry's body knew what the taxi driver, watching them in the rear-view mirror, couldn't see. That this physical gesture was one of sadness not intimacy. There was affection too, but it was tired and resigned – maybe it was the passive weight of April's head; the mindless, almost autistic back and forth of her thumb on the back of his hand; the exaggerated sound of her exhaled breath . . . but Henry's head, and shoulder, and hand – every part of him in contact with April – could feel the inevitable sitting silent and lumpen between them.

It wasn't until they were in bed and the lights were off that April had sat up and announced into the darkness: 'I think we need a break.' Nothing as final and clear-cut as *It's over*, but they both knew it amounted to the same thing. They declared their mutual sadness, reassured each other of their enduring affection, and made love with a passion that had been absent for close to a year. It was no one's fault; it was simply a sad fact of growing up and growing apart.

The following morning, after dressing with her back to him, April had kissed Henry goodbye, and told him she loved him, he would always be special to her, and everything about them was right except the timing. After she left the bedroom, Henry heard another door open and the muffled sounds of his mother and April talking in the corridor – reassuring sounds, soothing coos, a kiss. April worked in his mother's salon full time now, and where the relationship had once projected the cutesy feel of stepmother and surrogate daughter, it had matured into a deep, almost sororal friendship. And Henry had no doubt that his mother knew his relationship was over well before he did.

It took Bobbi less than a week to contact Henry in the wake of his break-up with April. The first text simply asked if he was okay, she called him 'hon' and signed off with a single 'x'.

Henry had been immediately aroused by this brief and fundamentally innocuous message. He replied that he was fine, making a pragmatic and open-ended reference to his newfound freedom. Within a week they were talking on the phone. No longer about April and Henry's break-up – they had exhausted that line of enquiry within a few short texts – but about small town life, student life, their degrees, the books they were reading, the colour of the sky. Three weeks later Bobbi stayed in Sheffield for the weekend – two days of long walks, late night talks and greedy sex. It was the first of several visits that summer, and on only her second stay in Henry's small student room, Bobbi allowed him to do something to her that April never would: she let Henry cut her hair.

Since the age of twelve, Henry had worked in his mother's salon, Love & Die. Perhaps the signwriters had never been employed by a hairdresser or a fish and chip shop before this particular commission, but they had taken it upon themselves to correct the perceived misspelling of Die. And so, instead of a pun on the universal connection between love and appropriate hair colour, his mother's salon had been given a more philosophical identity. As it happened, Sheila Smith had been quite taken with the name, and besides, the signwriter had offered her a fifty per cent discount.

Initially, Henry's duties were limited to sweeping and picking up dropped pins with a horseshoe-shaped magnet that looked like something from a *Roadrunner* cartoon. From there he graduated to washing hair, applying dye, rollers and perming solution. The first time he wielded scissors was to trim his mother's fringe, her coaching him on how to pull the hair tight with the fingers of his free hand, to cut with clean confident strokes of the scissors. Next, she taught him to use thinning scissors, then how to cut over a comb. At fifteen his mother let him cut her hair into a short retro crop; he learned to cut choppy layers, clean angles and feathered textures. By sixteen he was – to the profound disappointment of his father – cutting paying customers' hair on Saturdays. A little over ten years ago, the most popular haircut in the village and surrounding postcodes was a graduated bob. Not because the style was in fashion, but because Love & Die was offering the cut for free plus a cup of instant coffee and a biscuit. 'If you can cut a grad-bob, you can cut owt,' Henry's mother claimed, and in the summer between the lower- and upper-sixth form, she was determined her son would master this holy grail of women's hairdressing. More than once, Sheila Smith had to step in and salvage her son's handiwork, but by the time Henry returned to school for his final year, he could style a grad-bob with geometric precision, choosing a severe decline or gentle descent depending on the set of his client's features. For more adventurous ladies, he had created an asymmetric variation that his mother found a little showy, but nevertheless impressive. And despite this, April would not let Henry so much as tidy her split ends.

Lying in his single student bed, with his fingers twined in Bobbi's chaotic curls, Henry had been thinking of the various ways he might tackle such a head of hair, when Bobbi, seemingly reading his mind, had said, 'Anything but one of those Lego bobs.' Henry found a pair of sharpish scissors in a first aid kit in the communal kitchen, and borrowed a pair of clippers from a guy on the floor below. With these less than perfect tools, he styled her a punky undercut and choppy fringe that looked fine in the campus nightclub, but was going to be as conspicuous as a lesbian kiss in their mutual hometown.

When the summer term ended, Henry stayed on in Sheffield for the first time since leaving home. He found work on a building site, and pulled pints in a rough local three evenings a week. Bobbi visited more weekends than not, and the relationship developed a layer of cosy intimacy and familiarity. Henry enjoyed Bobbi's garrulous, playful attitude; but at the same time he found it slightly contrived – the rom-com kook – and a little exhausting: the constant jokes, and twirls, and 'do you think?' The sex was fantastically – almost pornographically – satisfying, but also had an element of performance about it; something he yearned for on a Thursday while they made arrangements for the weekend, but tired of by Sunday afternoon, as he looked at the clock waiting for the time when he could walk her to the station.

To her friends and family at home, Bobbi claimed her weekend excursions were trips to visit a girl befriended on an open day at Edinburgh University – a fictitious character called Penelope, whose name she adopted as a pet moniker for Henry: *Where shall we eat, Pen? Penny for your thoughts, Penny. Fuck me, Penelope!*

The affair ended, as they both knew it would, in September, when Bobbi began her course in Edinburgh. There were continued phone calls, but these tapered off through the autumn term. Bobbi travelled south to see Henry once in October, and he made the trip north the following month, but he saw little of the university campus. It was clear from Bobbi's demeanour that there was another man on the scene. She didn't introduce him to her friends, and appeared furtive when they left her room, eschewing the student bars for more touristy spots in the city. Even so, it was a beautiful weekend; the theat-rics had gone from the bedroom, but it had been replaced with an unostentatious intimacy. Perhaps because they both sensed this relationship – *fling* – had run its course, and were both fine with that. In many ways it had been a perfect affair; perfect in its timing and duration. Henry knew Bobbi was not the one for him; that she would drive him crazy for anything longer than a week, let alone a lifetime. But she picked him up; and it was her not-Aprilness as much as her own nature that had moved him past the disappointment and sadness of splitting up with his childhood sweetheart.

'Look after yourself, Penelope.' And when they kissed on the platform, Henry felt a small warm lump in his chest.

When Henry went home for Christmas, it was the first time he had returned to his hometown in seven months. When eventually he did bump into April (Tesco's: her buying a bottle of wine and a tub of Ben and Jerry's ice-cream; him buying a twelve-pack of toilet rolls) it had been less awkward than he had feared. They had talked easily; April seeming pleased to see him and genuinely interested in how he was getting on at university. Henry had nodded at the wine in April's hand. 'Quiet night in?' he said, his expression making the deeper enquiry.

'Something like that,' she said, blushing. They laughed off their embarrassment, but Henry also felt a pinch of sadness. Or maybe jealousy. He didn't imagine for one second that April wouldn't have seen or dated other men in the half year since their break-up, but here was the confirmation – and at Christmas, too. They kissed on the cheek and wished each other a Happy New Year.

It was inevitable they would get back together, April liked to tell people. 'We just needed some time and perspective to appreciate how lucky we were, didn't we, Henry?'

Three years, it turns out, was sufficient.

Fate – *good or bad?* – nudging them back towards each other.

Henry was qualified and working in Sheffield when his mother called to say Big Boots had been in an accident. The call came past midnight, waking Henry from a deep sleep, and before he even picked up the phone, he had a sense that something serious had happened. His father had been rushed to hospital with fractures to both wrists and three ribs, the latter precipitating a collapse of his right lung. Henry's first thought was that his father had been assaulted, whereas the reality – a drunken tumble into the cellar – was both more mundane and, somehow, more frustrating. Henry left a voicemail at the surgery, cancelling his list, then jumped into his car and broke the speed limit all the way to the hospital.

Big Boots' injuries required a chest drain, two surgeries and intensive rehabilitation. And despite his determination to prove the quacks wrong, the old fighter was barely able to feed himself, let alone run a bar and throw out drunks. As he had several years before, Henry fell into a routine of weekly trips home, this time so he could help to run the pub and care for his father. Since April was working full time in Love & Die, it was a natural step for her to help out in the Black Horse at this difficult time. Frequently, Henry found himself tending the bar with his ex-girlfriend, the old affection coalescing around them, a more mature and meaningful thing now. Sometimes he would walk April home after a shift, occasionally sneaking up to her room before returning to the pub to clean the tables and help Big Boots brush his teeth the following morning.

There were complications, both medical and romantic. April was in a relationship, but unhappily so, and the extent of her affections were uneven and unpredictable. But on the other hand, she did save his father's life. After successful treatment on his lung, his symptoms deteriorated. Unknown to anyone but the man himself, Big Boots was in constant and worsening pain – experiencing a stabbing sensation in his chest every time he drew breath. During a lull behind the bar one weekday night, April had popped upstairs to make him a cup of tea, only to find the old man on his knees and sweating glass beads. Refusing to take no for an answer, April drove Big Boots to the hospital where it was ascertained that he had developed empyema – a collection of pus on the lung. Left untreated for much longer, the outcome would very likely have been fatal. Further surgery was required, and Big Boots' recovery was pushed back further still. Towards the end of October, some seven months after the initial accident, Big Boots was finally and fully discharged. April, always doted on by Henry's parents, was by now as much a family member as Henry himself. And having fallen in love as smoothly as they had fallen out of that same state three years ago, the expectation was that he would make it official.

As well as pulling pints and flirting with the locals, April took great care and pride in what passed for interior décor in the Black Horse: spray-can snowdrifts in the windows at Christmas, patriotic bunting for internationals, poppies and flags for Remembrance, coconuts and plastic palms in the summer. With Big Boots back on his feet in time for Hallowe'en, April took to her task with unprecedented enthusiasm: cobwebs, lanterns, haunted bed sheets and plastic critters. When Henry came home one weekend with pots of alginate normally used for taking impressions of teeth, he told April they were making severed jelly fingers. And as she pressed her small hands into the goopy compound, she did not for one second suspect Henry was measuring her finger for a diamond ring.

When Henry thinks back to that Hallowe'en night, the memory doesn't make him smile the way it should. Maybe April sensed something was coming, there were too many familiar faces in the pub; friends from school, both sets of parents. Henry's mother as excited and awkward as a toddler on Christmas Eve. Even April's brother, Mad George, was in attendance. Of course she knew. So when Henry knelt on the sticky carpet, and the chatter died away, April's eyes went wide in expectation rather than shock. Her hands going to her heart, the way they do it in the movies. 'Will you marry me?' Henry had asked, presenting the ring that would fit April's finger perfectly.

And as the question floated in the air, he watched April's eyes flick towards the ring. For a fraction of a second he registered a trace of disappointment on her face. And then it was gone – her eyes found Henry's, her smile pulled wide. 'Yes,' she said. 'Yes.'

The following day they caught a train to Liverpool, exchanging the ring for another, larger and more expensive one. The difference in price wasn't extraordinary, and Henry didn't begrudge spending the money. But even so, he couldn't shake the feeling that he had made a mistake.

And this is the problem – he can't be trusted with himself. He cannot be relied upon to intelligently sift his emotions and find the truth beneath all the layers of thought and doubt and indecision. Henry loved April, right up until he didn't. And then back the other way, changing his mind like a kid in a comic shop. Changing his heart. April never asked how he had known what size ring to buy, so Henry never told her.

He has finished his tea and the clock tells him it is now 3.31 a.m. Tomorrow morning he will wake up next to his wife in the four-poster bed on the other side of the castle. Their suitcases are packed, passports and sun cream all in the appropriate compartments of their luggage. The newlyweds will take a ten-minute taxi ride to the train station, a train to Manchester airport, an internal flight to Heathrow then a long wait before a two-hour flight to Ibiza. They will arrive at their hotel close to midnight, fatigued and clammy with travel. There is an earlier flight, arriving at a more civilized time, but to make all the connections they would have to catch the 5.28 a.m. from the local station – the first train of the day. It is Saturday morning now and Henry wonders whether the trains run to the same timetable today as they will tomorrow.

He estimates the station is six miles from the castle, a cold walk along dark twisting lanes. On foot it would take ninety minutes, maybe as long as two hours. He looks at the clock as it clicks over to 3.33.

Zoe

Fingers To Shred

Of course he had a girlfriend.

Zoe all but laughed when he told her.

Alex was already in the pub when Zoe arrived, drinking what she guessed was a gin and tonic. He spotted her walking towards him and immediately stood up, waving a short salute across the room. She was surprised to see DJ Lexx wearing a suit, but before she had a chance to make a glib comment about it (scrolling through her mind: *Been to court? Been to a wedding? Blimey, is this what all DJs wear on their days off?*), Alex had stepped away from the table, gesturing for Zoe to sit while he asked what she was drinking.

The pub Alex had suggested turned out to be a charmless cave tucked away in a knot of narrow cobbled streets with names – Ludgate, Newgate – that reminded Zoe of

Dickens and his city of urchins, riots and Victorian gaols. They were a stone's throw from St Paul's Cathedral, and this grotty boozer seemed a peculiar choice in an area replete with far more salubrious wine and cocktail bars. Perhaps Alex thought it was cosy, or characterful or intimate.

When he returned to the table with Zoe's drink, Alex was visibly awkward. If they'd been dating already she would have sworn he was about to dump her. She'd been planning what type of kiss to greet him with (cheek or lips; peck or subtly lingering, delicately foreshadowing), but the moment had gone and Alex's discomfort was contagious.

'Cheers,' she said, raising her glass, air-clinking and taking a sip of generic red wine. 'So, is this what all DJs wear on their days off?'

'Sorry, what?'

Zoe thumbed invisible lapels. 'The suit.'

'Ah, oh, right, yeah. Actually, I . . . I work in the City. Well, kind of, oil and gas. It's a bit . . .' Alex made an apologetic shrug and blew air through his lips. 'Well, it's oil and gas.'

Zoe nodded, trying to hide her disappointment. 'Cool. I mean . . . great! That's . . . people always need oil and gas. Do they?'

'Well, let's hope so, otherwise I'm out of a job.'

'You could always DJ?'

Alex laughed. 'That would be nice.'

'So . . . at our party thing, what was that?'

'Favour for a friend. Well, I got paid, but . . . not much.'

'And free champagne.'

Alex smiled. 'Yes, and free champagne. But not enough to give up the day job, unfortunately.' He seemed to hesitate a moment before saying: 'I did play at a fairly big club in Thailand for a while.'

'Thailand?'

After graduating, Alex had secured a job at the firm where he still works today. He had managed to defer his start date for twelve months, planning to DJ his way from Asia to Australia to America and anywhere else the wind blew him. But finding gigs that paid anything other than alcohol was easier imagined than realized. Alex was running dangerously low on money and optimism, when various circumstances aligned and the DJ gods span him in the direction of a regular set paying paper wages. The location was less idyllic than Koh Lanta or Rai Leh, but it was a good opportunity to bank some much-needed cash. Four weeks into Alex's Phuket residency, however, the club owner accused him of stealing, threatened him with a machete, and said if Alex was still in Phuket by the weekend something 'crinical' would happen to him.

'*Crinical*?'

'I didn't know if he meant criminal, critical or what,' Alex continued. 'I mean, considering the mad bastard was waving a machete around I guess it all amounted to the same thing, but – have you been to Thailand? – I'd had a bunch of diet pills, speed basically, and a magic-mushroom milkshake, and, well, I was having trouble processing it, danger and all, so I'm saying to him: "*Crinical*? What's crinical?" And he's practically foaming at the mouth, shouting: "Crinical. I send you to the doctor's crinic. You understand me now?"'

Something – besides the vaguely Alex Garland plot – didn't ring true about Alex's story; he was fidgeting with his watch and seemed reluctant to hold eye contact. On the other hand, the detail ('crinical') felt too specific not to be authentic. But if Zoe doubted him, Alex didn't seem to notice. He went on to tell Zoe how the club owner not only refused to pay his four weeks' outstanding wages, but also 'confiscated' his record collection and headphones. So with neither money nor music, Alex had little option but to return to the UK. A friend put him up on their sofa, and through various contacts Alex was able to land a couple of 'eighty-quid gigs' in large pubs and small clubs.

'What about your records?' Zoe asked, trying not to sound like she was interrogating a flimsy story.

'Borrowed some off a friend.'

The answer felt deliberately terse, something in its delivery seeming to say: *Can we leave it at that?*

Zoe nodded.

Alex laughed. 'Sorry, it's a mad story, I know. I tend not to bring it up because it sounds like so much bullshit. Like *The Beach* with DJs.'

Zoe laughed now. 'The thought never crossed my mind.'

Alex took a sip of his drink and continued. 'And so I played a few gigs in London, but by the time September rolled around I had two hundred quid in the bank, a ten grand loan, and so . . .' he pulled at the lapels of his very nice suit, '. . . oil and gas.'

'At least you got a good story out of it.'

Alex nodded as if this was fair enough. Then he sighed. 'There's something I should tell you.'

Zoe closed her eyes, took a breath. 'If you tell me you're married or you've got a girlfriend, I swear to God' – she raised her glass of wine – 'you're going to need a dry cleaners.'

Alex smiled at that, briefly. He reached across the table, took hold of Zoe's wrist and lowered her glass-holding hand to the table.

'I don't believe it.'

'It's not . . . it's not exactly . . .'

'Well, aren't you just full of surprises.'

'L—'

'Let you explain. Is that what you were about to say? Wh . . . do they give you a handbook?'

'Zoe—'

'You can't sit here with your hand on my wrist all night, Alex. For one thing, what if your girlfriend walked in?'

'She's not. She's . . . I'm going to end it.'

Zoe glanced pointedly down at the table, the glass still in her hand, Alex's hand (nice watch, clean fingernails) still firmly gripping her wrist.

'Do you promise not to throw it on me?'

'I haven't decided. If you'd bought a better red, I'd be more inclined to drink it. But this tastes like someone's gran made it in a mop bucket.'

'You're funny,' Alex said, smiling. 'Almost as funny as a bloke.'

'Yes, I'm a laugh a minute, me. Zoe Bubbles, they call me.'

'Is that a joke?'

'Nope. And I don't know why I'm telling you. My flatmates at uni came up with it; called me Zoe Bubbles, Zoe Bubbs, Bubbs, ZeeBee. God, I'm wittering.'

'I like your wittering. ZeeBee.'

Zoe unpicked Alex's fingers from around her wrist. They both looked at the glass. Zoe shook her head in resignation, took a sip, winced. 'Never call me that again. You know what "Bubbly" is a byword for, don't you?'

'Fat.'

'First things first, I was not "fat", I was . . . bonnie. But I was young and we drank pints and ate a lot of chips.'

'Nothing wrong with bonnie. Although I prefer "cuddly".'

'Cute doesn't suit you. And second things second, my nickname had nothing to do with the *former* size of my bum.'

A look from Alex: *Really?*

'Like I said, it's because I'm a laugh a fucking minute.'

'I like you,' Alex said then. A flash of the cool confidence she had seen at the summer party, and it was impossible not to fall for it. She smiled thinly as her anger (at least one-quarter contrived, after all) cooled.

'Right, here's the plan. You go to the bar and get me a decent glass of red. Then we can get to the bottom of this "not my girlfriend" business and decide where we go from there.'

Alex nodded, stood and reached for Zoe's glass. 'I'll keep it,' she said. 'I still might need it.'

Alex came back from the bar with a bottle and two glasses; the glibness had gone, replaced with an expression of nervous sincerity. He filled their glasses, then backtracked to Phuket.

The 'thing' he had allegedly stolen from the Thai club owner turned out to be a German girl called Ines. Ines was also taking a year out after graduating and before embarking on a career in London; in her case, out of Heidelberg University, and into a large American bank. Alex and Ines 'got together', which would have been fine, but for the fact the club owner had formed the idea that Ines was already taken – by him. Zoe had many questions, but Ines (no doubt privileged and beautiful) was the competition, and it didn't do to appear too interested in the 'other woman'. 'Coke,' was pretty much all Alex offered by way of explaining this pivotal misunderstanding, and Zoe allowed it to remain it that. For now, at least.

Alex had no money and Ines had no agenda, but she did have friends in London and a house off the King's Road, paid for (confirming half of Zoe's assumptions) by her father. They flew back to London and shacked up in the pastel blue two-bedroom mews house in the heart of Chelsea. Their neighbour on one side was an investment banker; on the other a gruff gentleman who had played bass in at least two bands Alex had heard of from the sixties. After two weeks of eating in restaurants with heavy cutlery, and drinking expensive coffee from small cups, Alex took the train north to visit his mother and brother in a now defunct mining town. He made the return trip carrying two suitcases full of clothes, books and photographs, and by Sunday evening he and Ines were living together.

Sipping her wine a little too quickly, Zoe did not particularly want to know which members-only clubs Alex and Ines frequented, or how much Ines spent on clothes, or which socialites they befriended. But this was how Alex chose to tell his story, building up to the point in his own sweet way. And, okay, she was maybe a little interested.

'Have you ever felt trapped by a bad decision?' Alex had asked.

Zoe thought about the patches of eczema on her shins. She thought about pulling her hair in the bath, and the Sunday night blues that had seeped backwards so far she had come to dread the entire weekend, leaving work on a Friday depressed because she would be walking back through the revolving doors all too soon. Shredding a document at work earlier today, she had wondered how much sick leave she would get if her fingers became accidentally jammed in the mechanism. Two weeks, had been her guess, and the exchange had felt worryingly tempting.

Zoe nodded.

'I knew on the train back to London that I was making a mistake.'

'Why?'

Alex sighed. 'Ines isn't exactly . . . dazzling company.'

'But you went to all those cool clubs and ate in all those fancy restaurants.' Laying on the sarcasm a bit thick, but what the hell. 'So it took you how long to figure that out? A month?'

'Thailand's weird. Everything's . . . it's different . . . weird.'

'Is she beautiful?' *Damn*.

Alex swirled his wine and watched the drops run down the inside of the glass. He nodded without looking up. 'Yup.'

Annoying. And Zoe felt suddenly self-conscious about her nose – cute, it's been called, *cute as a button*, but the phrase has always made her think of mushrooms. And now the damned thing was itching. Even so, there was something flattering about being courted over a beautiful German woman.

'Rich, beautiful and . . . a banker, did you say?'

Another nod from Alex.

So that's why we're drinking in a back-alley ale-house. So we don't get spotted by Ines or any of her City colleagues.

'Rich, beautiful and intelligent,' said Zoe. 'That's the fantasy, isn't it?'

Alex looked up and laughed. 'Actually, that's rich, beautiful and dumb.'

'So which am I?'

Alex smiled but resisted the bait.

'Long story short,' he said. 'It was wrong – is wrong – but I stayed too long. It was too easy, too convenient, I guess.'

'How long?'

'About eighteen months.'

'So you chat up girls at discos—'

'Discos?'

'Invite them out for a drink in a dingy pub, bare your soul, then catch the last tube home to the rich, beautiful, boring girlfriend on the King's Road.'

'That's about the size of it.'

'Well . . .' Zoe felt suddenly tired, exasperated. 'Glad I could be of assistance. But I've got a busy day tomorrow. Meetings to pretend I'm interested in, fingers to shred, and all that.'

Zoe pushed her chair back from the table.

'Wait,' Alex said, apparently amused, looking like he was about to laugh. 'Did you say . . . *fingers to shred*?'

Zoe closed her eyes, sighed. 'Things,' she said, blushing. 'I meant *things* to shred.'

Zoe laughed, laughed so abruptly, in fact, that she snorted; and there's nothing cute about that. She has always done it, and long ago learned that any attempt to stifle this sinus gurgle only exacerbates it from little-piggy grunt to great big snotty hog-sized bellow. So she let it go. Good, cathartic, tears-in-the-eyes laughter. Alex laughed too, but not as hard. He sat back, sipped his wine and smiled as Zoe pulled herself together and wiped her eyes with the heels of her hands. Her button-mushroom nose would be red and swollen now – the complete antithesis of poised Teutonic beauty. But . . . well, fuck it.

'Feel better?'

Zoe nodded.

'Has anyone ever told you that you look beautiful when you laugh?'

'Don't push your luck. Seriously d . . .' and like a crazy woman, she was laughing and snorting all over again.

They talked. About bad decisions, work, ambition, disappointment, university, family, the seaside, the Fens, kids' TV shows from when they both grew up. They talked about love and sex; Zoe and this man she barely knew. But she felt like she did know him, or perhaps understand is a better word. A two-way thing. They held hands across the table as they talked about first times and funny times, Alex's thumb stroking the back of her hand. They extended their

66

legs towards each other, letting their feet and shins connect beneath the table like their hands above. Zoe told Alex he should leave Ines, and he told her she should quit her job. You have to do what makes you happy, they told each other; you only live once, they confided across the table, lapsing into cliché, but embracing its truth without self-consciousness. Yes, they agreed, absolutely, life is way too short to waste a moment with the wrong person, in the wrong job, in the wrong place. And so, when Alex told Zoe she had a beautiful laugh, a sexy smile, and – yes – a cute nose, she chose to believe him. They kissed in the pub, her initiating by leaning across the table and – she felt it would be wrong to ignore the impulse – putting her lips against his as he talked with infectious enthusiasm about his love of music. They kissed again outside, less inhibited now in the glow of the streetlights; each pushing hard against this other body and whispering statements of desire and intent; they kissed against the glass façade of Blackfriars Underground station where anyone might see them. Their teeth clashed and she could feel the physical proof of Alex's muttered frustrations pressed hard against her as the city filed past them out of the rain and into the station for the last train home. They laughed when a gang of drunk men heckled and jeered and told them to *get in there*. They ran down the escalators, Zoe precarious in her heels, and then – the guard warning *stand clear of the closing doors* – one more kiss before she jumped onto her tube, travelling north to the flat she shared with Vicky; leaving Alex to make his way west to the bed he shared with Ines.

There were more dates, more kisses, more last trains home. Arguments, too, when the promises and pledges went unfulfilled. 'Complications,' Alex said. He did broach the subject of moving out, but Ines cried, refused food, threw things, threatened to swallow a bottle of pills. And what do you say to that: *Let her; She's lying; She's manipulating you*? What if Ines were telling the truth? What if Alex left her and the German bitch jumped off Waterloo Bridge? 'Do what you need to do,' was all Zoe could say; neither condoning, nor making any demands of her own. 'It's your life, your call.' They continued to meet in the same dingy pub, but the energy changed. There was still a physical attraction, still flirting and revealing and laughing and sometimes kissing, but there was drama, too. Exciting in a way, but exhausting, and eroding the candour and empathy that had seemed on their first meeting to be so special. Zoe came to feel foolish, like a distraction, a fling, while Alex agonized and beat his breast and lamented his life before going home to rent-free Chelsea and the beautiful Ines. Zoe stopped answering texts and emails. Not all but some. She made excuses when Alex suggested meeting, she went on a date with another guy and – instant regret – screwed him because, well, he had no German to go home to and it was easy. She never told Alex about this distraction (and to this day doesn't intend to); not his business while he had a woman at home. They sent emails at Christmas; polite, succinct and, probably, final. And then, midway through January, Alex sent a text:

> Single guy seeks disgruntled lawyer for bad
> wine, public snogging, naughty talk and
> snorty laughter. Beautiful smile preferable.
> Germans need not apply.

Two years and nine months ago now.

Zoe sits on the edge of the bed in her underwear (a matching set, peachy pink, no loose threads) applying make-up. She glances at the clock and sees that it is past eleven. Whatever time Alex left, he's been gone for more than an hour, maybe as long as two. Zoe experiences the mental equivalent of a flinch, pulling back from a thought she doesn't want to acknowledge.

Alex has been ... what? ... off, lately. Not himself. He's been quiet, distracted and ... uncharacteristically attentive, is how it feels – volunteering to cook, clean, fetch ('let me bring you breakfast in bed'). Almost as if he feels

69

guilty for something. When he came in from the pub last Wednesday, Zoe was an hour into a chick-flick and had expected him to be loud, smelly, kissy, irritating, but he'd come in quietly, whispered an apology then kissed her on the cheek before going through to the kitchen and microwaving a bowl of leftovers. Zoe had turned up the volume on the TV, but Alex had eaten quietly on the opposite end of the sofa, checking his phone periodically, but going out of his way, it seemed, not to distract her. Ironically, Zoe found this more distracting than the anticipated barrage of interruptions, questions and snide commentary on the film. Before the film finished, Alex had washed the dishes and gone upstairs to brush his teeth. When Zoe went up after him, she found him in bed, reading. They talked for five minutes, and while Alex wasn't exactly remote, neither was he overly forthcoming. He answered her questions and enquired after her day, but he was just ... *off*. In the dark of the room, with Alex sleeping beside her, Zoe recalled a scene from the movie, in which the heroine discovers her reliable, faithful – boring, even – boyfriend had been cheating on her for almost a year. The thought presented itself, like an unwelcome guest at a party, and Zoe had found herself holding her breath as she studiously ignored it.

Because that was a film and this is her life and Alex would never do that.

Do what, Zoe?

She looks at her reflection in the compact mirror.

Is Alex cheating on me?

Zoe doesn't believe he is, but of course it's possible. More likely is that after nearly a year of living together, he has simply become complacent. Or bored. He could be; after all, hasn't Zoe been guilty of complacency, too? *And we all know what bored men do*, says the unwelcome guest.

And what if he was cheating on her? How would she feel about that? The truth is, Zoe isn't entirely sure. Of course she would feel betrayed, embarrassed, angry . . . But – and maybe this is why she has been reluctant to address the idea – maybe she would be relieved. Because there would be no second chances. Her brain – independently of its owner, it seems – presents the consequences and logistics: the mortgage; the dishwasher; the sofa; the cushions; the Scrabble-print mugs, a single A and a solitary Z. The details move freely through her consciousness, rapid and scattered and unushered. *He left his girlfriend for you. Not true: he left her for himself. But he cheated on her for you, didn't he?* She considers the wine decanter, a moving-in present from her parents – surely she has the claim on this item, even though it's Alex not her who ever bothers to use it. The bedding – someone has to take it; to sleep alone under the covers they bought together. Whereas the other will have to spend ninety quid on a new set of linen. And what of the bricks and mortar? Could Alex afford the mortgage on his own? Maybe; but Zoe certainly couldn't. Would he buy her out, or would they sell, and can she force the issue if he resists?

So what is this, Zoe? Is it cold feet, or something more significant? She doesn't know, and worse than that, she doesn't know *how* to know. *And why now?* Why now and not before you signed up to a twenty-five-year, six-figure mortgage?

When Alex had first suggested buying a house together, she had been in her new job for over a year. And again, she reminds herself that it was Alex who supported her – in pocket and morale – through this frightening transition. She was riding high on the excitement of seeing her first picture book in print. The author had even taken on board one of Zoe's suggestions and given the bumblebee a pair of love-heart sunglasses. While they were promoting the book, the author had given several readings at bookshops and book fairs, and they had given away pairs of love-heart sunglasses to the children in attendance. Seeing these delighted, fat-faced children sit, fidget, giggle and cry through these events had made Zoe incredibly broody, and whenever she picked up a copy of the *Busiest Bee* she imagined reading it to her own child (a girl), and telling her *Those sunglasses were your mummy's idea*. And so, when Alex had said *Let's buy a place of our own*, parenthood was the first thing Zoe thought of. Before a mortgage or a wedding or where they would live or what types of plates they would buy, she had imagined a nursery. Because isn't that what happens in a new home? Maybe that's why she had agreed so readily.

That or the smell.

They had been together for almost two years and were already renting a small two-bedroom flat together. The couple in the house next door argued and banged doors on a daily basis, and the Nepalese family in the flat below cooked fish-head stew at least twice a week, suffusing every cubic centimetre of air with an almost palpable seaside stench that would swell and fade but never fully clear. She suspected the smell had impregnated her clothes, but she had become so accustomed to the pong, it was hard to be sure. And then one November night, with the sound of an argument blasting through the walls and the smell of fish guts wafting up the stairs, Alex had said why didn't they buy a place of their own?

Zoe had laughed, assuming Alex was merely passing comment on their various domestic pollutions.

'Is that a fish joke?'

'What?'

'The smell. Cod, haddock, a *plaice* of our own.'

Alex laughed and kissed her like he loved her. 'P–L–A–C–E. We've got the multiple.'

'Multiple?'

'On our salaries. We could do it; we could borrow enough to buy a flat, maybe a small house.'

'You're serious?'

'Here's the thing. I've got enough saved for about half a deposit. But . . .' He raised his eyebrows.

Alex was earning good money by now, including a sizable annual bonus. And he'd been prudent, saving and investing, since the day he began work. Zoe, on the other hand, had a lot of nice shoes and expensive handbags.

'I don't have more than a couple of grand.'

'What about your folks?'

Zoe took a deep breath, blew it out in a long steady stream. She already knew she would ask, and that her parents would agree to lend her the money. It would be a loan, of course, but there would be no rush and no interest. Still, it felt appropriate at least to pretend that it wasn't a foregone conclusion. Alex's father had died when he was twelve, and his mother had struggled to raise him and his brother, working several jobs, taking in ironing and buying groceries at the end of their shelf life or in bashed packaging to make their meagre means go further.

'I'll ask,' Zoe had said.

But even with the loan from her parents, their options were limited. For months, they spent their weekends and evenings viewing neglected flats and squashed houses at the far reaches of the various tube lines. 'Doer-uppers' in estate agent speak; places where a couple with vision could 'place their stamp'. But despite the peeling paint, bad wallpaper and worn carpets, it was an exciting time. They drank in a variety of oppressive pubs, scribbling notes on the property sheets and exercising not so much their vision, but a pragmatic blindness towards the scowling locals and depressed high streets lined with poundshops, bookmakers and whitewashed windows. Balancing the variables in their small equation – size, setting, squalor – they settled on a 'cosy' house in tired but serviceable repair, two tube stops or a good walk from a fashionable area with trendy bars. There was no Starbucks or organic deli, but they did have a Sainsbury's Local and two pubs that it felt reasonably safe to drink in. They were further encouraged by the high proportion of what Alex called 'PLUs' – People Like Us: young professionals in nice shoes, returning home from gainful employment, who would, with their collective optimism and need for good coffee, drag the area up to par with its near neighbours.

The baby hadn't happened. Not that it would; you needed to stop taking the pill first, and before you did that, it was considered polite to discuss the matter with the man donating the other half of the genetic goods. And Zoe wasn't ready for that conversation; the maternal pangs had passed, replaced by more practical concerns – a pay rise, new windows, taps that didn't drip. A clearer sense of herself, perhaps. Neither had they discussed marriage in anything other than an indirect fashion, but then, they had only been living together for nine months. And, again, a conversation Zoe was in no immediate hurry to hold. She wants these things – a husband, children, family – but ... well, she'd at least like to sort out the carpets first.

She remembers clearly the day they moved in, and the memory makes her smile. They had a supper of fish and chips, and champagne out of coffee mugs. She remembers Alex saying he would 'wash the dishes' before scrunching up the chip paper and tossing it nonchalantly over his shoulder. She remembers sleeping on an inflatable mattress for two weeks before their bed arrived; Alex inviting her every night to 'climb aboard the Love Boat'. The airbed would deflate slowly overnight, so that if they slept for more than seven hours they would wake to find themselves grounded on the floorboards. It took them half a day to assemble the new bed; Alex giving himself blisters from gripping the handle of their cheap screwdriver. That evening, sitting in front of the TV, Zoe had kissed his sore hands and one thing had led smoothly to another. They had laughed afterwards at the irony of spending four hours assembling a bed only to make love on a lumpy sofa. She feels nothing but love recalling these moments of simple affection and spontaneous intimacy. *Focus on the positive*, she tells herself. Forget the patches of paint on the bedroom wall, the creaky floorboard, the toothpaste on the bathroom mirror – focus on the way he kissed you this morning, the way he looks at you when he's horny; think about the romantic gestures (a Valentine's Day trail of M&Ms leading from the front door to the bedroom where her man lay waiting with a bottle of fizz on the bedside table. Laughable really, but she knows that's part of the point.). Focus on his hair, his footballer's bum and the fact that he got out of bed to fetch breakfast in bed. Wherever that got to.

Henry

The Stone Stairs Don't Creak

He saw Bobbi tonight, out there beyond the croquet lawn. She lives in Spain now, but has come back to be one of April's bridesmaids. Henry wonders what her dress will be like; will her cleavage be on display? Her toned back and shoulders?

At dinner Brian had insisted it was part of the best man's responsibility to drink anything the groom didn't. By ten o'clock he was bouncing off the walls and in danger of putting his elbow through a priceless vase. Henry and his father – a professional in the art of manoeuvring drunks – escorted Brian up to bed. As they walked back down the stairs to join the rest of the party, his father put a heavy arm around Henry's shoulders. Henry remembers asking his father to show him his muscles when he was a boy. He recalls his awe at seeing his old man's bicep contract into a hard mass that conjured the image of nothing less impressive and destructive than a cannon ball. Clive Smith cupped the side of his son's face and stroked his cheek. The gesture seeming to say, *You'll be alright, son. Everything will be alright.*

As his father detoured into the gents, Henry found himself alone for what felt like the first time in a long time. All day he had been surrounded by people, posing for photographs, organizing, smiling. And this small moment of solitude felt like a glass of cold water. Instead of rejoining the dwindling party, Henry doubled back on himself and slipped out of a side door into the castle grounds. He wondered if April might be having the same idea, and hoped not. But he imagined she would be in bed by now, face stripped of make-up, hair plaited to keep it free from knots. It was cold and Henry shivered as he walked around the front lawn, staying close to the perimeter where he would be less noticeable against the bordering hedges. As the castle receded behind him, Henry wondered how long a person could survive outside in this cold – it can't have been more than two or three degrees – wearing nothing more than a pair of jeans and a t-shirt. It was refreshing, though, and Henry enjoyed the sharp sensation of cold in his scalp and across his back; he embraced it and walked on towards the koi carp pond at the far end of the grounds.

Looking out of the window now, Henry imagines he sees himself sneaking across the wide lawn, the idea of absconding forming in some sub-cellar of his mind. Cold wind leaks around the old diamond-shaped panes. Beside the window is an armchair, upon which Henry's wool jumper sits like a grey, curled-up cat. He pulls it on, continuing to stare out into the dark.

As he had approached the pond, Henry saw a shape and stopped walking. Someone, a woman, was sitting at a bench and he wondered if April had ventured out after all. He stood still, breathing silently, contemplating a slow retreat when, his eyes adjusting to the dark, the shape at the bench resolved itself into the familiar form of Bobbi. The varsity undercut grown out now, her indecisive ringlets once again rolling free in a thousand different directions. Henry exhaled and Bobbi turned to face him.

'Penelope,' she said. 'What you doing out here?'

'Freezing.'

Bobbi, wrapped up inside a thick coat, patted the bench beside her. 'Snuggle in,' she said. Henry sat and Bobbi put an arm around his shoulders, kissing him firmly but chastely on the cheek. 'God. You're like ice.'

'I'm a tough guy.'

'In your dreams. Nervous?'

Henry laughed. 'Too late for that now.'

'You said it, Penelope.'

And what he wanted to do was fuck Bobbi right there on the soft, cold mud. He imagined that her body was communicating the same need to his. He felt certain that if he were to turn to her, thread his fingers into her curls and pull her face to his, she would respond fully – pushing her tongue into his mouth, pressing her face hard against his own. He would unbutton her jeans, push them down past the curve of her arse and around her legs and – without a word said by either of them, neither caution nor encouragement – they would fuck with no one but the moon as witness. They would pull their clothes on, kiss like old friends, and never talk about or acknowledge what they had done. When he saw her in the morning, she would smile as if nothing had happened, and Henry might even wonder if it had.

Sitting beside her, feeling her heat radiate into him through their layers of clothes, Henry said, 'It's late.'

Bobbi made a sound at the back of her throat – *uh huh*.

He wanted to kiss Bobbi goodnight, just a kiss on the cheek, but didn't dare. He walked away from the bench, back to the castle, back to his wedding party. He drank two large whiskies in quick succession, forced a big idiot grin, said goodnight to those still hanging on and trudged upstairs to 'get my beauty sleep'. 'Too late now,' the men chorused, and everybody laughed. No doubt about it now, though, he is going to look awful today. He glances at the clock – 3.49 – and his eyes feel raw and swollen with fatigue.

Again, he asks himself the question: *Which is worse, marrying the wrong woman, or jilting her on her wedding day?*

The question begs another: *Who is the right woman?*

Not Bobbi, he knows that much. She is too ... transient, perhaps. Insubstantial, maybe. But whatever Bobbi lacks, she has something April doesn't. She does something, moves something, kindles something that his fiancée doesn't. And whatever it is, it diminishes April.

Not sleeping with a bridesmaid on the night before your wedding is, Henry knows, nothing to be proud about. But he is nevertheless glad that he didn't. It would confuse things. Guilt encouraging him to stay; an illicit orgasm urging him to leave.

Besides the clothes he wore yesterday, Henry has a clean t-shirt to wear in the morning and then his rented tux for the ceremony. Hanging on the back of the bathroom door is a new white shirt, never worn. He has a coat, his phone and his wallet. He has keys to the brand new front door he is supposed to open in two weeks' time before carrying his new bride across the threshold.

Sitting on a low antique desk is a pad of paper, printed

with the castle's letterhead. Henry takes a seat at the desk, picks up the complimentary biro and begins to write. He covers a single sheet of paper without looking up, then folds it neatly in half, resisting the impulse to read his unspeakable words. He stands from the desk, rolls the stiffness from his neck and pulls on his coat.

Walking towards the door he looks at Brian, as still and quiet as the hills, sleeping the sleep of a contented, uncomplicated man. He puts his hand to his friend's head, not sure what the gesture means or why he is making it. Daring Brian, perhaps, to stir in his sleep and ask Henry what the hell is he doing?

Brian snuffles, groans and rolls onto his opposite side, turning his back on Henry.

The windowless corridor is pitch black and Henry holds a hand to the wall, feeling his way as he creeps forwards to the top of the staircase. At school they had read *Great Expectations*. Henry hadn't enjoyed it, but a few images remain. He recalls Pip sneaking downstairs to steal something – food, he thinks, the image of a pork pie making Henry's stomach rumble. As Pip crept, the stairs creaked, seeming to shout 'Stop thief!' at every step. Henry remembers some dark character threatening to gut the boy – to remove and cook his liver – if he failed in his task, and Henry suspects he will suffer a fate no less gruesome if he is discovered on these stairs. The other memory is of Pip's benefactor, Miss Havisham, jilted by her betrothed, and now as pathetic and ruined as her decaying, infested wedding cake.

Henry pushes the thought away.

The stone stairs don't creak and Henry finds himself in the entrance hall of the castle. The double wooden doors are bolted top, centre and bottom, but he is not sure if they are also locked with a key. The bolts slide open with no more noise than the cracking of a knuckle – one, two, three. Henry glances about the hallway and up the stairs but sees no one, hears nothing. He takes hold of the door handle – a heavy iron hoop wider than his fist – and twists. The sound of the lock's mechanism echoes loudly in the open space, a heavy three-part *ka-ka-klunk*. Henry and the castle hold their breath, and the absconder fancies he can hear his own heartbeat. And then … the sound of movement.

Very slowly, Henry turns his head to the right, towards the room allocated to the Smith party this past evening. Through the open door the room is still and dark. Dark except for a single pool of light cast by a table lamp adjacent to a deep, wing-backed leather armchair. His father leans forwards, his shadowed face expressionless, the black hair falling across his forehead in messy strands.

His parents fought again last night and Henry wonders if his father harboured any doubts before his own wedding night. And if he could turn back the clock, would he act on them?

Father and son stare at each other with such calm stillness that Henry wonders if it couldn't be a dream, or its dark cousin. Henry takes a deep slow breath; he nods towards his father. Big Boots raises his hand and Henry sees he is holding a cut-glass tumbler a quarter-filled with amber liquid. His father tilts the glass in Henry's direction – a gesture of farewell – and relaxes back into the shadow of his chair. Henry steps out into the cold night, the first suggestions of grey infusing themselves into the black sky.

And he is gone.

Zoe

He Used To Be A DJ

Her stomach groans and she feels suddenly nauseous with hunger; too hungry to wait for Alex to bring her breakfast in bed. Zoe shakes out the duvet, plumps up the pillows and finishes dressing: a pair of knee-length shorts and the t-shirt Alex says makes her boobs look nice.

As she walks down the stairs, Zoe stops in front of a framed black and white photograph – one of five hung along the incline of these thirteen steps – showing her and Alex surrounded by boxes on the day they moved in. They had positioned Alex's camera on the mantel-piece and set the timer. When the mechanical shutter on the fifty-year-old Leica had eventually snapped open, it had caught Zoe laughing at some comment – she can't remember what – made by Alex. He was looking at her, amused and in love, while her face was creased with the beginnings of laughter – mouth partially open, eyes half closed. Knowing they had missed their cue, they reset the camera to take a 'proper' picture. But when Zoe had looked over the prints some weeks later, this was the one she chose to have enlarged and framed. *Our place*, she thinks, smiling.

'You home?' she calls, as she takes the last few steps at a trot. 'Alex? Babes?'

Although Zoe hadn't really expected to find Alex hidden inside his headphones, she is still disappointed to find he is not in the living room. She looks through the kitchen window into their 'yarden', but he is not home. She flicks on the kettle then opens the fridge to see what she can rustle up for breakfast. They have eggs, but no butter and no milk. There is a jar of jam and a tub of hummus, but they have no bread and the hummus looks worryingly bubbled. Half a cucumber, a single red pepper, a block of cheese, dry and cracked where someone – it could be her – failed to wrap it properly, and half a jar of olives. Mustard, anchovies, pesto, a swig of apple juice and a bottle of champagne. Zoe thought they had finished the fizz, but it seems Alex has found what must surely be the final bottle from their moving-in haul. Maybe they'll take it with them on their bike ride this afternoon. She notices the freezer door has not been closed properly and her first instinct is to be annoyed, but this is followed quickly by a pang of guilt. Her shins had been itching in the night, and when she'd told Alex, he had got out of bed to fetch ice cubes for her to hold against her skin. It had worked, too. *And how many men would do that for you on a Baltic October night?*

She puts two eggs in a saucepan full of boiling water and goes out into the yarden to extract the bicycles from the shed. The sun is out and despite the month it is warm, so Zoe eats her breakfast and drinks a mug of black tea, sitting on a folding chair outside. When she has finished, Alex is still not home so she finds her phone and calls him. She calls twice, but each time it rings through to voicemail, so she leaves two separate messages asking – with good humour, because the rest of this glorious day is still ahead of them and she doesn't want to spoil it by starting an argument – where the hell he has got to with her breakfast. She paces the living room, trying to recall exactly what he said before leaving:

I'll bring you breakfast in bed?

Or was it *I'll be back before breakfast?*

Either way, he's late. She seems to remember him saying he had to 'get some stuff', but maybe he'd said '*do* some stuff' – although what stuff she can't imagine. The thought suggests itself again: *What if he's cheating on you?*

But repeating the question does nothing to clarify the answer.

It occurs to her that he might be playing football. She checks the cupboard where he keeps his kit but everything appears to be there, mud-caked boots and all. Angry now, she calls his phone a third time, but when he fails to answer she resists the impulse to leave a message – the thought that something has happened to him has occurred to her and her anger is mixed with anxiety. She calls Darren, his best friend, but Darren hasn't heard from Alex since Wednesday. When Zoe says she hasn't seen him since around ten, Darren laughs and says, 'Typical. Probably bumped into someone and lost track of time, you know what he's like.' And while it rings true, it feels wrong. Darren wants to chat, he starts off on a 'Remember that time—' but Zoe is too distracted – too worried – to listen to an Alex anecdote, and she cuts Darren short, saying she has to go, then hanging up before he has finished a protracted goodbye.

Her heart is beating quickly, and Zoe realizes she is holding her breath. She forces herself to stand still, stop pacing, and breathe. If she stays in the house she'll drive herself mental, so Zoe makes the decision to walk up the road and see if, as Darren suggested, he's fallen into a coffee shop or the pub. Maybe there's a game on. Zoe has no clue when the football season starts or ends, but it seems there's always a match to catch. She has lost count of the times when, walking past a pub, Alex has stopped to look through the window at the big screen, 'Just checking the score, babes.' And more than once – the boyish smile, the funny head wobble – he has convinced her to go inside for a drink and watch the rest of the game.

Feeling a little exposed in her tight t-shirt, she pulls on a jumper, picks up her keys and phone and heads outside. When she hits the high street, Zoe has two options: up the hill towards the tube station is the new organic deli and the refurbished real-ale pub; downhill (she has never before made the connection) is the Aldi and the slightly scary locals' pub. If Alex were fetching breakfast provisions, would he have gone to Aldi or the deli? And if he were watching the game, would they show it in the downmarket drinker, the hipster ale-house, or both? Zoe turns right, heading up the shallow incline. The traffic on her side of the road is flowing freely, while the vehicles on the opposite side of the street are backed up halfway down the hill.

Maybe fifty yards from the deli, she sees the parked police car. A uniformed officer is leaning casually against a white van, talking to another man, this one wearing a fluorescent orange boiler suit. Her heart rate increases, and she quickens her step – trying not to think, but simply to cover the distance between here and there without running. The men appear relaxed, there are no flashing lights and no sirens, but a section of road is cordoned off with striped blue and white tape. She looks for an ambulance, but doesn't see one. A female police officer wearing a high-vis jacket is standing in the road, waving traffic past, and a second man wearing a boiler suit is sighting down a tripod-mounted device. Zoe wonders if a pipe has burst, or something similar – but then why the police?

As she draws closer to the area, she becomes aware of people standing on the pavement, talking solemnly and looking in the direction of the zoned-off area. There are fragments of broken glass, orange and white, scattered across the road; chalk marks have been drawn around a short quartet of skid marks. A splash of liquid, not blood, but it seems ominous and conspicuous on the dry tarmac.

As if coming out of a dream – *or a nightmare* – Zoe realizes she has stopped walking. She turns to the police officer leaning against the van and starts towards him; he sees her approaching and stands up straight, as if suddenly found out. He watches Zoe approach, and the man in the orange boiler suit goes to join his colleague at the tripod.

'Can I help you, Miss?'

'What happened?'

'There was an accident.'

'What accident? Was someone hurt?'

'You're shaking, Miss. Would you like to sit down?'

'My boyfriend,' she says. 'He left the house, a few hours ago I think and . . . what happened here?'

The man takes hold of Zoe's elbow and walks her to the police car; he opens the passenger-side door and Zoe sits inside without being asked. The officer walks around the front of the car then climbs in beside her.

Zoe turns to the man; he's removed his hat and she notices he is prematurely bald. Alex is beginning to recede in the same area; in two years his hair will look like this man's.

'Was somebody . . . did somebody get . . .' She can't finish the sentence, but the police officer understands. He nods.

'Can you describe your boyfriend?' the man says.

'He . . .' Zoe's voice sounds as if it belongs to someone else. 'He used to be a DJ.'

PART 2

Henry

A Ribbon-Wrapped Brick

It's past midnight and the surrounding fields are black and silent, disturbed only by me. Eight days ago I left my fiancée at the altar, but already it feels like an event that happened to someone else; an actor in a play, an other, a *him*. Not me. Surely I could never do a thing like that. A fox's eyes or maybe a cat's flash in the headlights, *Oh, it's you alright, we see you, Henry Smith*.

That's me; sneaking home undercover of the night, the way I snuck out on April just over a week ago. As the rental car emerges from a tunnel of old oaks reaching towards each other across the single lane, the road forks. To the left it curves back towards the castle; to the right, the village via the train station. Cold nauseating anxiety floods my empty spaces.

What were you thinking?

What are *you thinking?*

I turn off the engine and the silence envelops me like a dropped cloak. We tore down these lanes in this dark at this hour – me, Brian, and whoever else. Five or six to a car, taking the black corners at idiot speeds on old tyres. If anyone had been coming our way it would have been a busy week at the funeral co-op, but nothing ever did. We came out here in Mad George's Cortina once, April's big brother taking his hands from the wheel and holding them over his eyes. As the car veered towards the edge of the road, I went to grab the wheel and George lashed out, punching me in the ear. And then he was laughing and passing around cigarettes like nothing had happened.

Walking down these monotone lanes last week, I was breathing so heavily the sound filled my ears like surf and I wondered if I would hear an approaching car before it smashed the guts out of me. I closed my eyes and counted twenty-three steps before I slipped on something wet, and fell into a patch of gorse, scratching my cheek and twisting my ankle.

Sitting in the quiet car now I depress the brake as far as it will go and experience a jolt of pain in my ankle. I turn on the engine, put it into gear and turn right, towards home. If that's what it still is.

Last week I caught the first train from the station

without worrying about where it went. It was a new day, eight-thirty in the morning, when it arrived at Liverpool Lime Street, and from there – not on a whim exactly, but something similarly automatic – to Manchester airport. I've had time and solitude since to wonder why I went there, and the best I can come up with is simply that it was the next place I was meant to be. As if I could mitigate my failure to turn up at the altar by at least arriving at the airport. Our honeymoon flight was due to depart in a day and a half, and while I had no means or intention of taking the flight, neither did I have anywhere else to go. So I booked myself into the airport Hilton, punched the wall and opened the minibar. When I stepped out of the shower an hour later, my phone was fit to crack the glass with messages and missed calls from Brian and my mother. The messages progressed from concern to anger to incomprehension to threat. I listened to them all twice. It became apparent Brian had slept in, and when neither he nor I showed up for breakfast, the general consensus was that we were doing 'groom and best man things'. It wasn't until Big Boots all but knocked the door off the hinges that it was discovered Henry Smith had left the building. The note had been discovered but, so far, the only people who knew about it were Brian and my parents.

I sent the same message to Brian and my mother:

I'm sorry, but I can't go through with it. Am safe, will call in a day or so. Sorry.

One of them was going to have to break the news I was too much of a coward to break myself. But there was no turning back now. My phone started ringing within seconds. It would ring all day and nothing would change. *And Jesus Christ, can't they trace your whereabouts with these things?* I wrapped the phone inside a towel and smashed it against the corner of the sink, again and again until I heard the glass break and the device folded in on itself. And then I threw up the two minibar beers and packet of peanuts I'd eaten for breakfast.

As I pass the train station, I let the speed drop to below twenty. Eight days felt like a long time while I was isolated in the Manchester Hilton, eating room service and working my way through the minibar. But now, approaching the village in which I must surely be the most hated resident, it is obvious that one week and one day is no time at all.

As I pull into the car park at the back of my parents' pub, the headlights of the rental pick out my own car, parked in one of the three spots reserved for staff. I am relieved and surprised to see that – as far as I can tell – the windows are intact and the wheels appear to be inflated. There is also something balanced on the bonnet – a single house brick wrapped in a pink ribbon. And it's as if the temperature all of a sudden drops by ten degrees. After I've parked the rental at the far end of the car park, I walk back to my own car, a three-year-old Audi that felt like a foolish indulgence at the time, and feels even more so now with my almost-father-in-law's wedding present balanced on the hood.

I lift the brick slowly and rub my finger lightly across the uncovered paintwork – it appears to be unscratched. It's not until I move around to the side of the car to check the tyres that I see the twin gouges running the length of the car from front to back wings, gouged, at a guess, with the corner of a red house brick. The same has been done on the opposite side, two sets of parallel score marks reminiscent of the racing stripes on Mad George's Cortina.

'Time you call this?' says a gruff voice, and I whirl around to find my father standing in the doorway at the back of the pub kitchen. He's dressed in pyjamas, his hair messy.

'Dad.'

Dad holds a finger to his lips and beckons me inside with a movement of his head.

'Drink?'

I nod, and place my brick on the bar while Dad pours

two large whiskies. He hands one to me and taps his glass against mine before taking a drink.

'So,' he says, regarding the ribbon-wrapped brick, 'I would have brought it in for you, but your mother . . .' He shrugs. 'She thought you should see it.'

'Sleeping?'

Dad nods, swallows half of his drink.

'How's it been?'

Dad laughs quietly. 'How'd you think?'

'Fucked up a bit, haven't I.'

'Just a bit. Nice girl, too.'

'I know, but . . .'

My father appears to stare through me, the way he did on the night I left the castle. He will have gone to bed with the knowledge of what would unfold the following day. The following morning, as my mother flitted about the room in a state of high excitement, he would have shaved, combed his hair and dressed in his tuxedo knowing – or at the very least suspecting – that it was all in vain.

'That night,' I say.

Dad nods, three slow, solemn movements of his thick neck.

'I'm sorry I put you through that.'

Dad widens his eyes sardonically.

'The morning must have been . . .'

He opens his mouth, but the floorboards creak upstairs and he closes it again. Dad glances towards the ceiling, puts a hand on my shoulder and squeezes. He finishes his drink then nods at mine, and when I've drained the glass he takes them both to the optic and refills them with tall measures.

Feet on the stairs, then my mother's voice: 'Clive?'

'In here.' He looks at me, nods, mouths the word *Okay?* And I nod back.

The door at the foot of the stairs opens. As if her still-waking brain has decided it's not yet ready to process the situation, Mum directs her attention to my father, standing behind the bar. 'What are you doing?' she says, rubbing her eyes. 'I heard . . .'

And then her brain catches up.

She freezes for a second, then slowly lowers her hands from her face. I've seen tapes of my father's fights and the way he would stare down his opponent before the referee told the boxers to touch gloves and protect themselves at all times. My father never looked away, and the threat and menace he was able to project with nothing more than his eyes was unnerving. I have stood across the ring myself, looking into the eyes of an opponent who is doing his best to conceal his own fear and dial up mine; sometimes it worked, other times I could see through the scowl to the doubt. None of it comes close to the way my mother looks at me now.

'Mum.'

'You.'

'I . . . hi . . .'

'You.'

Dad clears his throat and my mother turns slowly to face him. 'You'd better put something in a glass for me,' she says.

'Wh—'

'I really don't care, Clive,' she says, walking towards the bar. 'Anything.'

Dad selects a tall tumbler and mixes a gin and tonic complete with ice and a slice of lemon. The whole process is ludicrous. He puts the drink down in front of my mother, who is sitting two stools down from me, as if she can't trust herself to be within arm's length of her son.

'Where have you been?'

'Hotel.'

My mother snorts derisively. '*Hotel*. Alright for some, isn't it? Have fun, did you?'

I almost answer, but Dad catches my eye and shakes his head slowly.

Mum takes a sip of her gin and tonic, turns on her stool and throws the rest of the drink at me. Typical of a landlord's wife, she is an excellent shot, and pretty much every drop of cold liquid hits its mark. One of the ice cubes catches me on the lip, another bounces off my forehead.

'Jesus, Mum!'

And she's off her stool and on me before I can raise my arms to defend myself. She is hitting me about the face, neck, chest and shoulders, slapping me, hitting with her forearms and the sides of her fists. She's shouting, too, an incoherent garble of *you*s and *stupid*s and *bastard*s and *poor poor girl*s. When she runs out of breath she stops, and how I have managed to remain on my stool is a miracle. My mother's face is red and wet with sweat and tears, strands of hair stuck to her cheeks and forehead.

Like a fighter at the end of a round, my mother returns to her stool. Big Boots puts a fresh gin and tonic in front of her, and I note that this one contains considerably less ice. We all sit in silence while my mother regains her breath and decides what to do with her drink. She takes a sip, and my father refills my glass.

'How could you?' she says.

My mother looks me in the eye, and when she continues to hold my gaze in the echoing silence, I realize that the question is not rhetorical. It crosses my mind to shrug, to try and communicate in a simple physical gesture the confusion, sadness, regret, hopelessness and complexity of my dilemma and actions. But it might be interpreted as indifference.

'It wasn't right,' I say.

My mother's jaw clenches. She pushes her hands through her hair, brushing it back off her face and twisting it into a rough ponytail. With no make-up and her cheeks livid with blood, she is mesmerizingly handsome. So much so I almost comment on it.

'Not right?'

I shake my head.

'What exactly wasn't right, Henry? My God, that girl. She's gorgeous, kind . . .' As if answering her own question, my mother's list of April's qualities trails off into silence.

'It's like in those films we used to watch.'

Mum takes a drink and then, very carefully, sets down her glass on the bar top. 'Films?'

'Cary Grant,' I say.

'What are you talking about?'

'Cary Grant and Rosalind Russell,' I say. 'They had . . .' The word I want to say is 'chemistry', but I have a strong feeling that it won't fly. I glance at my father and he winces as if reading my mind, as if braced for an impact. '. . . something,' I say.

'Cary Grant?' my mother says again. She glances at her husband behind the bar, paunchy and tired, his thin pompadour hanging in strands. 'Let me tell you something,' she says, giving me the full heat of her attention. 'This is real life, not a fairytale.'

'I'm sorry, Mum, I just . . . I'm sorry.'

She slides down from her stool, puts her arms around me and hugs me tightly, kissing my neck and stroking my hair. 'I'm sorry I hit you.'

'I deserved it.'

'You deserve a damn sight more than that,' she says, disengaging. 'And you'll probably get it before this is done with.'

'Probably.'

'So,' says Mum. 'What's the plan?'

I shake my head.

'Where will you go?'

'What do you mean?' I say, looking around the empty pub. 'I don't have anywhere to . . . I thought . . .'

My mother looks at me as if I've just said something funny.

'You're not planning on staying here?'

'Well . . .'

'Henry, love. That's just not going to work out. I love you to death, son – to death – even if you are a stupid,

stupid bastard. But ... here?' My mother shakes her head sadly but emphatically. 'No. That just isn't going to work, love.'

'But ... what about my job?'

She laughs. 'Do you really think anyone within twenty miles of here is going to let you near them, Henry? God, they wouldn't take a pint off you, let alone a root canal. Son, you can't be here.'

I turn to my father. He shrugs. 'Don't see how you can stay, son. Sorry.'

'I ...' I hold up my glass. 'I've been drinking.'

'I'll set the alarm,' Dad says.

'Set it early,' says my mother.

Zoe

Triple On The I

We're at three thousand metres, my parents and me, playing Scrabble in a faux-log chalet and drinking thin red wine (although not as much and as fast as I want). The mountains are thick with snow, but the ski season hasn't officially started yet and the lifts don't open until December. Even so, Mum thought the scenery and fresh air would be good for me.

'I'm suffering from vowel obstruction,' my dad says – a familiar joke around this dog-eared board – then, nervously, glances up from his tiles, checking whether this mild humour has upset or offended me.

I harrumph a short laugh, and while Dad drops his eyes back to the board I take a long sip of my wine, aware of my mother watching me from the corner of her eye.

'Have some of mine, I think I've got all of them,' I say.

Mum laughs lightly, putting her hand on my wrist.

It's been almost three weeks; a fragmented and disjointed sequence of grief, shock, guilt, compassion and bureaucracy – as random and incomprehensible as the seven letters sitting in front of me.

E-E-E-I-G-L-V

One letter short of L-O-V-E. One shy of L-I-K-E. Funny how the two words begin and end with the same letters, identical on the surface, entirely different at their core. Live, too, ironically. This tragic coincidence should jolt me into spontaneous tears, but it doesn't. In the first days after Alex's accident, I cried myself to sleep and cried myself awake. I cried myself sick, literally; sobbing hysterically until I dry retched and tasted bile mixed in with the snot and salt of my tears.

Less so since the funeral, though. Since the slow mechanism wound Alex's coffin towards the flames, the main thing I feel is numb. Numb and guilty.

They say you grieve for yourself. Although no one has said it to me personally. But it's one of those things we trot out in the days following death. To your face, they say, *I'm sorry for your loss*, which amounts to pretty much the same thing – the idea that we cry for our personal loss, more than for the lost themselves.

What else they say is, *You were so good together*. And I

nod and say *Yes*, and *Thank you*, and I let them hold my hand while I cry. But they're wrong; we weren't *so* good together. We were *okay* together, and as much as I try to live up to the role I've been thrown into, I'm not crying for me, I'm crying for Alex.

He was kind, sensitive and considerate more often than he wasn't. He was a good man. Funny, clever, cool. He loved his mother and brother, was loyal to his friends, loved me, I think, and it breaks my heart that his life was stopped short. But a part of me (a cold, dispassionate part I don't like very much) knows that Alex's death has given me a way out of a bad situation. It's a thought I try very hard not to think, and if I could bring Alex back, I would, but not for us to be together again.

'Here we go,' says Dad, laying down two tiles on the back end of a dormant word. '*Wrongly*, what's that ... fourteen, not too shabby, considering.'

If I woke up now to find it were nothing more than a dream; if I woke to the sound of Alex returning from the shops, clattering through our front door with a bag full of provisions, then I would cry into my pillow with relief. We would eat breakfast, ride our bikes, drink a bottle of wine and maybe have an early night. And then the next day, or week or certainly not longer than a month later, I would tell him it's over. Certain in the cold knowledge

I had acquired during this nineteen-day nightmare of death and grief, I would break his heart, and it would be horrible. We would fight, call each other names, cry and drink and make accusations and let our worst qualities bubble up to the surface and we would come to loathe each other. But his death has spared me that, so no, I don't cry for me, I cry for Alex. I have cried my eyes dry out of grief and guilt and relief.

'Just going to get another,' I say, picking up the empty wine bottle.

'I could make hot chocolate,' Mum says. 'Marshmallows!'

'Thanks, but I'll stick with wine. Anyway, it's your go.'

Mum glances at Dad. 'I'll make it,' he says. 'Just don't go looking at my tiles.'

'Sure,' I say. 'Thank you.'

Mum rearranges her tiles while Dad moves through to the kitchen. 'You okay?' she asks.

'Yeah, I'm fine. Numb, you know, but ... just a bit numb.'

'Did you speak to work?'

I nod. 'I'm going to go back in on Tuesday. Start off with short days.'

'That sounds sensible.'

'Means I don't have to cry in front of the other commuters,' I say, still not sure how much humour is appropriate two and a half weeks after your boyfriend was killed while crossing the road.

Mum wraps her hand around my fingers and squeezes. 'Damn letters,' she says.

My mother is a fiercely competitive Scrabble player, taking longer than everyone else over her turn, playing tactically and challenging frequently. But looking at the board now with its primary school vocabulary, I'm pretty sure she's going easy on me.

'Will someone stay with you?' she asks.

'They would if I asked, but ... I think I'll be okay on my own now.'

'Are you sure, Zoe? You've had a dreadful shock, a ... a heck of a shock.'

I nod – *I'm sure.* Of all the emotions I'm going through, loneliness is not one of them. The compassion that people have gently wrapped around me, I don't deserve it. While Alex lay dying on the side of the road, I was lying in bed thinking unkind thoughts. Maybe he was already dead as I curled up under a warm blanket, cataloguing all of his faults and indiscretions. I don't deserve sympathy, and the weight of it is suffocating. I don't want to be protected and hugged and looked at like I'm about to break. I want to be by myself. I need space – not to think, necessarily, I've done too much of that – but just to breathe.

Rachel met me at the hospital, held my hand while the policewoman – the family liaison officer – asked me to describe Alex: his hair, any scars, any tattoos or distinguishing marks. My friend for more than ten years, Rachel was the first person I called after Alex invited me on a date. She put her arm around my shoulder while the policewoman showed me a photograph of a tattoo taken from the body they had removed from the road several hours earlier. Alex's tattoo, a Thai character on his left shoulder meaning love. When I'd teased him about its significance – *Was it for Ines, your German girl?* – Alex had denied it, saying the tattoo was a snap decision made high on weed. But I was never convinced.

When they took me to Alex's body, the man pulled the sheet back just far enough to show me one half of Alex's face. His eye closed, his stubble in need of a shave.

We spent that night at Rachel's, staying up late, drinking, scrolling through photographs, crying. Her fiancé, Steve, cooked supper, kept our glasses full and did his best to stay out of the way. On Sunday Vicky went over to the house and filled a bag full of clothes, underwear and toiletries, and in the evening the three of us went through the same vigil on the sofa. A far cry from our university days, alternately crying and laughing at weepy movies, never imagining these fictional dramas could ever reach out into our own worlds. They took alternate days off work, so I wouldn't be alone. My parents wanted to come up immediately, but the prospect of too much sincere compassion filled me with a hot destabilizing dread. They arrived the following weekend; bags of food and an inflatable mattress in the boot of the Land Rover. They insisted on sleeping in the spare room while I slept in *our* bed. I'd have preferred it the other way around, giving me a good reason to change the sheets Alex and I had made love on just seven days previously.

On Tuesday morning, we set off early and drove to Yorkshire for the funeral. I sat in the back, pretending to sleep so I didn't have to speak. After the service, at Alex's mother's house around a buffet of over-buttered sandwiches and dry sausage rolls and too much wine, the other thing people say is: *I can't imagine how you feel.* And you think to yourself, *No, you really can't.*

Remembering how I sat on the bed in Alex's old room on the morning of the funeral, crying with his mother and telling her how much I loved him and how devastated I was, I feel hot with embarrassment and shame. As we cried with our arms around each other, I underwent something like an out-of-body experience, and I wondered how long it would be before I could stop calling or returning her emails.

'Three *chocolat chaud*,' says my father, setting a tray down on the table.

'Thought we'd lost you,' says Mum, the short laugh dying on her lips as she realizes what she's just said. She glances at me and I pretend not to have noticed. A strategy I have had ample opportunity (*dead even, heaven help us, you're killing me!*) to perfect since the accident.

'Right,' says Mum, clicking down four tiles. 'And all through the house, not a creature was stirring, not even a M-O-U-S-E. Double on the S, eight points.'

After the funeral my parents stayed one more night, during which arrangements were made to reconvene in France the following weekend. I promised that one of my friends would be staying with me, but after eleven days of constant watch and pity I was desperate for space and silence. I changed the sheets the minute my parents drove away, waving and blowing sad kisses through the Land Rover's window. I cleaned all day and all night and well into the morning, dusting every square inch of the house, vaguely aware that dust was human skin; mine, my parents' and my dead boyfriend's. For reasons I'm not sure I understand – momentum, perhaps – I emptied every item of food from the fridge and then the cupboards. Vegetables, milk, packets and cans and jars of condiments. Every consumable item, with the exception of a single bottle of champagne, consigned to bin bags. I vacuumed the carpets, cleaned the windows, the mirrors, toilet, sinks and the tiles on the bathroom floor. I pulled the cushions from the sofa and the armchair, vacuuming up the dust and crumbs and pennies and pen tops. I polished door handles, light switches, the banister and every lampshade in the house before falling asleep on the sofa sometime in the early hours of the morning.

On Saturday, the night before we flew to France, Alex's London friends met for drinks in his memory. No one used the word 'wake', but that's what it was. I realized early on that my presence was killing the atmosphere, so stayed as long as was decent before making my excuses and calling a taxi. Besides which, I had to leave for the airport at eight the next morning. So this was not Zoe the magnanimous, this was Zoe the knackered with half a pizza and an entire bar of chocolate in the fridge.

As I opened the door to the taxi, a voice called my name. One of Alex's closest friends, Tom.

'Tom, hey.'

'Zo, I . . . I'm sorry we didn't get to talk. It's a bit . . . you know.'

I noticed Tom had his coat on. 'Are you not staying?'

Tom shook his head. 'Hugh's doing my head in, to be honest. The whole overdone grief thing. "To Al!"' he said, raising an invisible pint, mocking Hugh's loud and repeated toasts. 'Sorry.'

'It's fine,' I said, smiling, then, despite myself, laughing. I know how close Tom and Alex were, and I don't doubt his grief. 'I don't think Alex liked him all that much.'

'Well,' said Tom, rubbing a hand over his stubble, 'I'm afraid that if I stay much longer I might twat him.'

'Share a cab,' I said, and I knew exactly what I was doing.

'It's not really on your way, Zo.'

'I know. I . . . I don't feel like being on my own tonight. Watch a movie with me?'

We didn't even turn the TV on. Instead, we opened a bottle of wine and sat at opposite ends of the sofa with the bar of chocolate sitting on a cushion between us like a gradually diminishing barrier. When we started kissing, with instant and urgent intensity, I stood up from the sofa, taking Tom's hand and motioning for him to come with me.

He shook his head, 'Let's stay down here,' and pulled me back onto the seat beside him. Maybe it made him feel less guilty; fucking me on the sofa instead of his best friend's bed. But Alex and I had made love on those three cushions more than once, so there was no such leniency for my conscience.

'We can't sleep on here,' I said afterwards, the wine, the chocolate and the urgency finished.

'I'll take the bed, you take the sofa,' Tom said, laughing. And I was grateful for that; that he chose not to give the guilt any oxygen. That he didn't call a cab and leave me on my own like a coward.

'I'll get you a blanket,' I said, throwing a cushion at him.

We ate breakfast together the next morning, the final wisps of whatever had happened in the night lingering (an overlong good-morning kiss), before dispersing gradually over coffee (a touching of hands) and toast (a complicit, apologetic smile). We were embarrassed enough to satisfy decency, and both understood – I think – that this one time was forgivable and understandable and possibly even natural, but that it would never happen again.

'Zozo?'

'Sorry?'

'Your go, sweetheart.'

My parents are both smiling at me, attempting to project amusement instead of concern.

'Sorry, miles away. Blame the hot chocolate.'

I don't really know what that means, but my parents laugh and I make a show of examining my tiles.

E–E–E–I–G–L–V

117

From the minute I picked my last few tiles from the bag, I knew I could hang GRIEVE off the end of WRONG. But triple letter score on the V or not, I can't bring myself to do it. LIVE is slightly more bearable, but it'll only net me seven points, so is hardly worth the discomfort.

'R-E-L-I-E-V-E,' I say, 'triple on the I, twelve points.'

Henry

The Answer, I Think, Is Love

My hair is a mess.

Not just untidy or unkempt, but an erratic, uneven, split-ended disaster area. I've seen bus drivers with better hair. That said, I haven't had it cut since the week before my scheduled wedding, so this shouldn't come as a shock. A lot can happen in fourteen weeks. Looking at my reflection, if I had to guess my profession going by nothing but the chaos attempting to escape my scalp, I'd probably conclude I was the drummer in a pub tribute band – *Less Zepp, Deep Mauve, Bums N' Roses*, or something similarly cringeworthy. Or maybe I'd mistake me for a brilliant academic, an alcoholic mechanic, or a drug-dealing taxi driver. Not a dentist. Certainly not a hairdresser's son.

The man massaging my shoulders is called Gus, and he is the proprietor of this establishment. I haven't asked him to do this, and he didn't ask if I minded, but he's doing it all the same. Kneading the muscles of my neck as we both regard my cartoon mop. What I've asked this man to do is cut my hair, but he clearly doesn't know where to start. Nothing about Gus suggests a sexual inclination in any particular or exclusive direction, but he is certainly sexually *present* – confident, uninhibited, coiffed yet rough, ruggedly masculine yet somehow effete. If he has an orientation at all, I'd guess it's a three hundred and sixty degree humankind kind of thing. I wouldn't trust him with my girlfriend, if I had one, or my mother, or grandmother if I had one that was still breathing. Paradoxically, though, despite his palpable sexual readiness, I don't detect anything aimed at me. I'm probably below his radar. No, this massage, this deep, insistent full-handed mauling, seems to be the physical manifestation of Gus's thought process as he considers the quantum problem of my hair.

'I'm in your hands,' I told Gus after he sat me in the chair and asked what I wanted. Who knew he'd take it so literally.

'Let's give it a wash,' says Gus. 'Might make more sense once it's wet.'

In a peculiar variation on the great unfathomable tradition, the place is called The Hairy Krishna; the sign above the door features a fat Buddha with rock star locks, a pair of scissors in one hand and a hairdryer in the other.

After a hurried breakfast in the Black Horse three months ago (leaving the rental car under my old man's care), I pointed the brick-gouged Audi south, hitting London shortly after lunch. Following the path of least resistance, I found myself on a busy high street south of the Thames, with nothing more on my mind than a pee and a spot of lunch. After an overpriced pie and pint, I found a room in a guesthouse across the street, booked two weeks' accommodation and went back to the pub to watch the boxing. By the following Tuesday I had four offers of work and took the one closest to the guesthouse; eight weeks' paternity cover at a dental practice five minutes from my front door.

I have barely stepped beyond the triangle formed between the Red Lion, the Lavender Lodge and 32 White since. Within that roughly one mile isosceles are more amenities and distractions than in the entire village I called home for the majority of my life. Amongst others, there are bars, restaurants, gyms, a cinema, a supermarket, launderette and Gus's bohemian hairdressing salon. Not that I've availed myself to any great extent of the local attractions; I have worked every shift offered to me, including on-call duty over both Christmas and New Year's Day.

We also have two charity shops, one of which sold me fifty jigsaw puzzles for twenty-five pounds. The puzzles range from five hundred to two thousand pieces printed with detailed images of the countryside, the sky at night, and everything that lies between the two. I have even bought myself a specifically designed jigsaw mat, so I can roll up my work before turning in for the night. After my first four weeks in a single room in the Lavender Lodge, the 'premier suite' became available – double bed, TV, toilet, shower, bay window, mini kitchen and folding table. So I packed my bag and moved up one flight of stairs. Occasionally I venture beyond my small triangle to hit pads, jump rope and shadow box at a shabby boxing gym nudging the southeast border of the borough. Otherwise, I work, watch old movies, assemble poster-sized jigsaw puzzles and think.

I think about how I have exiled myself from my family and my home, how I have escaped to one of the most vibrant cities in the world, only to live like a hermit, shuttling between work and the sofa where I eat meals for one in front of old black and white movies I've seen dozens of times before. If I measure my life now against the one I ran out on, the significant differences are that I am now crushingly lonely but much improved at jigsaw puzzles. It's depressing.

I call my parents once a week, my mother alternating between tearful hostility and weepy melancholia, Dad talking about the pub, the weather, the fight if there's been one. In the first few weeks following my exile I called Brian, too, but we'd never talked on the phone before, other than to name a time and a pub, so our cross-country phone calls were awkward, tentative affairs. Maybe because the default topic was so uncomfortable. In the immediate aftermath of the ruined wedding, anyone even closely associated with me, meaning Brian, meaning my parents, was contaminated with the fallout. There was a general belief in the first wave of hysteria that the best man must have been complicit, and Big Boots had to physically restrain both Mad George and April's father as the mania turned into physicality. The Black Horse was boycotted, the way the home of a serial killer might be; a local embarrassment fit only for demolition or burning. Small pubs operate on a precarious profit margin at the best of times, and if it hadn't been for April's intervention, my parents could easily have gone out of business. Hearing this – how she would drink defiantly at the bar with my mother, and stand beside Big Boots in front of the big screen on fight night – I felt myself admire and . . . maybe even love her, more than I ever had before. This realization has caused me more than once to doubt the wisdom of my early morning flit, but I would never say as much to Brian. With stubborn parochial elasticity, village life appears to have contracted back into shape and routine, returning more completely to its old form the longer the irritant has been removed.

And if a year from now, I were to walk into the village, whistling a jaunty tune with a bindle over my shoulder and a cheeky apologetic grin on my face ... what then? Certainly no fatted burgers would be thrown on the barbecue. No, the obstinacy that keeps small towns constant comes with a long memory. The can of old vitriol would be opened, stirred and thrown over me and all within splashing distance. Probably, this is why Brian and I no longer talk. All for what? How, when and where does it end?

I think about this a lot, and I think I have the answer.

The answer, I think, is love.

Gus towels my thatch semi-dry and transfers me back to the chair in front of the mirror.

'Date?' he asks, running a comb through my hair.

I'm reasonably sure this is an enquiry rather than an offer, so I nod cautiously.

'Nice one,' says Gus, frowning at a hank of my hair.

If there's one thing the movies I watched with my mother have taught me, it's that love justifies everything. In *His Girl Friday*, Cary Grant schemed, lied, stole, kidnapped, and demonstrated a sociopathic lack of compassion and conscience – but it's okay. He did it for love. Dustin Hoffman in *The Graduate* stormed a wedding, assaulted the congregation with a crucifix and ran off with the bride. But it's fine, we get it, he was following his heart.

Love conquers, explains and excuses all. Love heals, too, and I want it to heal April. I hope she finds a better man than me, a better man for her. I doubt she will ever fully forgive me, and neither would I blame her, but she may at least come to tolerate me. And my mother will surely appreciate that it was all for the best once she sees April fulfil her own happy ending. And what about me? Would she wish anything less for her only son?

Last night I signed up to an online dating agency.

For the greater good, I told myself.

I was approximately fifteen hundred pieces into a two-thousand-piece haystack and finding it less exciting than you might imagine. The devil will find work for idle hands, they say. And, apparently, for fingers that do jigsaws. I opened my laptop and typed the word 'dating' into the search bar. Just to see what came up, of course. I clicked on the first link, out of nothing more than idle curiosity. A free trial, it said. So I filled in my name, chose an old picture, answered six inane questions. Clicked the red, heart-shaped button. Just for something to pass the time, really. Before I'd managed to assemble another twenty pieces of identical beige, I had three offers. The speed with which these responses came in might suggest a certain ... eagerness. But as I brushed my teeth before bed, one thing was glaringly apparent. No amount of romantic optimism could compensate for my hair.

'Undercuts are in,' says Gus.

'Hmmm, I dunno.'

'I know,' says Gus. 'Between me an' you, I find 'em a bit ...'

'Shit?'

'Yeah,' says Gus, slapping me on the back. 'Shit. Exactly.'

'Any ideas?'

Gus shakes his head. 'Jojo would know what to do.'

'Who's Jojo?'

'Genius with a pair of scissors. I'd be lost without her.'

'Where is she?'

Gus shrugs. 'Australia.'

'Maybe we should just start over,' I say to Gus.

'But we only just met,' he says, giving my shoulder a squeeze.

I reach up from under my gown and pull a length of

hair away from my head. Gus nods at me in the mirror, then inserts his hands into the depths of my hair, pushing and threading them through the dense mat until his fingers find my skull.

'Nice-shaped head,' he says.

'Thank you.'

'No birthmarks full of sixes?'

'None that I know of.'

'Fuck it,' he says. 'Let's find out.' And he moonwalks across the floor to retrieve his clippers, pirouettes and moonwalks back. 'Local?' asks Gus, examining my head and deciding where to start.

'Ish,' I say.

'That a northern accent?'

I nod.

'Whereabouts?'

'Middle of nowhere,' I say. And then I smile apologetically, hoping it will take the edge off my curt response to a friendly enquiry. This might be the longest face-to-face conversation I've had in the last two months that didn't involve teeth, and I don't want to ruin it.

'Sweet,' says Gus, and it looks like I'm off the hook. 'Grade one?'

'In for a penny . . .'

Gus adjusts the clippers, takes my head in his free hand

127

and ploughs an inch-wide furrow from the nape of my neck to my forehead. 'Country road,' he sings, laughing, 'take me home.'

To the place I belong.

'Work round here?'

The dental surgery is maybe a mile from The Hairy Krishna. But in contrast to my hometown, this triangular slice of South London is swarming with humans, and I am just one more anonymous shape.

'Out of work,' I say, which is eighty per cent true.

My eight-week contract at 32 White finished on Friday, but the new and thoroughly modern dad I covered for has decided he only wants to work a four-day week from now on. They have offered the other day – a Friday – to me. It's a friendly well-run practice, so I was happy to retain a slither of continuity in my new life. But one day a week isn't enough to pay the bills. I have savings, but they are dwindling, and I need to find something else to keep me occupied for the first four days of the working week. The only slight hint of urgency comes in the form of a thus far uncashed cheque to the tune of seventeen thousand, six hundred and forty-six pounds. One lunch hour, around two weeks after landing in London, I found myself gazing through the window of a baker's transfixed by a three-tier wedding cake. I might have stood there all day, but the sound of laughter from the other side of the glass snapped me back into the moment. What I'd been thinking was how much April's father had spent on cars and flowers and violinists and beer and wine and cake, just for me to go and turn it into his daughter's worst nightmare. That evening I wrote a cheque then drove all the way to a village outside Luton to post it. Six weeks later the money hasn't left my account, and even though I sincerely want it to, the uncertainty has taken on the form of a dark shadow, roughly the shape of a dangling anvil.

'What d'you do?' says Gus, starting now on the western hemisphere of my skull.

'Hairdresser,' I say, smiling at his astonished reaction in the mirror.

'You're kidding?' he says.

I shake my head: *Nope, I'm serious.*

'You any good?'

'I can cut the second-best graduated bob in the middle of nowhere,' I tell him.

Gus points his clippers at my mad reflection. 'For real?'

I nod. 'For real.'

'Wicked,' he says. 'Wick*id*. Sixty quid a day or thirty-five per cent of your chair, whichever's highest. And' – he rubs his hand over the shorn side of my head – 'staff cuts are free. Just like that whale.'

'Willy,' I say.

'Who can tell,' says Gus, laughing.

Zoe

All Over The Place

Rachel is making a gin and slimline tonic last longer than should be legal, and Vicky – normally so reliable in these matters – has pulled the old palm-on-glass manoeuvre as I tried to top up her chardonnay. The second Tuesday in January was never going to be a wild night in the boozer, but I'm beginning to regret suggesting this 'quiet drink'. But it's an anniversary of sorts and I don't want to drink on my own.

Three years ago today Alex sent a message that I still have on my phone: **Single guy seeks disgruntled lawyer for bad wine, public snogging, naughty talk and snorty laughter. Beautiful smile preferable.**

There are more dates heading my way: the day we first met, our first kiss, the day we moved in together, his birthday, the day he died. Others, too, and if I'm not careful I'll ruin my calendar. But this one – the day it began properly – feels significant. I haven't told the girls; they're still treating me like I'm made of glass and it makes me want to scream or flash my boobs just to get a reaction.

'How's the first week back been?' Vicky asks.

'Okay,' I say, topping up my glass. 'It's been okay. Be better if everyone wasn't tiptoeing around like ... well, like my boyfriend had just ... you know ...'

Vicky doesn't exactly wince, but her features make all the preparatory contractions. Rachel takes a good swallow of her drink, which is something of a relief.

Things were less awkward in the immediate aftermath of Alex's death. The grief was a thing we could share and address and examine. But as that fades and we transition back to normality, it's hard to know exactly how to behave – how *okay* it's appropriate to be.

'I read a story about a pirate that wants to be a ballet dancer,' I say, and the girls turn their eyes back to me, talking over each other in their relief to be on sounder ground.

'That's awesome.'

'Sounds brilliant.'

'I love pirates!'

'Your job's *so* much more fun than mine.'

Work told me to take as much time off as I needed, but really, what else am I going to do? All my friends work, and after a week up the Alps in November and two weeks on the coast over Christmas, I've had as much of my parents' care and concern as I can handle for a while. The start of the New Year served as a neat opportunity to begin the process of picking up where I'd left off three months previously. Although where I'd left off, in any meaningful sense, I'm not sure. But work seemed as good a place as any to start.

I've never drunk so much coffee – it seems that no one can walk past my desk without asking if they can make me a drink, and they look so bloody uncomfortable, I don't have the heart to say no. I'm on light duties, which is just as well because I spend around half my day in the loo on account of all the coffee. Not that anyone has put it that way, 'light duties', but I'm being well insulated from anything too demanding or stressful. The majority of my day revolves around reading manuscripts, but when they seldom run to more than a thousand words, I take care to read slowly.

'What's it called?' asks Rachel.

'*Pirates and Pirouettes*,' I say, and I laugh reflexively at the ridiculousness of it all. The laugh catches, everyone relieved to have a legitimate outlet, and it feels like the air around us lightens a little.

Vicky reaches across the table and places her hand on top of mine. People do this a lot. And more than the tears and earnest sympathy and flowers, lasagnes and casseroles, more than the sleepovers and messages of support, it's this, this quiet articulate contact that gets me the most.

I have become reasonably good – competent, at least – at holding myself together. Learning the knack of composure, of controlling my irregular beats of grief and guilt. There are songs, situations and places that bring on the memory of Alex and all that comes with it. I avoid them when I can, and brace myself when I can't. On Monday nights Al used to put the bins out. I do that now. The trick, I've found, is not to overthink it – I put the kettle on and listen to the water boil as I remove and knot the bag. As I carry it outside, I think about the coffee I'm going to make: a spoon and a half of instant, milk on the granules, water on the milk. And before you know it there is a new liner in the bin and you don't have to reapply your mascara. People, too, have their own tells. Reacting to a faux pas, perhaps, or an item in the news, someone will exhale through their nostrils and turn a small sympathetic smile towards me. Seeing this, I fix my own smile, control my breathing and prepare myself for whatever – a touch, a word – comes next. I hold myself together. But this, this gentle contact that says: *It's good to see you doing better, Zoe*; it comes without warning and feels like a hard mass between my lungs. It triggers a reflex of despair and I simply melt into quiet uninvited tears.

'Oh, Zo,' says Rachel, squeezing my hand tighter and wringing out a fresh pulse of tears. 'Zo.'

'Hey,' says Vicky, placing her hand on my shoulder, 'are you okay?'

I withdraw my hand, ostensibly to wipe my eyes, but essentially because if I allow myself to be held a moment longer I might dissolve.

I nod: *Yes, I'm fine.*

'Was it something I said?'

'No. Just ... caught me off guard ... I'm fine. I'm fine.'

'Are you sure?'

I fan my face and nod.

Vicky is looking at my hair again.

You hear stories about people's hair turning white overnight, but it doesn't happen that way. The change takes as long as it takes for your hair to grow through. If you were Sinead O'Connor, I suppose, you might turn white over the course of a day or two, but my hair hangs down to my shoulders. Small mercies; my hair has only lost its pigment in a localized patch three fingers wide at my right temple. Where I used to twist and pull it back in my hair-pulling days, as a matter of fact – so maybe it's my own fault. At the moment it's around an inch long, but by summer I'll have a full-length streak like some kind of Disney villain or B-movie vampire.

I run my hand through my hair and Vicky looks away.

'How's the wedding prep?' I say to Rachel.

Rachel shrugs. 'Oh, fine. I'm mostly looking forward to the honeymoon now.'

This, I am certain, is a lie for my benefit. In the three months before Alex's accident, Rachel could barely talk about anything that didn't involve flowers, lace or something blue. But in the three months since, she has swerved every attempt I've made to discuss her upcoming wedding. As if she feels guilty for having a still-breathing boyfriend. The big day is seven months away now, and I'm supposed to be a bridesmaid, but knowing Rachel I'll bet she's agonizing over whether or not this is still appropriate. Not for her sake, but for mine. Watching her face trying to settle on a suitable expression, I know that I have to pierce this fog or choke on it. So, before I've thought it through, I hear myself say: 'I snogged someone on Christmas Eve.'

'Oh,' says Rachel.

Vicky nods. 'Blimey.'

'Wow,' says Rachel, 'that's ... good,' her face saying something subtly different – *that's odd*, maybe, or *that's quick*. 'Right?' she says, turning to Vicky.

'Yeah,' says Vicky, pouting with sincerity. 'I mean, it's only a snog, isn't it. Christmas Eve, and all that.'

Well, the snog was the least part of it, but I'm not sure my friends are ready to deal with all of that right now.

'Anyone we ... know?'

'Old school friend,' I say. 'A bunch of us meet up in the pub every Christmas Eve.'

'Oh,' says Vicky smiling with relief. 'Great.'

'Yeah,' says Rachel. 'Great.'

'So,' I say. 'Do I still get a bridesmaid's dress, or what?'

Rachel surprises me by throwing her arms around me and kissing my ear. 'Oh, Zoe. Really? Do you still ... really?'

'Of course. I mean, come on – free dress!'

'Oh, thank God,' she says, reaching for her gin and tonic and finding it empty. 'You have no idea how much I've been ...' She stops, puts a hand to her mouth. 'Zoe, I'm sorry, I sound so selfish.'

'Of course you don't; it's your wedding, for God's sake. I'm happy for you.'

'We just thought, what with . . .' and now it's Vicky's turn to try and stuff her own words back into her mouth. 'What I mean is . . . we weren't talking about . . . oh bloody hell, Zo.'

'It's okay,' I tell them, 'honestly. This is weird as hell, I know, but . . .' I have a tingling urge to confide in my friends that while I am in every other way upended, I am not necessarily heartbroken in the romantic sense of the word. I take a sip of wine and swallow the impulse.

'Will you do something for me?'

Vicky and Rachel drop their hands from their mouths.

'Of course.'

'Anything.'

'Can we just be normal?'

They nod in mute, bewildered agreement.

I raise my eyebrows.

'Oh, yeah, right,' says Vicky. 'Normal.' She forces a smile. 'I . . . have a date on Thursday?' She clenches her teeth at the end of the sentence, as if checking that this is okay.

'That's great,' I say, and Vicky looks both relieved and surprised. 'Anyone we know?'

Vicky shakes her head. 'Just some, you know . . . bloke. Probably be rubbish.'

We all sip our drinks and nod.

When it becomes clear that this topic has been exhausted, Rachel takes a breath and says, as if telling us about a new recipe, 'I, er . . . I had sex last night.'

'Sex?' I ask. 'With Steve?'

Rachel nods uncertainly, as if sleeping with her fiancé might be some kind of moral transgression.

'And this is you being normal?' says Vicky.

'I didn't know what else to say. Sorry. I thought I'd sort of . . .' – and here she illustrates her point by sliding a coaster across the table – 'push the envelope.'

'Any good?' I ask.

Rachel wobbles an equivocal palm. 'Not bad for a Monday.'

We all nod as if this makes some kind of sense, sip our drinks, nod again.

Vicky tops up her glass. 'This is going to take some practice, isn't it?'

'It's going to take more than that,' says Rachel, standing up from the table. 'Three tequilas?'

'That's better,' I tell her. 'And some crisps.'

Normality creeps back into the evening as the empty glasses and crisp packets stack up. Vicky opens up on the details of her impending date (French, handsome, primary school teacher, triathlete), and it turns out that Rachel really is more excited about her honeymoon (elephants, tree house, waterfall, diving) than her wedding. It's wonderful and it's cathartic, and I only wish I could give it my full attention. The problem is, I have an ulterior motive for dragging my best friends out on a school night in the middle of detox season but what with this outpouring of normality, it's fast approaching chucking-out time, and if I don't say my piece now, I'm in danger of losing my nerve.

'I'm going travelling,' I blurt, cutting off Rachel halfway through a catalogue of Maputaland's indigenous sea life.

'A holiday?' says Vicky. 'Lovely. Where?'

Rachel, a little quicker on the uptake, whispers the word 'Travelling?'

I nod.

Vicky adopts the role of disapproving parent. 'Hold on a what now? Who's travelling? Where?'

'Me,' I say, indicating myself with a forefinger. 'All over the place.' And the double meaning isn't lost on me.

I've had more time to think than is probably good for me, and I have thought hard and repeatedly about what I am doing with my life. And one of the few conclusions

I have come to with any confidence is that I don't know what I'm doing, where I'm going, what I want or who I even am. Three years ago I accused Alex's ex-girlfriend, Ines, of being spoiled. But I'm not sure that doesn't apply to me, too. My parents have always given me everything I've needed and pretty much all I wanted. I passed my own exams, I earn my own wages, but ... I'd hesitate to call myself an independent woman.

'You know that cliché about *finding yourself*?' I say, giving the phrase its requisite air quotes.

Vicky nods, Rachel looks like she's about to cry.

'Well ... I can't think of a better way of putting it than that. I need to find myself,' I say, and I make a squeaky snorty noise that is halfway between a laugh and a cry.

'How?' says Rachel. 'How are you going to pay for it?'

How many twenty-nine year olds make wills? Not me, not Alex. He only had life insurance because it came with his job, and the person he named on that policy four years ago was his mother. She also inherited his savings, pension, premium bonds, the clothes hanging on his side of the wardrobe if she'd wanted them. Six weeks after the funeral his brother Pat came to London to help take care of various morbid formalities. We put items into boxes for Alex's mother: pictures, books, DVDs, a football mug that he never drank out of. After first offering them to me,

Pat took Alex's watch and cufflinks. I asked if he wanted
the Xbox, decks and vinyl, but Pat didn't want anything
he might enjoy. Suits, clothes, shoes, we took to a charity
shop – leaving the bags on the pavement because we were
crying too hard to face anyone. Everything else went
into bin bags and we drove in silence to the tip, where
we heaved the sacks into their relevant skips. I miss the
presence and weight of these items now and feel I was too
quick to tidy his life away.

When you take out a joint mortgage, they give you two
options. One where, in the event of your death, your half
of the property passes on in the fashion of your watch,
cufflinks and football mug – to whoever is named in your
will, or in the absence of that document to the relevant
legal beneficiary: a parent, sibling, child or spouse. Not
a boyfriend or a girlfriend. The second way, the house
passes to the other person named on the mortgage papers.
We had laughed awkwardly at this mortal distinction,
quickly agreeing to the more romantic of the two choices.
Although a part of me wishes we hadn't.

Rachel and Vicky know that the house is now mine.
And the fact I can barely afford the mortgage, bills and
everything else that comes with it.

Vicky frowns. 'I thought Alex didn't leave ... I
thought ... aren't you skint?'

'As a church mouse,' I say.

'Travelling's a big . . .' Rachel reaches across the table to hold my hand. 'Are you sure you're ready for something like that, Zo?'

'Not exactly,' I say. 'But . . . did I tell you about the bank? About Alex's bank?' My friends shake their heads, looking worried, braced. 'You met Pat?' I say to Rachel. 'When he was down, helping me with Al's stuff, all the admin, he had to go to the bank, to Alex's bank. You have to actually go in, hand over his cards. So Pat – such a sweet guy, did I tell you he offered me money?' Vicky looks aghast, and now it's my turn to lay the consoling hand on top of hers. 'He was embarrassed about the will, the lack of a will. Said that if me and Al had been, you know, married . . . then the money, the life insurance, it would have been mine. And did I want, you know . . .'

Rachel looks conflicted, agitated. 'And did you?' – I shake my head – 'Because, well, he had a point, don't you think?'

What I think is *No*. I think we never would have been married, never should have been married. And I think that his mother, who bought bread on the day of its sell-by date and who ironed the neighbours' shirts to look after her sons, I think the money is hers and I know I'm right.

But I don't want to go into it and I don't want to play the martyr. And besides, it's off the point.

'The point is,' I say, 'Pat asked me to go to the bank with him. Partly, I don't think he wanted to go on his own, and partly, I think he felt bad – guilty – that it was him, and not me – like he was prying. I don't know. Anyway . . .' I look at my glass and see there is one mouthful of wine left, so I leave it where it stands for now. 'Anyway . . . we went to the bank. And they give you . . . they give you his . . .' And I can feel the heavy invisible fingers tugging at the corners of my mouth, pulling at my cheeks; I feel a hard pressure behind my eyes and now the tears are coming and coming hard. I finish my wine, and when Vicky slides her glass towards me, I take a big gulp of hers too. 'God! Sorry, sorry. They give you his . . . they give you his statements and then they leave the room, so you can go through them in private and check that everything's as it should be. And you know how . . . the statements, how they go backwards? Last purchase first?'

I can tell from Rachel's expression and her tear-glazed eyes that she is one step ahead and sees what's coming. 'Oh God,' she all but whispers. 'Oh God, Zoe.'

'What?' says Vicky. 'What?'

I take a deep breath. 'It's silly, really. The first thing on the statement, the last place he . . .'

'The deli,' says Rachel.

'And before that the florist on the corner.'

'Flowers?'

I nod, and damn it if I can't stop myself from crying again. Vicky offers her wine, but I slide the glass back to her. 'Thank you, I'm . . . I'm fine.'

'You poor thing,' says Rachel.

'So me and Pat, bloody hell. We just folded the statement in half and waited until the woman came back into the room and asked if everything was "in order". We said yes, then went back to the house to finish packing up Al's things.'

The three of us sit quietly for a while before Vicky leans forwards, clears her throat delicately and says, 'Travelling?'

'Oh, right. Sorry, lost my train of . . . you know. It sounds silly, I know, but Al going out to get breakfast and stuff, it's typical, isn't it. It's typical of me, of people doing things for me, taking care of me – my mum and dad, Alex – carrying the heavy bags, throwing out spiders, fetching me breakfast. I can't even wire a plug.'

'A plug?' says Rachel.

'You know what I mean,' I say. 'I've been spoiled.'

Vicky shrugs like this is to be expected and is nothing to be ashamed of. 'You're a woman.'

Rachel shakes her head. 'Right on, sister.'

'Find myself,' I say, finishing where I began and finding the two words far more articulate and pertinent than my effort at expanding.

'I think it's a great idea,' says Rachel, and Vicky nods in agreement. 'But when?'

'I haven't really thought it through,' I tell them. 'To be honest, it only really came together as a notion on the train home this evening. It's been brewing, I think; going to France with my folks, the bank, the map on the tube . . . soon, though.'

'You're not missing my wedding,' says Rachel, and it's not a question.

'No, God!'

'So after August, right?'

'I don't want to be here in October,' I say, and thankfully I don't have to explain why. 'So I suppose that means September.'

'Give you time to save up,' says Rachel.

'It'll take longer than that,' I say, 'I can barely afford the tube.'

'So what's the plan? Work your way around?'

I take a sip of Vicky's wine, after all. 'I'm selling the house.'

Rachel gives me a hard, almost angry stare. 'Over my dead fucking body, Zoe.' And then she realizes what she's just said and her face crumples like a tent freed of its guy ropes. 'Oh my God, oh my God, Zoe, I'm sorry, I'm so sorry, I didn't mean ... I didn't ... oops?'

'It's okay,' I say. 'Normal, remember?'

Rachel nods. 'In which case, Zoe Goldman, you would be out of your mind to sell a property in London in a rising market.'

'She's right,' says Vicky. 'Out – of – your – mind.'

'I don't see how else I can do it. I'm not going travelling to work, I don't have any savings, the mortgage is a big fat pig, and ... and I don't see how else I can do it.'

'Get a lodger,' says Rachel brightly.

I shake my head. 'God no, I couldn't, it would feel ... just ... no.'

'Right,' says Rachel, holding up a finger and reaching into her handbag for a pen. She peels a beer mat in half, creating a clean square of white card. 'How much is your mortgage?'

I tell her. I tell her how much my bills cost, my travel, my lunch, my phone, the gym, the repayments on my credit card. We estimate the rental value of the house as a vacant, furnished premises, we guess at the cost of a ticket to somewhere hot and exotic, tickets to various onward locations across the globe, how much I will need to keep me in beer and noodles and accommodation. We do a lot of mathematics and by the time Rachel has finished she has dismantled three beermats and has ink on her lip.

'The good news is,' she says, circling a number on one of the impromptu pages, 'the rent should cover the mortgage and bills, and give you a few extra quid a month for spends.'

'Bad news?'

'The bad news,' says Rachel, 'is you'll still need to save up to buy your ticket, cover sundry expenses and give yourself a buffer in case your tenants run off or smash the place up.'

'I'll get nice tenants.'

'And you'll have to drop the gym—'

'Done.'

'—cycle to work, shop in Aldi, and take a packed lunch to the office.'

'Can do.'

'No more new clothes,' she adds, and Vicky winces as if I've been told I'll need to sell an eyeball.

'Clothes schmoves,' I say, warming to the idea of noble austerity and Zoe the independent woman.

'eBay your handbags and shoes.'

'Click,' I say, doing exactly that to an invisible mouse.

'And,' says Rachel, 'you're still fucked.'

'What?'

'Unless you want to put if off until next year, you're still about three grand off target.'

'But what about Aldi? The clothes? The egg sandwiches?'

Rachel shakes her head, taps a beer mat with the tip of her biro. 'The numbers don't lie.'

'Listen,' says Vicky, 'don't be offended or anything, but I could lend you—'

'Vicky,' I say, leaning across the table and hugging her hard, 'thank you. Thank you, but ... I can't.'

'Of course you c—'

'No, I can't. That's the whole point, isn't it. I have to do it on my own. On my own.'

'So I suppose you're going to sell the house, after all?'

I look to Rachel, as if for approval, and she shakes her head emphatically. 'It's your house,' she says. 'But, Zo, as a friend, I've got to tell you I think it would be a huge – *huge* – mistake.'

And if my trust in Rachel weren't enough, my lack of faith in my own judgement is a powerful voice. After all, huge mistakes are my speciality. Vicky must read the essence of this in my body language.

'So,' she says, 'next year, then.'

Now it's my turn to shake my head. 'Over my dead body,' I say, but it doesn't get the laugh I'd hoped for. 'One way or another, I'm going in September. Even if I have to stow away.'

Zoe

Click

The camera weighs more than a bag of sugar. Over half a kilogram of dials, levers and buttons that mean little more to me than nothing. Apparently it's a classic, but hanging around my neck it feels like a brick and the strap cuts hard into my neck.

I lift this marvel of German precision to my eye and point it at Henry, the guy cutting Rachel's hair. As I adjust the lens (a 35mm F/2 Summicron, apparently), the bruise around his left eye comes into focus. The colours are magnificent – yellow, purple, orange – but this heavy hunk of metal is loaded with black and white film. I press the button, listening again to the solid mechanical click that so excited the geeks at my photography class.

Henry turns around, visibly awkward at having his photo taken. He angles his body away from me, working the scissors through Rachel's hair with rhythmic, staccato movements.

Rachel gets married in three months and is having something of a hair crisis; still undecided on how to have it and who will cut it. Henry came highly recommended by one of Rachel's colleagues – as well as cutting in a salon, he will cycle to your house and drop your split ends onto your own carpet.

'Put that thing away,' says Rachel. 'I look like a bag lady.'

'No film,' I lie.

'Then what are you playing at?'

'I like the sound of the spring.'

'You a photographer?' asks Henry. Despite the bruising he has nice eyes. No, they're better than nice, more interesting than nice. Blue mostly, but not the kind to make a fuss about – nothing evocative of sea or sky. Zooming in further until I can see flecks of green and grey and black, the effect is diminished. It's the way he looks when he's concentrating, the way he looks when he looks at you – there is confidence, but also something . . . guarded it seems. They say you can learn a lot from someone's eyes, but Henry's aren't telling. He'd be magazine handsome if it wasn't for his broken nose, but there's definitely something about him. And it gives me butterflies; quick, struggling wings beating in my stomach.

Rachel thinks he's gay, but the butterflies disagree.

I shake my head. 'Just a hobby.'

'So you're going back?' says Rachel, referring to the photography class.

We talked about apertures, shutter speeds, ISO numbers – the holy trinity of photography. And even without the pervasive smell of body odour, I doubt any of it would have clicked my shutter. In the pub afterwards, some guy with bits of crisp in his beard cornered me and talked at excruciating length about the 'honesty of film and the purity of black and white', and all I could think was that it was a shame he cared less about the purity of his breath.

'Maybe,' I say. 'I dunno; it's a bit . . .'

'Pretentious?' tries Rachel.

'Hold still,' says Henry, placing a hand on top of her head and rotating it back into position.

Alex bought the thing off eBay, drunk one night, bored and disgruntled with work. 'A hobby.' Typical Alex; rushing into something full of enthusiasm and good intentions. I remember the look of disappointment when we collected his first roll of developed film from Snappy Snaps. A flimsy cardboard wallet containing twenty-four mostly out-of-focus prints of trees, brick walls, railings and a dog. Undeterred, Alex decided the solution was to develop his own film and print his own photographs. He ordered chemicals, gizmos, and a scanner to convert the negatives into digital images. I should have let him get on with it, but couldn't resist pointing out – and ridiculing – the preposterous irony of spending eight hundred pounds on a manual camera, turning the spare bedroom into a darkroom, hanging up dripping rolls of film and then converting them into a format I can take on my mobile phone. He used an analogy of baking bread – saying you can buy it, bake it in the oven or make it in a bread-maker. What he was doing, Alex said, was akin to the latter, 'getting your hands dirty, but with a bit of assistance in the final step.' And when I still refused to let it go, he called me a killjoy and suggested I might be better getting a hobby of my own instead of 'pissing all over' his. And don't I feel like a bitch. He took the camera out only once after that, and never did get around to setting up his darkroom. I tried to be encouraging, inviting him and his camera out for walks, but the Leica remained on a shelf and the scanner stayed in its box. For his last – *final* – birthday, I bought him vouchers for a photography class, but then October happened.

I put the camera down and pick up the remote, flicking through the channels, stopping on a young Meg Ryan.

'Love this film,' says Rachel. '"I'll have what she's having."'

'Did you know that the woman, the lady at the next table, she's the director's mother?' says Henry.

'Ha,' says Rachel, flicking me a look, which I interpret to be her presenting evidence that Henry is, indeed, gay. 'I did not know that.'

Henry lifts a handful of Rachel's hair. 'Maybe we could go for something a bit Albright,' he says.

'Alright?' says Rachel.

'Albright,' he repeats, nodding at the TV. 'Sally Albright.'

'Of course,' I say, '*All bright*, I never noticed that before.'

'Yeah,' says Henry. 'Bit obvious, but ... well, amazing film, so what do I know?'

Again, that look – *gay* – from Rachel. 'But her hair's a bit ... eighties, isn't it?' she says.

'God yes. But you know at the start, when she's in college – we could go for a shorter, toned down, less *Charlie's Angels* version of that. I'd bring it in here' – he holds her hair in towards her cheeks – 'show off those cheekbones.'

'What'd you think, Zo?'

'Yeah,' I say. 'A bit of Albright. Definitely.'

'I won't take any more off tonight,' says Henry.

'Tease,' says Rachel, smacking him on the arm, and if I

155

didn't know better, I'd swear she was flirting with Henry.

Henry shakes his head as if it isn't the first time he's heard this, and I can't help but wonder if it's ever led anywhere. 'We'll keep it neat and healthy,' he says, 'but we could use a little more length—'

Rachel sniggers at the back of her sinuses. 'That's what I keep telling my fiancé.'

'Okay,' says Henry.

'Sorry about Rachel,' I say, 'she's an idiot trapped in an accountant's body. They go a little crazy when you let them out in the evening.'

Henry laughs. 'I've had worse,' he says, brushing hair from her shoulders and carefully removing the gown from around her neck.

'Give me five minutes to rinse my head and I'll sort you out,' Rachel says to Henry, popping her eyes at this last turn of phrase.

'Take your time. I'm not in any rush.'

'Zoe,' says Rachel, 'keep Henry company while I jump under the shower, this hair's making me itch. Make him a coffee, yeah. There might even be some biscuits.'

I glance at Henry and he smiles awkwardly: *Why not.* 'Milk and none, if that's okay.'

When I come back into the living room with two cups of coffee, Henry is perched on the arm of the sofa, watching the movie. Harry and Sally are watching *Casablanca* together down the end of a phone line, each in their own beds.

'You know,' I say, 'I've never watched that movie.'

Henry points at the TV. '*Harry Met Whatsit*?'

I laugh. '*Casablanca*.'

'You should,' he says. 'It's excellent. I used to watch it with my mum . . .' Henry trails off at the end of the sentence, his eyes going to the scissors still in his hand. He looks at me, as if he's about to say something, then smiles and looks back to the TV.

'She does have amazing hair,' I say. 'Bit bouffy for me, but, hey.' I blow my fringe out of my eyes and shrug. As well as economizing on groceries, clothes, travel and leisure, I haven't had my hair cut since February and it's beginning to look a little feral. Particularly now that my white streak has grown through.

Henry spins his scissors around his index finger, and points them at my hair. 'Want me to . . .?'

'No, thanks, I'm fine.'

'Sure? I could just take the split ends off, if you like.'

'I'm flattered.'

'You've got nice hair,' he says, smiling. 'Is this' – he pulls at an invisible lock of hair, where my own has turned white – 'natural?'

I nod, feeling myself flush slightly.

'Sorry, professional . . . you know. Come on,' he says, beckoning me towards the chair in the centre of the room. 'Sit down.'

The word *forceful* forms on my tongue, but I keep it caged. 'Thanks,' I say, 'honestly. But I'm . . .' I mime turning my pockets inside out, 'skint.'

'On the house,' says Henry, pointing his scissors at the chair. 'And I promise to do a lousy job.'

'You better,' I tell him. And I think to myself, no way is this guy gay. I don't think he's flirting with me, exactly, but . . . well, neither is he not flirting with me.

Rachel has taken the mirror down from above the fireplace and balanced it on the seat of another chair in front of this one. In the reflection, I watch as Henry lifts, bunches and weighs my hair, his fingers sliding through the neglected curls, making my scalp tingle. He piles the mess of hair onto the top of my head, then lets it drop like tangled wool. Beside the chair is a plastic spray bottle half filled with water, and without a word, Henry starts wetting and brushing my hair.

'Any requests?' he says.

'I'm in your hands,' I say, and for some reason Henry laughs.

'What's funny?'

'Last time I said that to someone they . . .' He runs his hand over his shaved head.

'Suits you,' I say.

Henry nods, not in agreement necessarily, but acknowledging the compliment. 'You'd really suit a graduated bob,' he says, using his hands to indicate hair slanting in towards my neck at a forty-five degree angle.

'Really?'

'You have a nice neck,' he tells me.

'What about my cheekbones?' I ask.

Henry makes a fifty-fifty gesture with his scissor hand, but he's smiling.

'Fair enough,' I say. 'Do your worst.'

On screen, the film breaks for one of those interludes with the cute old couples telling how they met all those years ago. The lady explains that her husband – a young man at the time – walked across the room at a dance, and introduced himself. She thought he was going to hit on her friend, people always did, but he introduced himself to her. Just walked up and told her his name. 'And I knew,' she says. 'I knew the way you know about a good melon.'

'Sweet,' I say. 'I always like these little clips.'

Henry hum-haws, not convinced. 'I always thought Harry and Sally were one of the most . . . convincing couples, you know. I absolutely believe they're meant for each other.'

He pushes his fingers downwards into my hair, then rotates his palms outward so that the tips of his fingers are pressed into my neck, pulling my hair tight so that there's a not unpleasant tension at the roots. And then he cuts the hair up to his hand and repeats the process.

'In *Casablanca*,' he says, 'it's chemistry between Bogart and Bergman more than the characters they play. For me anyway.'

'I really need to see it,' I say, watching Henry in the mirror, his hands working through the layers of my hair with a smooth hypnotic rhythm.

'But Sally and Harry,' he says, 'I don't think there's ever been a more convincing couple.'

I murmur my agreement as Henry walks around to the front of me, blocking my view of myself. He reaches his hands towards me, one on either side of my face, and gently touches my cheekbones, measuring their line and level, the way a painter might measure the horizon. There is a moment of eye contact matching the contact of his fingers against my face, and then he looks away and continues cutting.

Henry points his scissors at the TV. 'These stories with the old couples, though, they're all about . . .' he doesn't wink when he looks at me, but there's a flutter of movement in his cheek that could be taken as a close relative of a wink, '... physical attraction.'

'Like the melon?' I say.

'Exactly,' says Henry, becoming worryingly animated with his scissors. 'Their decades of marriage is founded on nothing deeper than instant physical appeal.'

'They seem happy to me,' I say.

'You know they're actors, right?'

'Sure,' I say, lying.

'Real stories, apparently. But actors.'

'Well, there you go. Real stories. And anyway, you've got to start somewhere. Physical attraction seems as good a place as any to me.'

Henry smiles, finds another layer of hair and continues cutting.

If forty years from now, a man with a camera were to ask Henry and me how we met, I'd say to the guy:

He was cutting my friend's hair, and there was ... there was just something about him. And then he offered to cut my hair.

For free! Henry adds. *I cut it for free, remember?*

I tap his hand, smile. *I remember. It wasn't quite so white then, either,* I say, putting my hand to my perm. *There was a film on the TV.*

Casablanca, says Henry.

That's right, I say, our memories failing but adjusting to preserve a mutual truth. *And as he cut my hair, I looked into those eyes – careful blue eyes – just inches from my own. And I thought, yes, there's definitely something about that boy.*

When Henry met Zoe, I think.

'What?' says Henry, and I realize I've laughed under my breath.

'Nothing,' I say, shaking my head. Because there won't be any forty years from now. The reality is that four months from now I am getting on a plane to I don't know where. But I do know I am going alone.

Henry

If I Liked Her Less

There is something about this girl.

Although exactly what, I'm not sure. Maybe I'm imagining it, but there seemed to be a chemistry between us for a moment. But now, for no reason I can detect, she has become suddenly awkward and quiet. Maybe it was all that dopey talk of physical attraction.

While I had been hoping Rachel would take her time, it's a welcome relief when she comes downstairs, towelling her hair, and dispelling the tension.

'My God, Zo,' she says. 'Your hair!'

Zoe grimaces. 'What? Is it . . . what?'

'It looks amazing. I love it!'

'Almost done,' I say, 'hold still.'

'Honestly,' Rachel says, handing me a fold of ten-pound notes, 'you turn your back for ten minutes. Do I get commission?' she asks.

'Sure,' I say, winking at Zoe, and I'm relieved to see her return it with a smile. 'Fifty per cent.'

'Deal,' says Rachel. 'I'm making tea. Anyone else?'

'I'd love to,' says Zoe, 'but I'm flagging and I've still got to ride home.'

'Henry?'

'Riding too,' I say.

'Where to?' Rachel asks. I tell her. 'That's near you, isn't it, Zo?'

It's an innocent enquiry, but Zoe seems discomfited by it. 'Well, kind of,' she says. 'Not exactly.'

'And you're done.' I lift the mirror so Zoe can better see her hair, watching her reaction as she inspects her reflection from various angles. Her hand goes to the white streak flowing from her temple, she pulls it through her fingers and smiles, but there's something behind her expression that's hard to read. 'I've had better reactions,' I tell her.

Zoe appears to come back to herself. 'I love it,' she says, and she turns from her reflection to me. 'Thank you. I love it.' And then, almost as if she doesn't trust herself to speak, she mouths the words again: *Thank you.*

The sound of a boiling kettle echoes through from the kitchen. 'You two sure you won't join me?' says Rachel's disembodied voice.

I wait for Zoe, and when she answers in the negative, I

do the same. I brush the hair from her shoulders and help her remove the gown.

'Suit yourselves,' says Rachel, walking into the room with a steaming mug of something herbal. 'So, Henry, what are you doing in August?'

'Excuse me?'

'Thursday the fifteenth of August.'

'Nothing as far as I know.'

'Good, because I'm getting married on the Saturday, and if I don't look exactly like Meg Ryan, I'll be holding you responsible.'

Weddings, even the mention of them makes my feet itch. The thought of being associated with one makes me feel vaguely bilious.

'Right,' says Zoe, bending at the waist and shaking her hair over the pile of clippings. 'I had better be going.'

'I'd ask you to come on the day,' Rachel says, and I all but heave, 'but it's in France, so . . . no offence.'

'None taken.'

It's a cool spring evening, so despite it being a little out of my way, I offer to cycle Zoe home. We're both heading south of the river, so she has little option but to accept.

I'm unsure of the proper etiquette when cycling with a lady for the first time, but the sun has set, and the traffic is easing off, so for the most part we are able to cycle two abreast. I try not to fall behind, because I don't want Zoe to think I'm checking out her bum, although this is occasionally unavoidable, and whether it's the cycling or not, she does look good out of the saddle. At the same time, I don't want to forge on ahead, forcing the pace and intruding my own backside upon Zoe's view. We cycle at a speed easy enough to allow conversation, but say little besides commenting on the occasional landmark, oddity or idiot driver. Whereas I'm inclined to hop up the curb, squeeze between cars and sneak through the lights, Zoe abides by the rules, signals correctly and stops on amber.

As we approach the river, Albert Bridge twinkles above the water as if it's waiting for Christmas. Two months after I started working with Gus, I bought a bicycle so that I could follow up on recommendations beyond his small shop in the South West Triangle. I must have covered hundreds of miles, criss-crossing the river in the shortening nights, and there's something magical about all of London's bridges after sunset. But this one, like something out of a fairytale, is my favourite. My clients live on both sides of the dirty water, east and west, but whenever I can, I cross here, riding slowly and imagining the air isn't thick with fumes.

The bridge inclines deceptively, and tonight, as we crest the centre, the light thrown from its constellation of strung bulbs bounces up to meet us, reflected back from a loose mass of glass and polished metal. Parked on the opposite side of the road are maybe a dozen or two dozen motorcycles, all chrome cylinders and fat gas tanks. Without discussing it, we slow to a roll as we approach this gathering of ostentatious hogs. The riders are standing around, talking, comparing gaskets and drinking coffee from a nearby burger van that I have never seen here before.

'Buy you a coffee?'

'You think it's safe?' says Zoe, laughing.

'We're bikers, ain't we?'

'Sure,' says Zoe, steering her bike across the road. 'Let's do it.'

And this is no mean measure of burnt instant in a Styrofoam cup. To our mutual amazement, this small snack van on the Albert Bridge offers five varieties of beans and three kinds of milk, covering everything from a flat white to a decaf soya mocha. We order two white Americanos and take them to the railings so we can look at the lights reflected in the water.

Zoe unclips her helmet and runs her fingers through her bob. 'Is it ruined?' she asks.

'Nothing a wash won't fix. You look . . . it looks good. Really good.'

Zoe smiles, looks away. 'On the road again tomorrow?' she asks.

Tomorrow I am swapping my scissors for a drill; I have appointments from 9 until 6.30 including three root canals and a tricky filling. But I'm not about to admit it; it's too complicated. Too weird. 'I only do the mobile stuff in the evenings.'

'You work in a salon, too?'

I nod.

'What are you, a workaholic or something?'

'Hah! No, not really, but I do need to pay the rent.'

'Tell me about it,' says Zoe. 'Does it have a' – air quotes – 'funny name? The hairdressers.'

'The Hairy Krishna.'

'That's just weird. Is it a Buddhist thing?'

'It's a Gus thing. He's the owner.'

And all of a sudden I experience a nudging impulse to tell Zoe about my mother's salon, the mix up with the name, the way she taught me to cut a graduated bob. It might endear me to her; it might even make her laugh. Her mouth has a natural pout, and there is something both cartoonish and seductive about the way she smiles while she's waiting for an answer. Full in the middle, her lips taper towards the corners, where they curve gently upwards, giving her an air of wry amusement. But there's something else; something held back, and it's magnetic and ... something more, sad perhaps. But if I tell Zoe about Love & Die, what then? What if she laughs and asks where I'm from, what if she asks what it's like and why did I leave? How do I answer that line of enquiry? If I liked her less, perhaps I'd risk it.

'What about you?' I ask. 'What do you do?'

Zoe shrugs. 'Kids' books.'

'You write them?'

'No, no, publishing. I'm an editor. But ... I did have an idea for one once.'

'Tell?'

Zoe appears to think about this for a moment, leaning over the railings and staring through the black water. A light breeze ruffles her hair and she shivers back to herself. Zoe takes off her backpack and removes the camera. 'One for the album?'

'I thought there was no film,' I say.

Zoe shrugs, grimaces apologetically. 'Well, it's only black and white,' she says, aiming the lens at me.

'Make sure to get my good side,' I say, and I cringe a little at the obviousness of it.

'Which one would that be?'

'Anything that hides my nose.'

'In which case,' says Zoe from behind her camera, 'I guess you're all out of luck. Anyway ... gives you character.'

'Fine. How do you want me?' I ask, hoping she'll miss the inadvertent double entendre.

'Just try and look cool,' she says, laughing. 'Just drink your coffee and look at the river.'

I do as I'm told and listen to the solid click of Zoe's camera as she moves around me, finding her angle.

'What happened to your eye?' she asks.

'A plumber hit me.'

'Seriously?'

'He does it every week,' I say, still staring out over the Thames. 'Boxing.'

'Tough guy, huh?' Zoe says, trying out what is probably meant to be a New York accent.

'Yeah, that's me.'

'Show me your tough guy face,' she says, closing in with the camera.

And when I laugh, I hear the shutter click.

Zoe packs away her camera, fastens her helmet and climbs onto her bike. I follow her over the hump of the bridge, and then she surprises me by popping up the pavement and veering left into Battersea Park.

'I thought you were straight on.'

'Detour,' she says, following the path east along the line of the river.

'Where are we going?'

'Japan.'

'Isn't that a little out of our way?'

'Yes,' says Zoe, smiling at me over her shoulder. 'But only a little.'

I am both literally and figuratively lost, but I have nowhere better to be, so I pedal on to wherever Zoe is leading me. After no more than a minute, the silhouette of a structure – angular, layered and almost as tall as the trees – comes into view.

'It's a peace pagoda,' Zoe says, circling clockwise around its perimeter. 'Sometimes in the morning, if you're early enough, there's a monk.'

About twenty pedal pushes in circumference, the pagoda is accessible by about a dozen steps on each of three sides. At the centre is a broad white column, inset with four gilded panels or statues, each as big as a man and glowing warmly in the lamplight.

'What does he do? This monk.'

'Walks, bangs a drum. Monk stuff, you know. I cycle past here if I'm going in early, but I've only seen him once.'

'It's beautiful.'

'I thought you might appreciate it. What with you working at a Buddhist hairdressers, and everything.' She smiles at me teasingly.

'I do.'

On our third revolution, Zoe peels away, heading back towards the traffic and the bustle of late night London. I make one more circuit of the peace pagoda then follow after her.

I've had more dates in the last four months than in my whole life leading up to them. Some have ended in bed, one in tears, and one or two have resulted in brief follow-ups. Confident, ambitious, funny, attractive women for the most part, but no one I'd walk out on a wedding for. And on more than a dozen of these dates, I've gone home wondering if I didn't suffer some kind of synaptic malfunction seven months ago in that cold castle. But these last two hours with this funny, reticent, awkward editor – I've enjoyed them more than all those dates and drunken fucks placed end to end. Maybe because this isn't actually a date; no contrivances and no expectations.

After ten minutes of slow riding, Zoe coasts to a stop. 'This is me,' she says, pointing her handlebars in the direction of a long side street disappearing into a pinpoint of converging street lamps.

'Right,' I say, stopping beside her. 'You want me to . . . will you be alright?'

'Thank you. And thank you again for the . . .' She flicks her eyes up towards her helmet.

'You're welcome. Look after it for me.'

'Okay,' says Zoe.

'Plans for the weekend?' I ask, a little abruptly.

Zoe takes a deep breath and lets it out slowly. 'Not much; working.'

'The books?'

Zoe shakes her head. 'Pub. The Duck and Cover,' she says, swivelling her handlebars so her lights point down the quiet high street. 'Got to pay the rent,' she says, playing my own words back to me.

'It won't pay itself,' I say inanely, buying time and trying to draw this moment out.

Zoe laughs politely. 'You? Plans, I mean.'

'I er . . . well, I'm supposed to have a date on Saturday.'

Zoe nods at this. 'Supposed?'

'Well, I could . . . cancel?'

Zoe winces. She actually winces, her teeth coming together, eyes tightening, head withdrawing away from me by maybe an inch.

'Sorry,' I say, 'I just . . .' but there's no easy way of ending that sentence, so I opt instead for closing my eyes and trying to make myself vanish. When I open them again, Zoe is still there, but at least she is smiling now.

'No,' she says, 'it's fine, I . . .' She nods her head from side to side, as if rehearsing a line inside her skull. 'I'm going travelling.'

'What, this weekend? I thought you were working.'

Zoe laughs. 'September.'

'Like a holiday travelling, or *travelling* travelling?'

'The last one.' She smiles apologetically at this. 'So . . . you know.'

'Sounds amazing,' I say, forcing a smile. 'Where to?'

Zoe shakes her head. 'I really need to decide.'

'You going there for long? Sorry . . . I sound like I'm interrogating you.'

Zoe laughs. 'It's fine. Maybe a year? More, less, I . . . I dunno.'

'Okay . . . well, I guess I'd better . . . cut and run.'

'I bet you say that to all the girls.'

My intentions are modest as I lean in to kiss Zoe, aiming for nothing more than a peck on the cheek. Perched on our bicycles, it's a slow, cautious approach requiring a good deal of balance and concentration. I put my hand against the side of Zoe's face, and the additional contact seems to ground and stabilize us; she leans into me, increasing the pressure of her cheek against my lips.

As my hand slides to the nape of her neck Zoe turns her head towards me and my lips glide across her cheek, bringing our mouths together.

Two seconds, maybe ten ... and Zoe – slowly – withdraws.

'I should go. I have to ... go.'

I'm inclined to ask Zoe if she's sure, but the look in her eyes has already answered. 'See you around ...' I say, trying to pitch it somewhere just west of a question.

'Yeah,' she says. 'Enjoy your date.'

Zoe

The Pleasant Awkwardness

Enjoy your date? Damn.

On the last two hundred metres of my ride home, I replay the conclusion to my unusual night. The pleasant awkwardness, that slow opportunistic kiss. And my smug sounding farewell: *Enjoy your date.*

Why didn't I go the whole hog and invite him to have a nice life? In the grand scheme – the scheme in which I travel the world, find myself, become independent, develop a deep all-over tan – I suppose it doesn't matter. Even so, I can't help but wonder how it would go if I'd met him two years from now – what the new, found, Zoe would make of Henry and his don't-ask eyes. What she would make of that kiss?

It's been seven months since I lost Alex and the small house still feels too big when I wheel my bike through the front door. For a while I found the silence terrifying, walking from room to room, checking behind the doors, in the wardrobes and under the bed for intruders. Sometimes waking up in the middle of the night and doing the same, clutching a broken banister rail that we never did get around to replacing.

There's mail on the mat and I pick it up with an acquired sense of trepidation. Mostly junk, but a postcard from my parents who seem to be visiting a different European city every month at the moment. So far this year they have done Rome, Madrid and – the origin of this postcard – Zagreb. They invite me each time, but I'm yet to take them up on the offer.

There is just one envelope addressed to Alex today. I can get them stopped, fill in some forms and enclose one of my remaining photocopies of his death certificate. But perversely, I like receiving these offers of low-interest credit cards, invitations to wine clubs, or, like this one, an opportunity to insure my property against damage caused as a result of a burst water main. I add the envelope to the small pile on the shelf beside the front door, slip off my backpack and hang up my helmet. My bike stays in the house most nights – after all, it's not like it's in anyone's way.

There's a message on my phone from Rachel, asking if I made it home okay.

I send one back, reassuring her that I'm alive, but keep the rest of the details to myself.

Walking upstairs, I pause in front of the photograph taken on the day we moved in, me laughing at some comment from Alex. I touch my finger to his face . . .

Goodnight, Alex.

. . . and in the moonlight hazing down the stairs through the open bathroom door, the glass is smudged with fingerprints. I'll clean it on Sunday. While Henry is waking up next to his date and wondering whether he made a mistake or not.

It has nothing to do with me, but as I inspect my new graduated bob in the bathroom mirror, I hope he decides that he did.

After I've taken off my make-up and brushed my teeth, I change into my pyjamas and climb into bed. Some mornings, but it's becoming less frequent now, I wake up expecting to find Alex lying beside me. On those days, I roll over onto his side of the mattress, feeling the cold of the sheets where they should be warm. Some mornings I cry, and on other days I simply feel a numb absence. Sometimes when I wake to the fresh realization that he isn't there, I experience an awful skewering guilt for not missing him more. I roll over onto his side of the bed now, open his bedside drawer and remove the iPad. I turn it on with the same sense of apprehension that I experience on finding a pile of mail inside the front door. Worse today, because she always mails him in the first week of a new month.

The iPad is set up with both of our email accounts, so it's not like I'm actually snooping. It's all just sitting there, available at a single touch. His inbox is filled almost exclusively with junk now, the electronic equivalent of the envelopes that drop through the letterbox – discount codes, special offers, concert dates. Occasionally, he will receive a message from an old colleague or acquaintance looking to reconnect, and I reply with a cut and paste explanation of what happened last October.

It wasn't until February, four months after his death, that I plucked up the courage – the defiance, maybe – to trawl through his message history. There were no emails to or from a lover; no evidence of the affair I had feared. Not proving Alex's innocence – maybe he was simply careful – but neither confirming his guilt. The only woman he wrote to with any regularity was his mother.

Within a day or two of a new month turning over, she would email her son, filling him in on a variety of domestic events, family news and local gossip. And Alex would reply in kind, long, warm, funny emails, about work, football, his lunch, a funny dream. About me. Expressing a simple affection and contentment that shines a harsh light on my own misgivings. Working forwards from last summer, I read the emails they exchanged in July, August, September and – the last time Alex wrote to his mother – October. He told her we had argued about the wallpaper, expressing his regret for acting like a 'complete pillock'. He told his mother that he would make it up to me at Christmas. But Christmas never happened.

Ready to delete Alex's account, I scrolled upwards through the junk correspondence of November and December. But when I came to January, my drifting eyes locked onto a single glaring dreadful email. Two short paragraphs of a mother's farewell to her dead boy, pouring out her pain and loss and incomprehension and telling him they would be together again one day soon. There was another, unopened and forever unanswered sent in February. When I checked again in March, there was another, and again at the beginning of April. The raw heartbreak gradually giving way to a more prosaic familiarity. Today is the fifth of May, and my heart tightens as I click on the familiar greeting: Hello Son.

May

May 5 at 10:04 AM

From: Audrey <audreywilliams56@mymail.net>

To: Alex Williams

Hello Son

   It's a strange thing typing those two words, they make me feel so sad and so close to you at the same time. It's as if I can see your face more clearly when I type them, and I get a feeling, like a small fist inside my chest. Not so strange, if you think about it, you and your brother, you're part of me in the most real way imaginable. So when I feel that tight hand inside me, I know it's you in some shape or form.

   It's the middle of spring now, or is it the end? Either way, the roses are beginning to come out, although we've had a lot of greenfly this year. I put a few of the better stems in a vase next to your urn. It's that blue vase you and Zoe gave me for Christmas and it always makes me think of the pair of you.

I write to Zoe too. She doesn't always have the time to write back, but we deal with our grief in different ways don't we. I think her friends are looking after her, and she seems to be busy with work. It's good to see her settling back into life. Such a lovely girl. I think you found a good one there son, it's such a shame the two of you never had a chance to build a life together. I've told her she's welcome to visit any time, but I haven't seen her since your funeral. It's a long way for her to come, I suppose, and not a very happy trip at that.

I was looking at your old football medals the other week, and it made my heart so terribly heavy pet. Quite took me by surprise, and I had to take a short lie on your bed. I'll be honest Alex, I could have laid there all day if I'd let myself, but life goes on doesn't it.

I'm going to the bridge club tonight with Maureen. She's very lovely, and has been so kind to me over the last few months. But between you

The Trouble with Henry and Zoe

and me son, she can go on if you let her. You'd
think no one had had a hip replacement before!

I think about you all the time son, and I keep
you in my prayers.

I miss you so much – all my love and all my
heart

Mum xx

Henry

All New

It's my job to look at bad teeth. Well, it is on Fridays. Even so, I have to suppress a wince when Jenny Tseung opens wide. Maybe working only one day a week at the chair has made me soft, but this dreadful collection of wonky brown enamel, more gaps than teeth, is painful just to look at.

Her skin is largely unlined, but it appears thin and delicate, stretched tight over unusually large cheekbones. According to her records, she is seventy-two and last visited the dentist nine years ago. Visibly nervous, she holds my hand in hers as we talk. Jenny speaks in broken, heavily accented English, and has a habit of speaking from behind her hand – but while her discourse can be hard to follow, it's easy to understand that her confidence is as shaky as her remaining teeth.

'Ha! You not look like dentist,' she says. 'My son shave his head too, you know.'

'Stylish guy,' I say.

'I don' like,' Jenny says. 'On my son, look like a . . . *a kei ji gwo*.'

'A ki . . . sorry, Jenny?'

'*Kei ji gwo*, what you say it . . . fruit, like a—' Jenny breaks off into what I assume is Cantonese before returning with, '. . . like hairy egg, haha! Green, innit.'

'A kiwi fruit!'

'Yah, that's it. Head like a green fruit. Your head good shape, though. Your head suit you.'

The dental nurse looks at me and raises her eyebrows.

'Thank you, Jenny. So, what can we do for you today?'

Jenny pats my hand. Her fingers are crooked and swollen with arthritis at the knuckles. 'Yes,' says Jenny, holding a hand to her mouth. 'You have gir'frien?'

Whether it's confusion, embarrassment, nerves or loneliness, it's not unusual for patients, particularly the elderly, to talk around the issue, and I've found it's often best to let them find their way to the point.

'Er . . . no, I have a date tomorrow, though.'

Enjoy your date, Zoe said last night.

As if drawing a line under my clumsy attempt at

flirting. But – and I've replayed it several times now – I felt she was drawing that line reluctantly.

'I married forty-seven year,' Jenny says.

'Wow.'

'Wow, haha! Yes, wow. I use be very pretty, you know. Maybe you don' believe, but—'

'I bet you were,' I say, and I mean it. Her hair is thinning slightly, but has kept its colour and hangs past her shoulders. Her wide eyes are yellowed, but alive with warmth and humour, and yes, I bet Jenny has turned a lot of heads in her time. The past tense of my declaration is floating and I'm inclined to correct it – *are, Jenny, you are* – but it would be patronizing, and besides, I don't think Jenny needs it. 'So . . . your teeth.'

She nods, pats my hand again. 'Is too late to fix?'

'Not at all. Do you have pain?'

Jenny nods. 'Very. You give me new teeth, though. Or new.'

'Or new?'

'*All new,*' she says, indicating the entirety of her mouth. 'All new, all white.'

'Jenny, that's a lot of work.'

'I have a money, you know. Is expensive, innit?'

'It will be, yes. But, it's also . . . it's a lot of work.'

I take x-rays, photographs and impressions. Some

teeth need extracting and those that are viable will have to be chopped down and crowned. Over several weeks and visits, Jenny will require nine titanium implants and twenty-eight pieces of porcelain. It will be the most complicated dental work I've performed, and as to who is more nervous – me or Jenny – well, toss a coin.

'Okay, Jenny, that's you done for today. Talk to the receptionist on the way out and she'll book you another appointment in about two to four weeks.'

'Good good,' says Jenny, shuffling off the chair. 'An' you enjoy date, innit.'

Zoe

Compactualized

I fear I have become compactualized.

Or maybe the proper word is condensified, it's hard to be sure. The world is out there doing Friday night, and I'm in here doing ... this.

The darkness is so complete my eyes could never in a thousand years adjust to it. Funny ... how we refer to absolute dark as a 'completeness', when it is in fact an absolute absence – if there is so much as a single photon in here, then it's a very determined little particle. I need to get out; I've done what I need to do and the air is heavy with my recycled breath. But it is kind of cosy, sitting here, drifting, in my ten-tog bubble.

When you work in a five-thousand-employee, cross-continent law firm, you become inoculated against corporate nonsense. You inhale and ingest words like diagonality and intellactual without coming out in so much as a rash, let alone throwing up. I thought I'd left all that behind when I moved to the faraway land of once upon a time, but publishing, too, it seems, is a breeding ground for bullshit. Approximately once a month we have a 'lunch and learn' – some industry somebody talks for an hour about the demise of bookshops, the rise of digital, harnessing the power of social media, whatever. This is the price of your 'free' lunch. You take a notebook, pretend to listen and eat as many sandwiches, wraps and muffins as possible before people start giving you funny looks. Today's price of admission was a slow hour on 'Adjusting the picture book format to digital constraints', or, in the words of our guest, 'compactualization'. I really could have done without, but last pay day is a distant memory and my purse is empty. So I took a seat near the sandwiches, and pretended to take notes while I worked out my budget – it's tight as a fat man's hat, but I have econominimized, scrimproved and budjettisoned.

On the way to work this morning I stopped at the post office and dropped off a parcel wrapped in brown paper; the last of my halfway decent handbags. Lucky bargain hunters up and down the country are stepping out in my Kurt Geigers, Alex McQueens and strappy Pedro Garcías. They are carrying their keys and lippy in my cast-off

Mulberry, Moschino and Max goddamn Mara handbags. But the proceeds will pay for hiking boots, a backpack and a whole bunch of tickets, so fair exchange. No one at work knows I'm planning on travelling, but I'm going to have to tell them soon. As of next week I have three more ends of the month before I board my plane to I don't know where.

Vicky and Rachel are going out for dim sum tonight, but I don't get paid for a week so I'll be having spaghetti hoops. Again. And I kind of like it. Not so much the Heinz product as the disciplined frugality. I've realized that getting there – on that plane to somewhere – is an important part of this adventure. And there is something satisfying about this minor act of self-denial. About this compactualization.

What would they think if they could see me now, sitting on the bed tented under my duvet with a pair of scissors, a bottle opener and a Paterson tank? Or Henry? That he'd had a lucky escape, probably. All day I've been wondering whether I shouldn't have let him walk me home – it's been a while since anyone has. I still have one hundred and seven days until the cabin crew close the doors. And God knows this bed feels awfully big some nights. Most nights. Less so, however, when you're cocooned inside a heavy duvet.

You don't need a darkroom to develop film. You need a dark space for five minutes, that's all – just long enough to transfer the film from your camera into the developing tank – a canister about the size of a cocktail shaker, or an urn, maybe. You can buy bags, like the things magicians use for storing rabbits and flowers and silk handkerchiefs, but Alex didn't buy one of those. Everything else, but not a black bag. His plan was to tape black card to the windows in the study (*nursery*), to somehow seal the gaps between the door and the frame. But he never did, didn't develop a single roll after I mocked him and his approach.

At widows' counselling they talk about having a 'bright place'. Somewhere you can return to in your mind, a happy memory of you and your dearly departed. Many of the women recalled their weddings, honeymoons, proposals, the births of their children. We didn't have those. Maybe that's why their grief seemed so much more real than my own. I've done the groups, the books, the blogs, the forums. Online I lied, claiming we had been married two years, but while the sympathy felt deeper and more sincere, it was more than offset by my feelings of guilt and fraudulence. In the counselling group we were told to bring a notebook; I couldn't even get that right. Twelve women in my group, with floral, pink, patterned pads and me with the only black book out of the dozen – as if

I were trying too hard to play the part. We wrote down memories good and bad, promises to ourselves, permission to smile, acceptance of what has gone, our bright places. On the third session I wrote in my book: *I will not come back here* – and I kept my promise. My notebook is now filled with numbers, destinations and scribbled pictures of cats, crocodiles and penguins.

Once you have removed the film from your camera, you go to your dark place and open the film canister. You can buy specially designed gadgets but a tin opener will do. Next you snip the corners off the leading edge of the film and – with nothing but your fingers to guide you – you feed all 1.4 metres into your Paterson tank. Screw on the lid and you're ready to go downstairs and add your chemicals. The first roll took me more than half an hour of fiddling underneath my blanket, and a part of me hoped I would get it wrong. If I exposed the film, then I wouldn't have to see the last pictures Alex took on his silly German camera. Of course there were no pictures of him; Alex was behind the camera. Instead there were twenty-one shots of shopfronts, litter, knackered fences, crooked goalposts – urban decay, I suppose. But instead of being interesting they were obvious, and cold and bland. At the end of the roll were three photographs of me, sitting on a bench on the common, unaware of the camera (or pretending to be, I don't remember) and staring into space. Whether I was happy or not, only that girl knows.

Inside my Paterson tank now are another twenty-four black and white pictures of strangers and shadows and textures. There are pictures of Rachel having her hair cut, and of Henry, looking out over the Thames. Maybe he was drumming up the courage to ask what I was doing this weekend. If I could have looked inside his head, if I'd known what was coming, maybe I'd have answered differently. But I didn't know, any more than the girl on that bench knew what was going to happen to Alex.

Henry

For My Sins

I've never met a Kirstine, never even heard the name before tonight, and my mouth insists on autocorrecting its phonetics. So far, I've called her Kirsten, Kristy and Christine. She laughs it off with the learned tolerance of the unusually tall, small and named. Fortunately, Kirstine is a talker, so the opportunities to mispronounce her tricky syllables have been limited. She's bright, confident and has it all mapped out.

'... and then, maybe a year after that, I should get promoted to junior director. Probably not a bad time to have a baby. Haha! Don't panic, we only just met. But seriously, babies *are* on my agenda, and if I get them out before I transition into the upper tier, then it shouldn't have too big an impact on my momentum. Maybe take ten months off then ...'

She has kale in her teeth. I'd never had kale until I came to London, but there must be a surfeit of the stuff somewhere, because I can't seem to open a menu lately without finding it in at least two places. Three, if you include Kirstine's teeth. I'm not sure what the protocol is here: if I tell her she'll be embarrassed now, but if I don't she'll only be embarrassed later. But I already know I won't be sticking around for 'later', so I fill up our glasses and let her keep talking. She has good teeth, there's a small chip on her left incisor, but they are otherwise white, straight and, from where I'm sitting, in good repair.

A waiter brings our desserts, and Kirstine – like she has done for the starters and the main course – takes out her phone to photograph her food and upload it onto Facebook.

'You on?' says Kirstine, tapping her phone with a highly polished fingernail.

'I'm a digital recluse,' I say, and Kirstine laughs quite convincingly for exactly two seconds.

I was never a social media enthusiast, but it became quickly and dramatically less entertaining after I left April on our wedding day. So no more Facebook, which could be considered a silver lining if it means I no longer have to look at pictures of my friend's puddings.

'You lost your hair,' says Kirstine, miming the haircut

from my profile picture. The last cut my mother gave me, in fact.

'I know,' I say. 'And I've looked everywhere.'

'Shame,' says Kirstine, either ignoring or entirely missing my poor attempt at wit. 'It was nice. So ... hairdressing?'

'For my sins.'

For my sins? As far as I know, I've never dropped this particular dollop of conversational grout before, and I'm only using it now because I cannot think of a single original thing to say. But as I replay my words, it does strike me that they are uncomfortably appropriate.

'Pay well, does it?'

'Not unless you own your own salon,' I say.

'And do you?'

'Er ... no.'

'Oh.'

If it weren't for my Fridays fixing teeth, I don't know how I'd survive down here. Move in with a bunch of Australians, I suppose, buy less meat, drink less wine, go on fewer dates. Which – with the exception of the Australians – may be no bad thing. It's occurred to me several times in the last few months how it would play out if one of my hairdressing clients turned up at the dental surgery, or vice versa. It's not illegal, of course, to cut hair and fill teeth, but some might consider it odd. As far as I can see, I would have two options: claim I have a twin, or flat denial. But I'm not overly concerned. When I'm cutting hair my clients tend to see me in reflection while concentrating on their own, and when I'm fixing teeth they stare at the ceiling and I'm wearing a mask. Besides all of that, I work at a posh clinic and a fairly grotty salon, so the chances of crossover are somewhat minimized. Even so, if I ever do find myself on a third date, or a fourth, or a twenty-fourth, then it's going to come up, and one revelation leads to another leads to *You did what!* Somehow, though, I don't think Kirstine and I are going to make it to date twenty-four. I'd be surprised, in fact, if we make it to ten o'clock.

'So . . .' I say, 'how's the sticky toffee pudding?'

'Yum. And the cheese board?'

'Great. Brie-liant, in fact!' And I wonder how hard it would be to bite out my own tongue.

At the dental practice we employ two receptionists, two hygienists and five dental nurses, all but one are women, half of whom are single, all of whom can send a text message blindfolded. I hear variations of the same story every week. If a date is going badly, they slip their phone out of a pocket, or purse or from under a thigh and, under cover of the table, they send a pre-typed text to their designated rescuer. Two seconds later your phone rings and the person on the other end informs you your cat has escaped, house burned down, granny exploded. I don't have a rescuer, so I eat my cheese, and wait for a waiter to pass within screaming distance so I can ask for the check.

Kirstine's phone rings.

'Oh,' she says, 'it's my ... do you mind?'

'Of course not.'

'Hi,' she says into the phone. 'Is everything okay? No,' – Kirstine holds a hand to her lips – 'you're kidding ... both legs! ... That's awful ... No, not at all, I'll be there as quick as I can.'

Zoe

Just For Tonight

Invention is the one we all talk about, but Necessity is the mother of an entire brood, including Desperation, Humility and Pragmatism. How else to explain my presence behind this narrow length of sticky timber? I'm pretty confident that if I were to wander into this pub off the high street, I'd never make it through the door, let alone all the way to the bar. More likely, I'd glance around, rapidly taking in the tatty décor and scowling faces, then pretend my phone had just rung, hold it to my ear with a look saying *Gotta take this*, then back out of the door and stride off looking for somewhere less authentic. Yet here I am, pulling pints and slinging peanuts.

The regulars are lovely, actually, even if they do look like the cast from some BBC2 crime drama set in Victorian *Lahndan Tahn*. Half of them would have your wallet given the chance, but they would spend your money behind the bar, buying drinks for their friends, and you too, if you happened to stick around. Plus, big bonus, no one knows my boyfriend died. People make tasteless jokes in front of me, they tease me about being single, ask 'Who died?' when I'm in a bad mood and snap at me when the cloud is over them. They treat me like a normal person. And as therapy goes, it beats the biscuits off the old widows' support group where, anyway, I felt like such a bloody imposter.

Even so, I'm still not convinced this is where I'd choose to spend my wages, which, by the way, are paid in cash at the end of every shift. And without which, I could forget about travelling in September. But besides the tax-free top-up, the Duck and Cover is also a welcome distraction; the locals have accepted me as one of their own – the 'token posh bird', according to Winston, the landlord. He struggles with the concept that it's not appropriate to pat me on the bottom ('I'm a product of me time, Duchess'), but he means well, and we're making progress.

What else I get out of the Duck and Cover is a free meal every shift. 'Anything off the menu, sweetheart.' Legend has it that this stained piece of card once featured such exotic items as halloumi cheese, Cajun chicken and 'them pies with just the lids', but after a sudden influx of 'ponces, puffs and prima donnas', the chef (Winston's nephew, Gary) reverted to the standard fare of bulk-bought burgers and steak 'n' kidney with a full casing of pastry. The Duck and Cover does a fine trade with home-grown custom, thank you very much. And while the 'trendy types' are more than welcome, Winston – 'to be quite frank, Princess' – doesn't need the earache if your romaine lettuce is a little limp.

The burgers are a long long way from wonderful, but with cheese, bacon and a ton of mustard, they're passable. And the chips are pretty bloody good. With a side of coleslaw, my Saturday night supper must come to fifteen hundred calories, and is generally enough to keep me going until the following evening, when I'll have a bowl of soup and a slice of toast. Lord knows what it's doing to my cholesterol, but I'm cycling about eighty miles a week and I've dropped a dress size since Christmas. You won't find it recommended by the NHS anytime soon, but it works for me.

Winston starts on the music round ('For which band did Stuart Sutcliffe play bass guitar? That's Stuart Sutcliffe.'), which means I have about seven more minutes to finish my supper before the pub quizzers drop their biros and run for the bar. Me and Winston will serve in the region of fifty drinks in a ten-minute window during which we really could use an extra pair of hands, but Janice has phoned in sick and there's no one else to cover her shift. It's a slog, but the upside is I won't have to listen to Janice catalogue every wrong her boyfriend has committed in the last seven days. Besides, when the rush is over everyone will return to their quiz sheets and I'll have precious little to do except polish the glassware. Silly night for a pub quiz, if you ask me, but Winston has found that a midweek quiz attracts too many 'bleeding students, graduates and whatnot, no offence, love'. Winston's theory is that having built up that huge loan attending university, the effing eggheads can't handle losing to teams of builders, plumbers, cashiers and market traders – which tends to generate all kinds of unnecessary agro and split lips. So it's rubber burgers, a Saturday night quiz, and everyone's happy, darling.

I'm struggling with a particularly tough mouthful when Henry walks through the door. He hesitates, taking in the décor, the locals, the 'Which artist wrote "Islands in the Stream"?', before spotting me, almost choking on my Duck and Cover burger.

There's nothing else for it, so I turn my back and cough a mouthful of burger into the bin. Please God, don't let him notice. It's bad enough that I'm wearing knackered jeans and a t-shirt so old it's forgotten what colour it's supposed to be. It occurs to me that I might have ketchup around my mouth, so I duck behind the counter and give my lips a quick once over with a licked finger.

And what the hell is he doing here anyway?

'Hello stranger,' I say, dialling up the nonchalance as I pop up from behind the bar. 'What's going on?'

'I was in the ... you know, neighbourhood,' he says apologetically, and whether it's deliberate or not, his awkwardness is gently endearing. 'I hope you don't mind.'

'Of course not. But ...' I lean over the bar, going through a small pantomime of looking for something on the other side, 'didn't you have a date?'

Henry smiles sheepishly. 'She er ... photographed her food.'

And damn it if I don't laugh so hard I snort. 'Hah! You should have brought her here, no one photographs the food here.'

'Sorry,' says Henry, pointing at my half-eaten burger, 'was I interrupting your supper?'

'What, that? No. I mean, I was, but I'm a bit, you know ...' I pat my stomach.

Henry slides up onto a stool, then leans forwards and whispers: 'Aretha Franklin.'

'I peg your pardon?'

He nods towards the tables of scribbling quizzers. 'Which soul sister contributed to the soundtracks of both *Bridget Jones* movies?'

'Aretha?'

'Franklin. "Respect" in the first, "Think" in the second. I think.'

'Very philosophical.'

Henry laughs. 'So . . . am I allowed to buy you a drink?'

'God yes. I'll have a large red, please.'

Winston gives his staff one free drink a night, and I'd finished mine by the end of the science and nature round. I pour a very generous measure of the most recently opened red, and tilt my glass towards Henry before taking a sip.

'Any chance I could have one of those?' he says, raising an invisible glass.

'Sorry, manners, Zoe!'

'Is it that good?'

I shake my head. 'No, but it gets better if you drink enough.'

'Best make it a bottle then.'

And as I pull the cork, it's as if someone has fired a starter's pistol. The sound of fifty chairs sliding simultaneously backwards sets my teeth on edge as I brace myself for the onslaught.

'Good luck,' says Henry, taking the bottle and a glass to a table in the corner.

Imagine a zombie apocalypse in which the insatiable dead have retained enough of their civilized nature that they are prepared to pay before taking a bite out of your frontal lobe. That's the half-time rush at the Duck and Cover quiz night; fifty thirsty punters, leaning over the bar, glass-eyed and frenzied, shouting orders, waving money in your face and giving you every impression that if they can just catch hold of your wrist, you will never see your arm again. Fending the buggers off is hard work, requiring concentration, coordination and stamina. I don't know what I look like at the end of this short ordeal, but it's a look you won't see on the front of *Cosmopolitan* any time soon.

As the undead traipse back to their tables, Henry returns to his stool. I place an empty glass on the bar, and Henry fills it silently. He waits until I've taken a good drink before speaking.

'How was that?'

'I won't miss it when I'm gone,' I say, instantly regretting the reference to my imminent departure.

Henry smiles awkwardly. 'September, right?'

'That's the plan.'

'In which film,' says Winston, 'did Donald Pleasance play Bond villain—'

'*You Only Live Twice*,' whispers Henry.

'God that annoys me.'

'I'm sorry, I was just . . .'

'No, not you, the film. Because you don't, do you. I know I'm being a twit, I know it's not meant to be literal, but it irritates the hell out of me. You live once and that's it; that's all you get. And it pisses me off when people take what they've got for gr— God, I sound like such a psycho. Sorry, I think I'm slightly pissed. Do you want to play Scrabble?'

Henry looks at me – quite rightly – as if I'm foaming at the mouth. 'Yes?' he tries. 'To the Scrabble part, that is. Not the . . . psycho bit . . . so much . . .'

'We're missing a few tiles,' I say, extracting the Scrabble set from underneath Monopoly, Buckaroo, Tumblin' Monkeys, Jenga and so on. 'But I think it adds an element of mystery.'

After the final round of questions and another zombie apocalypse, the board is crowded with tiles and, to my dismay, my hairdresser is a good fifty points ahead. So much for private school.

'*Put*' I say, laying down two tiles. 'Five points.'

'Nice,' Henry says, nodding in mock appreciation. As if I'd dropped *punitive*, *pupate* or *putative* instead of this puny three-letter disappointment. '*Putty*,' he says, laying down two tiles and holding eye contact for a second. His lips part, as if he's about to speak, then he looks away and smiles.

I don't know if this counts as a date, but if it had been set up that way, I'd have to count it as a success. We have talked and laughed, easily and for the most part about nothing, flitting from topic to topic, taking our conversation cues from the random words laid down on the board:

Yowl: How Henry came by the scar on his forehead

Fin: My favourite film

Ray: His favourite song

Shade: My first picture book

Something and nothing.

It has crossed my mind that if I ever do date, then at some point I will have to tell someone about Alex, and how will that play out? But Henry doesn't appear interested in the standard first-date inventory of where did I study, what degree did I do, why did I choose my career. So we paddle and splash in shallow conversation, avoiding all the rocks and dark shadows of the deeper regions. What we talk about isn't important; it's the way we talk that gives it value. Most men want to tell you about their job, their car, their plans, *this one time when*, but Henry doesn't talk about himself other than in anecdotes and abstracts teed-up from the letters in play. It's refreshing, amusing and – like Scrabble with a few missing letters – not without an element of mystery.

Henry upends the wine bottle over his glass, but the wine is done. 'What time do you finish?' he says.

'Depends how quick she can collect the glasses, wipe down the tables and put the empties out,' says Winston, appearing beside me.

I glance at my watch and see that my shift finished five minutes ago. The bar is mostly empty now. A few stragglers nursing their drinks; a couple necking in the corner; a table of regulars, arguing about football and showing no sign of slowing down.

'Shit, sorry, Winny, I lost track of . . . you now.'

Winston smirks. 'I noticed. We haven't been introduced,' he says, extending a hand to Henry. 'Winston, I'm the landlord.'

'Henry, I'm—'

'My hairdresser,' I say. 'He's my . . . hairdresser.'

'Pleased to meet you,' says Henry, still shaking Winston's hand.

'Hairdresser? What, like . . . hair?'

Henry nods, shows Winston a pair of finger scissors.

'Fair enough,' says Winston, shrugging – *each to his own*.

'Listen,' Henry says, looking out at the sticky tables, 'I could help.'

208

'Go on,' says Winston, opening the hatch, 'I'll take care of it tonight.'

'You sure, Winnie? I don't mind.'

'Get out of here before I change my mind,' he says. 'You owe me one.'

I kiss Winnie on the whiskers, and he pats me on the bottom as I make my way out from behind the bar.

'*Hands*, Winston.'

'Apologies, Duchess, force of whatssaname. And nice to meet you,' he says to Henry. 'Good job on the Barnet, by the way, suits her.'

'Does, doesn't it,' says Henry, and before I can quite figure out what's happened we're outside and all alone.

And then Henry is kissing me.

Did he kiss me or did I kiss him?

At my third meeting of the heartbroke widows, I had stubble burn on my neck. That evening I wrote in my black notebook: *No more meaningless sex.*

And while it feels in no way meaningless, this kiss is leading somewhere.

'We shouldn't,' I say.

'I know,' his lips not losing contact with mine as he whispers this.

'We can't stand here all night, either,' I say, even though I sincerely wish we could.

'Walk you home?'

I have had men back to my house before, but no one I intended to see a second time. So it didn't matter when they asked who was the guy in the photographs. I could lie, cry, laugh it off or ignore the question. But I don't know what I'd say to Henry, and I'm not ready to find out.

'House is a mess,' I say.

Something catches Henry's eye and he leans away from me, extending his arm. A taxi pulls to a stop beside us.

'Where to?' says the cabbie.

Henry

It's Everyone's Thing

Gus is looking at me out of the corner of his eye. He's paying more attention to me than his customer, but she, in turn, is too busy playing a game on her phone to notice.

'Ever cut anyone's ear off?' I ask.

'Only once,' says Gus.

My client's reflection stares at me, wide-eyed.

'So?' says Gus. 'How was the date?'

Now both customers and Gus are looking at me, waiting for an answer.

'Well?' says the girl with the phone.

I nod, smile.

'Sweet,' says Gus. 'Seeing her again?'

And my smile vanishes.

Gus shrugs. 'You gotta do, what you gotta do.'

'Men,' says the girl, turning back to her phone.

'So,' says Gus, 'I guess that means you're not busy tonight?'

'Well, I dunno, I mean . . .'

'Don't fight it,' says Gus.

'It's just . . . it's not really my thing.'

'It's everyone's thing, Henriqué.'

We have beanbags and blankets.

'Everybody comfortable?' says Gus, affecting something of the hypnotist's lilt.

The room above The Hairy Krishna is thick with incense and dim with flickering candlelight, the sound of waves and harmonic chimes plays on the speakers, and the beanbag is very plump. But I wouldn't say I'm comfortable. Besides cutting hair, Gus runs a once-weekly meditation group. From what he's told me, the hour-long sessions draw on a range of half-understood principles gleaned from Buddhism, late night TV and a yoga teacher with whom Gus once had a fling. There are five of us lying cushioned and cocooned on the floor; a big turnout for Gus's 'Tune Out Tuesdays'.

'We're going to slow it down,' says Gus, doing exactly that with his annunciation, which has more of a comic than a relaxing effect. 'Relax your toes . . . are your toes relaxed?'

'Uh hmm . . .' say several disembodied voices.

'Henriqué, are your little piggies relaxed?'

'Yes, I mean, Ah huhh . . .'

'Goooood. Now your ankles.'

And knees, thighs, bums ('Is your rump relaxed, Henroldo?'), tummies, arms, hands, fingers, necks and faces. And yes, I do relax; not as much as I might without Gus's diverting commentary, but I relax.

'Now for the noodle,' drawls Gus. 'If there's something on your mind, something weighing you down . . . Henry . . . bring it into your consciousness now.'

Zoe. Zoe's face looking at mine while I cut her hair. Zoe's heavy smile. Zoe travelling.

'Are we there?' intones Gus.

'Hmm hmm . . .'

'Now visualize a balloooon, any colour, just needs to be a ballooooon.'

'Ya hmm . . .'

'And attach that heavy thinking to your balloon. Mine's a red one. And let your balloon float that funk away.'

We are silent for a minute. My balloon floats away, Zoe clinging to its trailing string. And I don't want it to float away. I reach for Zoe's hand and pull her back towards me.

'How we doing, everyone? Have we floated our funk?'

'Ahh hmmm . . .'
'Henriqué?'
'Nuh huhh . . .'
'Gooood.'

June

June 6 at 8:43 PM

From: Audrey <audreywilliams56@mymail.net>

To: Alex Williams

Hello Son

I've been thinking about you a lot this last
week.

I think about you almost constantly, is the truth
of it. Sometimes it's a quiet thing at the back of
my mind, like a radio left on in another room.
And then there are the things that catch you off
guard. Like last week, I was in Morrison's and
they had a special offer on blueberries. Oobries,
you called them as a toddler. And remembering
that, I all of a sudden needed to be out of there
as quickly as possible. Just left my trolley half
full in the aisle and walked out the door. And I

215

just walked and walked until it was nearly dark.

In my mind you exist as so many different versions of yourself. From baby to boy to great strapping man. Maybe it's the summer coming on (you always loved those long school holidays!) but lately when I close my eyes, I see you as a lanky 11 year old, all skinny legs and grazed knees. It was hard without your dad around to help, but you and Pat were good boys – even if you did give me the run around! The number of nights I'd fall asleep exhausted on the sofa, probably I slept as many hours there as in my bed. But I'm not complaining son. I loved your energy and joy and noise and I wouldn't have wanted it any other way. There's gouges in the banister from where you and your brother would slide down, even though I told you a hundred times not to! They've been painted over a few times now, but I can still see the marks in the wood. And when I feel them under my hand, it's almost like I can feel you too. So no, I wouldn't have had it any other way.

Well, I think I'm going to turn in for the night. The sun woke me up just after five this morning, and I don't think I can keep my eyes open much

The Trouble with Henry and Zoe

longer. Every year I think I'll get thicker curtains, but for some reason I never do. Maybe I'll look at some in the shops tomorrow – no time like the present don't they say.

No time like the present son. I think you lived your life that way, and I'm grateful that you did. You should have had longer sweetheart, so much longer.

Sleep well beautiful boy.

All my love and all my heart

Mum xx

Zoe

Definitely In My Top Two

'Sure you won't let me treat you?' says Rachel.

'It's not that I wouldn't,' I say. 'It's just that I don't think it's possible.'

'Show me,' says the nail technician, an aggressive Thai lady who summons memories of intimidating schoolteachers.

'Really,' I tell her, 'I'll just watch.'

The woman's name badge identifies her as Molly. 'Hand,' demands Molly, extending her own to receive mine. Molly squinches her mouth to one side and tuts disapproval. 'Biter.'

'Blimey,' says Rachel, 'they are quite ...'

'Non-existent, I know. They'd look even worse painted – like child's hands.'

'Pedicure,' says Molly, indicating a leatherette chair beside the table.

'Great idea,' says Rachel.

'No, really, thanks.'

'Not bite feet?' says Molly.

'No. I not.'

Molly pats the chair firmly, and then clicks her fingers at another technician who scampers over.

'So,' says Rachel, as the nail techs set to work, 'how's my hairdresser?'

'You don't hang about, do you?'

Rachel taps her watch. 'I'm a busy lady. I've got meetings all afternoon, and I still need to sort out flowers, a band, a photographer and your bridesmaids' dresses. So . . . come on.'

'He's . . . *whoo*! What's that?'

'Chair,' says my tech, a surly girl with tight top-knotted hair. 'Vibrates.'

'Oo er!' says Rachel. 'Might get one of those for the house, get rid of Steve. Anyway, Henry – you were saying?'

'He's good,' I say, a slight tremolo to my voice now.

Rachel pouts at me in a way that communicates this answer is in no way close to acceptable.

'He's nice.'

Rachel dials up the pout to maximum.

'He comes to the pub on Saturdays, we talk, play

Scrabble ...' Rachel's pout has not softened, '... we have a little ... in-joke, I suppose.'

'In-jokes are good.'

'"My place or mine," he says, then we go back to his flat.'

'What's it like?'

'Well, it's weird; it's a shabby old guesthouse really. Feels kind of ... I dunno, temporary. Henry has a big room on the top floor. Got his own kitchen and shower, like a bedsit. Neat, but very basic. Maybe he's saving up for a place of his own. It would explain why he works so hard, I suppose. And he does jigsaws, which is weird, but ... I find it kind of sexy for some reason. His brow crinkles when he's concentrating.'

'Fascinating,' says Rachel. 'I meant what's *it* like? You know ...' and she waggles her eyebrows for emphasis.

'It's ...' Rachel is already pouting; making it clear she will accept no prevarication. I smile. 'Definitely in my top two.'

'Blimey,' says Rachel. 'Not quite a' – snapping her fingers – 'Ken, Ken Wood! Ha!'

'Not quite,' I say. 'But Ken was a freak of nature.'

'Colour?' This from the surly top-knot.

'Excuse me?'

The girl juts her chin at the colour chart in my lap.

'Oh, right, er ... red?'

'Cherry Red, Ruby Red, Red Apple, Red Devil, R—'

'She'll go Devil,' says Rachel. 'So, you like him?'

I nod.

'He knows you're travelling, though?'

Another nod.

'Tricky.'

'Yes it is.'

'Did you tell him about ... Alex?'

'No.'

'Zoe!'

'I know. I should have told him straight away, but it's hardly ... I mean, how do you drop that into conversation?'

'Very very tricky,' says Rachel. 'I'll go Midnight Satsuma,' she says to Molly.

'He wants to go on a date,' I say. 'Like a proper couple.'

'Awkward.'

'I know. But if I don't, then it's just a bit ...'

'Cheap?'

'Sad. But if I do, then it gets a bit ...'

'Fucked up?'

'Yeah ... fucked up.'

'Talking of which,' says Rachel.

'What?'

'Well, when we get back off honeymoon, me and Steve were going to start trying for a baby.'

'Okay.'

'So, I've been on the pill since I was fifteen. A *long* time. And they say you should come off it a few months before you start trying. Give your bits and bobs a chance to settle down and get ready.'

'Rachel?'

'Yeah, well, turns out I'm ready. Very ready.'

'As in ...'

'As in ten weeks yesterday, twenty big fat weeks when I walk up the aisle.'

'Holy shit, Rachel. Holy ... *shit.*'

'Yeah, that was me for about an entire week after I found out.'

'Are you ... happy?'

'Well, the honeymoon's kind of ruined. Not sure I'll be scuba diving or bungee jumping, and I certainly won't be drinking any piña coladas, but ... yeah, I'm happy. Very happy, actually. Are you crying, babes?'

'Only a little. Good crying, though. So' – I indicate a growing bump – 'twenty weeks?'

'Well, I've had a look online, and it could be anywhere from a bit bloated to the massive "oh my God the bride's up the duff" look. Probably that, knowing my luck.'

'Dress?'

'Well, the good news is I should have a decent pair of boobs by then. So, plenty of cleavage, and then' – Rachel indicates a wide A-line starting just below her boobs – 'away she goes.'

'Holy shit.'

'You like cake, don't you?'

'What?'

'I need to ask a favour.'

'Okay.'

'Great. And then you can explain all that nonsense about jigsaws.'

Henry

We Shouldn't

It's been a long day. A routine morning of simple pro-
cedures followed by an entire afternoon with Jenny. It
would have been easier under a general, but Jenny is old
and frail, and the risks outweighed the advantages. Instead
I have fitted nine titanium implants under local anaes-
thetic and a mild sedative.

'Are you sure there isn't someone who can come and
collect you, Jenny?'

It's been four hours of hard work for me, but it's been a
lot tougher on Jenny. Her mouth is going to hurt like she's
been kicked by tomorrow morning, but for the time being
she is still numb with lignocaine. Nevertheless, her hands
are trembling and she's been through quite an ordeal.
Despite this, and despite the crudeness of her temporary
crowns, her smile is transformed.

'Everyone busy,' she repeats. 'I fine. Taxi fine.'

'Well, let's give it another half hour or so, shall we? Then I'll call you a cab.'

'You're good boy,' Jenny says, patting my hand. 'Very good boy.'

'I'm really not,' I tell her. 'It's just that I don't have anything better to do.'

And even though this is in every way true, Jenny laughs, and smacks my wrist. This is my last appointment of the day and there's no more dentistry to be done; my nurse has gone for the weekend, so it's just me and Jenny in the consulting room.

'What 'bout that girl?' she says.

In addition to her full-time day job, Zoe works shifts at the Duck and Cover. As far as I can tell, Saturday nights are a repeat fixture; and for the last three weeks I have warmed the stool on the other side of the bar. Three dates, I suppose, sharing a bottle of wine, answering random questions in the Duck and Cover quiz, playing Scrabble, Kerplunk, Snakes 'n' Ladders. And then the long walk back to mine through largely empty streets, holding hands, talking trivia, laughing, anticipating.

On the Sunday morning after our first night together, I went out for papers and pastries. We placed two chairs in front of the bay window and drank a pot of coffee, the sound of turning pages loud in the bright room. We spent a strange two hours where it seemed the air around us consisted of discrete pockets; some heavy with an awkward tension, others light with familiarity and humour. In one of those clouds of charged atmosphere, we found ourselves kissing again, but as the kiss gained heat and pressure, Zoe stepped away from me, repeating her line from the previous night: 'We shouldn't.'

We left the house together: Zoe to go home and change before her Sunday shift, me to wield a pair of scissors at The Hairy Krishna.

We said we'd see each other around, but we didn't exchange numbers or make arrangements. Something in Zoe's body language – the way she kissed me, touched my cheek, squeezed my hand – felt like a subtle injunction. And then when she was gone from sight, I felt like a fake and a fool and almost ran after her, but something stayed my feet. She is travelling in a few months, after all.

The following Saturday night I walked into the Duck and Cover as Winston was handing out the quiz sheets. My reasoning went that I could order a drink, feel the temperature and then make my excuses or make myself comfortable.

'Hello stranger,' Zoe said as I took my seat at the bar.

'What's going on?' Taking down the Scrabble board as she said it.

At the end of the night we walked the forty-five minutes back to my flat, holding hands, kissing, walking slowly then fast, drawing the tension out, then letting the anticipation quicken our feet.

'We shouldn't,' Zoe said again, a small smile playing about her mouth.

She said it again last week, our own in-joke, losing humour and gaining truth each time it's said. And then in the morning, we kiss goodbye under that pocket of bad weather, and tell each other 'see you around', although we make no plans or promises. We have exchanged numbers at least, but they remain unrung. There is no doubt in my mind I'll spend tomorrow night in the Duck and Cover, sitting on the other side of the bar playing some game or other, drinking mediocre wine and having a wonderful night talking about nothing. 'My place, or mine?' I'll say, and Zoe will pretend to deliberate before choosing mine. And then the walk home, the familiar and surprising sex, the weird ecosystem of Sunday morning.

The longer this goes on, the harder the end will hit me when Zoe leaves. So let's hope it lasts as long as possible, and hurts every bit as much as I deserve.

After the second time – date, thing, call it what you

will – Rachel phoned. Just a short call to book a cut in a couple of weeks. She asked how I was, made small talk and then, before signing off:

'Listen … Zoe, she's … she mentioned that you and her had … met. A couple of times.'

I hadn't considered whether or not Zoe had told her friends about us, but I was still surprised to learn that she had. Surprised and pleased.

'You know she's travelling?'

'Yes, she said.'

'I know it's none of my … actually, she's my best friend so I suppose it is my business, but … sorry, rewind, I don't want to sound all …'

'It's fine, I understand.'

'Thank you, I … just be nice, yeah?'

'I'll try.'

'Do better than that, Henry.' Laughing a little. 'Just … be nice.'

'I will.'

'Good. I'd hate to have to stab you with your scissors. See you in two weeks, yeah.'

And God knows what the story is. I'd ask, but I assume that if Zoe wanted me to know she'd have told me by now. My guess is there's a man involved, maybe he cheated on her, or walked out, or maybe it's the other way around. But whatever it was, I'll bet it's the reason Zoe is working two jobs to buy a plane ticket.

'She's going travelling,' I say to Jenny. 'The girl.'

'Where?'

'All around,' I say. 'Going to see the world.'

'India!' says Jenny, jabbing a crooked finger towards the sky. 'She should go there, very nice.'

I'm always wary about guessing someone's country of birth; it's just too easy to come off sounding like an ignorant racist. I have a hard enough time with Aussies and Kiwis, let alone the whole of Asia. 'Aren't you . . .' I gesticulate nonsensically with my hands, trying to keep them from performing some involuntary reductive mime.

'Chinese, yes,' says Jenny. 'But my husban', India. I'm go in October.'

'To India? That sounds nice.'

Jenny nods. 'Yes. Scatter ashes.'

'You . . . you mean the ashes of . . .'

'Husban', yes. He die, innit.' There are tears in Jenny's eyes as she says this. In boxing, they say the punch that hurts most is the one you don't see coming, and Jenny's simple, matter of fact revelation has caught me with my guard down.

'Jenny, I'm so sorry to hear that. When did it happen?'

'March,' she says. 'Two week before birthday.'

'His?'

'Mine. Was going take me theatre. That one with dancing boy.'

'*Billy Elliot?*'

'Funeral on same day so tickets wasted.'

I look into her eyes for any hint of humour, but there is nothing but sincerity.

'So I get my teeth, innit.'

'Instead of *Billy Elliot?*'

Jenny laughs, pats my hand as if I were joking. 'Husban' family never like me. Chinese girl, see. Very cross when he marry, so never go back.'

'But you're taking his ashes.'

Jenny nods. 'I promise. When he get the cancer' – Jenny holds a hand to her tummy – 'I promise.'

'Does he have any family left there?'

'Only sisters. They nice, write letters, cards.'

'So, that's why you're here? For India?'

'Nice to have good teeth,' she says.

By my estimation, Jenny's teeth have been beyond bad for at least ten years, possibly twice as long. And the fact that she is having them fixed only now – after her husband's death – is nothing short of a tragedy.

'Don't worry,' I tell her. 'Your teeth will be perfect.'

Jenny nods. 'You love her?'

I laugh involuntarily. 'It's a bit early for that.'

Jenny shakes her head. 'I know straight'way. Husban' a very handsome man, you know.'

'I'll bet he was.'

'I work in hospital, in Chennai. Like my name, innit. And every day I go in bakery for sweet biscuit.'

'Bad for your teeth, Jenny.'

'Yes, but baker very nice man, see. Say to me, no money for biscuit, just beautiful smile.'

'Ah, I do see.'

'So I get sweet biscuit every morning to work. And lots of weeks. Then one day – biscuits in square box, like this – one day, open box and no biscuit. Just flat cake. On top is little lady and little man. Like on wedding cake, innit.'

'You're joking.'

'He follow outside, and say to me, "You marry me". Not even know my name.'

'But you married him.'

Jenny laughs. 'No, baker very fat man, hairy nose. I eat the biscuit in hospital, with handsome doctor. He buy tea, I bring biscuits. Then one day, he moving to England. And so I go with, get marry, have babies.'

'Blimey, Jenny, you are full of surprises.'

'Just know, straight'way.'

'Maybe you do,' I say.

'Why you not travel with girl?'

'It's not that easy, Jenny.'

Jenny shrugs. 'Not that hard, neither. I okay now, you can call taxi?'

'Sure. Just remember, don't eat anything hard tonight. And no sweet biscuits, you hear me?'

Jenny laughs and pats my hand.

As I take out my phone to call a taxi, I see that I have one new message. And it's from Zoe.

What you doing tomorrow?

Zoe

We're Getting Married

'So are you going to tell me where we're going yet?' Henry asks as our train pulls out of Victoria station. It's Saturday morning, and I've swapped my shift at the Duck, so we have the whole day and night together.

'Surrey,' I tell him.

Henry taps his ticket on the table. 'Yeah, I'd kind of figured that part out.'

'We're getting married.'

The colour drains out of Henry's cheeks as if someone has opened a tap at the back of his neck. 'That's a joke, right?'

'God, Henry, you really know how to make a girl feel special.'

'Sorry ... weddings, they're a bit ...'

'Relax, we're going cake tasting.'

'Cake?'

'Wedding cake, actually, but I promise not to propose.'

'Wh ...?' Henry begins, but the process of forming one question seems to raise nine more, and the enquiry dies on his lips.

'It's a favour for Rachel. She's ... can you keep a secret?'

Henry nods sincerely. 'Yes. Yes, I can.'

'She's on the nest.'

Henry glances out of the window, scanning the passing scenery. 'Nest?'

'Up the ... you know, family way.'

'Pregnant! What about the wedding? How pregnant?'

'Well, I'm pretty sure you either are or you aren't but ... she'll be twenty weeks when she walks down the aisle. *Biiiig* floaty dress.'

'Blimey. Have to make a bit more of her hair, hey.'

'Good idea. Massive beehive or something.'

'So ... cake?'

'Well, you did say you wanted to go on a date.'

'I was thinking more along the lines of a movie.'

'Well, Rachel has been a bit pukey, so ... loosen your belt.'

Henry has a very handsome smile. He relaxes back into his seat and again stares out of the window.

*

'What have you got for yummness?' I ask Henry.

'Hmm ...' He holds up a finger, finishes chewing, swallows. 'Definitely a seven.'

'Not an eight?'

'I'll give it an eight for scrummness,' he says, jabbing at the cake with his fork. 'But yummness is a seven; seven-point-five tops.'

'Remind me again what the difference is?'

'Yummness is taste, scrummness is—'

'Texture, darling,' says Janice – our Sherpa through this mountain of cake. 'The way I remember it,' she says, 'is scrummness sounds like crumbness, as in consistency. Whereas yummness is just, you know, yummy.'

Henry winks at me. 'And wowness?' he says to Janice.

'Eye appeal,' she says. 'How's it going to look in photographs when you two lovebirds' – she touches Henry's cheek with the back of one finger, pinches mine with the other hand – 'cut the first slice.'

'Remind me of the date.' She addresses this to Henry, and although I briefed him on the train ride out, he's clearly struggling.

'August ... the ... middleth?'

Janice laughs, as if Henry's hesitation is an adorable charade of male indifference.

'The seventeenth,' I say. 'Isn't that right, Poppet?'

As Janice turns her attention to me, Henry raises his eyebrows and mouths the word *Poppet?*

'Too cute,' says Janice. 'I see a lot, I mean *a lot* of couples and, trust me, I know. *Too*' – and she pinches my cheek again – '*cute!* Right, I'll leave you two lovebirds alone while I get the next selection. Be good!'

Henry seems to have recovered from his initial shock and has relaxed into this rather odd day, deftly fielding questions about the proposal, the honeymoon, and what happened to my engagement ring (at the jeweller's, being matched to the wedding band, apparently). If I'd met Henry six, or three or even two months ago, I don't know if I would have been ready for all whatever this is. But what about if I'd met him four years ago, before I met Alex? Would we still be together now? And – not that I'm getting confetti-headed, but I have eaten a lot of wedding cake today – if we had met four years ago, isn't it possible that we might be planning our own big day instead of Rachel's?

'Nearly there,' says Janice. 'I like to call this selection *the icing on the cake*. Because it is – haha! – literally, all about *the icing on the cake*. You've got eight different frostings so I hope you brought your sweet tooths with you. Or should that be sweet teeth? I never know.'

After a final platter of Italian cream, marbled coffee,

lemon poppy and spiced pumpkin, my jeans are cutting me in half and my tongue feels like it's been removed, tenderized, dipped in sugar and sewn back in upside down. Everything tastes like everything else, and I score the selection arbitrarily, already knowing we'll recommend the almond poppy sponge with fresh-fruit filling and peach buttercream frosting. Before we leave, Janice presents us with two sugarcraft souvenirs: a blushing bride for Henry, and a top-hatted groom for me.

'Good gosh and trust me,' she says, dabbing the corner of her eye theatrically. 'Just made for each other.'

Henry sleeps most of the way back to London, his head resting against the window as the passing scenery loses its space and colour. Maybe it's this situation, this part-time, while-it-lasts relationship, but there is always a trace of tension in his face. As if he never fully relaxes or lowers his guard. But it melts away now, and watching him doze with a half smile on his lips I feel a mixture of guilt, loss, doubt and frustration. Tangled emotions extending back towards Alex, and forward to the day I leave Henry. All connected, all pulling in different directions, distorting what might have been a simple uncomplicated thing. We both sense it, but it leaves Henry while he sleeps, and if I could change anything about today, this train would roll though London now and just keep on rolling.

'All change,' I say, stroking his cheek as we pull into Victoria.

'We back?' he says, massaging his eyes with the heels of his hands.

'Yup.'

'So,' he says, smiling, 'my place or mine?'

I lean across the table and kiss him. Passengers are heaving down bags from the overhead racks and filing down the corridor past our seat and off the train, but I kiss Henry hard and without inhibition.

'What was that for?'

'I don't have any right to ask this, but ... do you think that for the next twelve weeks ... do you think that while we're together, it can be just us?'

Henry puts his hands on my face and kisses my forehead. 'Did you think there was anyone else?'

I shrug. 'I don't know. It's just, we're not ...' and all I can do is shrug again.

'Yes,' says Henry. 'Just us.'

'In that case ... can I ask one more thing?'

'Sure, name it.'

'How would you like to be my plus one at Rachel's wedding?'

July

July 4 at 3:14 PM
From: Audrey <audreywilliams56@mymail.net>
To: Alex Williams

Hello Son

Well, your mum has finally turned 60. Pat and Aggy came to stay for the weekend, and they really spoiled me. They gave me vouchers for a health spa and Pat was encouraging me to get a massage – but good lord son! Just the thought of lying there in my underwear made me blush. Aggy said they put a towel on you, but even so ... no, I think I'll have a facial instead. Although I'm not expecting miracles!

I always thought when I got to 60 I'd lie about my age, but now that it's come around, I've changed my mind. I think growing old is a privilege – one you never had son. So I'm telling everyone I meet, I've even got a badge – big as the lid off a jam jar! I only wish you and your dad could have been here to celebrate with me. But I know we'll all be together again one day and the thought is a great comfort to me.

There's a shoebox under my bed with all the birthday cards you used to make when you were a boy, and I set a few out on the chest of drawers in my room. One of them has a finger painting of a flower on it. Six little red petals, where you pressed your fingertips to the paper. I think I'll take it to the framers in the week and hang it in the hallway. It can be my birthday present to myself.

All my love and all my heart

Mum xx

PS. I did it! I got the curtains! They're quite trendy I think, blue and white check! They almost totally block out the light and I've been sleeping quite well most nights. Should have done it years ago.

Mum xx

Henry

Are We Floating?

'Is everybody relaxed?'

'Uh huhh . . .'

Very far from it.

In place of waves we are listening to something repetitive on a cello. It brings to mind the string quartet April and I booked for our wedding.

'Excellent. Now relax your toes.'

I would be happy never to even hear the 'W' word again, but now Zoe has invited me to be her 'plus one' at Rachel's wedding in August. Last time I was a 'minus one'.

'Kneeees,' says Gus.

The girls are all travelling out by ferry on the Friday before the wedding; I'm in no hurry to be there, so I've played the work card and will fly out first thing on the

Saturday morning. I've even bought my ticket. All I need now is a passport. That essential piece of paperwork is in the front pocket of the suitcase I left in April's room eight and a half months ago. I assume she has unpacked our sandals, sunglasses and mosquito repellent and, in regard to my possessions, thrown them into the nearest volcano. And in a way, I hope she has. Better that than have the still-packed Samsonite standing in the hallway of our new home, gathering cobwebs like Miss Havisham's wedding cake. Whether April would deliberately destroy a legal document or not, I don't know, but I'd bet not. I could apply for a new passport, of course, but that feels cowardly. And besides, it would only be delaying the inevitable.

'Aaaand face.'

Face the music, people say. But I've never known what that means; what's so terrible about facing music? Music doesn't throw bricks or slash your car tyres. Grasp the nettle at least makes sense, but even that brief and shallow sting would be welcome compared to the reception I can anticipate in my hometown. Since walking out on April I have missed Christmas, my birthday and those of both my parents. It's their fortieth wedding anniversary at the start of August, and I would very much like to be there. Dad, for all his outward displays of antagonism, oafishness and indifference to all things romantic, has never forgotten to give my mother a card and a bunch of flowers on their anniversary. This year he's upping the ante and splashing out on a piece of ruby jewellery; he's been on the phone twice in as many weeks, calling when Mum's out so he can confer with me on what to buy: ring, necklace, earrings. But if I want to attend their anniversary party without ruining it, I need to first show my face and allow it to be slapped, punched and screamed at. Maybe even get my teeth knocked out. And wouldn't that be poetic.

'And let's bring out the balloons,' says Gus. 'This week I'm going with yellow, but any colour will do. Just so long as it flooooooats.'

Zoe is going to Brighton for Rachel's hen party a few weeks from now, and while Rachel parades along the beach in a veil and an L-plate, I will head north to grasp the nettle, take my medicine, face the music and grab my passport.

'Are we floating?' says Gus.

My passport can't weigh more than a few ounces, but it's giving my little blue balloon some serious problems.

Zoe

P Is For Prick

There are twenty-six letters in the alphabet; thirteen double-paged spreads in *The Elfabet*: A is for Antler; B is for Bauble; C, for Christ's sake, is for Carols. Christmas is almost five months away, but the way these things work, this book needs to go to print before the end of the month, so here we all are – me, my boss, the author, illustrator and art director – looking at the illustrator's roughs, checking the layout, and double-checking that, yes, Toys really is the best use of a T. We've been crowded around this small table since two o'clock and we've only just landed on V for Vixen, which has caused all kinds of innuendo and forced laughter.

Early on, Alex and I saw each other so often that people started calling us A-to-Z, an entity. I pretended to be offended, of course, but secretly enjoyed being one half of a complete and unified whole. It was our little joke: 'You complete me, Zee,' Alex would say. 'And you begin me,' I would answer. It's the anniversary of the day we first met, and I miss him today more profoundly than I have for weeks, more than I have since I met Henry probably.

I glance at my phone; it's 4.30 and Henry still hasn't been in touch. A needy little game, played every Friday, but I've lost track of whose turn it is to buckle.

We argued last Sunday. Henry all but called us fuck buddies, and although I was kind of affronted, it was good to see his frustration coming through. I almost told him as much, but felt it might be mistimed.

W is for Winter, by which time I will be on a beach somewhere.

I bought my ticket at lunchtime. Just walked into an old-fashioned high-street travel agent's and spent four hundred and forty-nine pounds and ninety-nine pence, one way to Bangkok. So, no turning back now. The man said I could get the ticket cheaper if I waited until August, or better still, September, but it felt like something that needed to be done now, today, that minute. Because the more I feel for Henry – and it's growing by the week – the more I feel my resolve wavering. *Maybe I should put if off for a month, two months, maybe until next year.* But I know that's just fear talking. I stayed with Alex too long; some of it was gratitude, some guilt, but mainly fear. Fear of being alone, of the unknown. When I decided to go travelling it terrified me, and that's how I knew it was exactly the right thing to do. And yes, there is something about Henry, but if I don't do this now, there's a good chance I never will. And I'll never forgive myself. So I took a deep breath and handed the travel agent my credit card, and he handed me a ticket. Or what passes for one. This is no gilt-edged piece of stiff card, my name and destination printed in slanting, curving script; this is a flimsy sheet of A4 paper with a QR code on the bottom. But it'll get me where I'm going.

Henry still hasn't tried to contact me. Five minutes and I'll excuse myself to the loo and send him a message: **What you doing tonight?** Or maybe I'll add a little joke; a peace offering: **You win! See you at 7.00**.

'Am I the only one who has a problem with Xmas?' This from our illustrator, Maggie, a small, unassuming girl who, from what I can tell, is doing ninety per cent of the work on this project for just fifty per cent of the cheque.

'I bloody hope so,' says the author, laughing awkwardly, 'I mean, it is a Christmas book, after all.'

'Well,' says Maggie, fiddling with her pen, 'that's sort

of my point. Isn't Xmas sort of, you know, crossing out Christ?'

Charles, the author – and God how I resent attaching that title to a pompous twerp whose book consists of twenty-six letters and twenty-seven words including Plum Pudding – sighs. 'Seriously?'

'It's sort of important to me,' says Maggie.

'You might have said that before agreeing to the sodding book.'

'I thought I did, sorry.'

'I kind of agree,' says Sunni, the art director.

'Claire?' says Charles, appealing to my boss despite this being my book.

'Zoe?' says Claire, as I was rather hoping she wouldn't.

I realize I'm sighing, and make a big show of stroking my chin, trying to disguise the outflow of air as an act of deep consideration. And at the same time, I wonder why the hell I'm bothering. 'How about Xylophone? I say. 'Xylophones are Christmassy, aren't they?'

Charles makes a loud, braying noise. '*Whonk whonk whonk!* Cliché alert!'

'What,' I say, 'and Toys isn't? Or Decorations or Snowman or Jack sodd–!'

'Okay,' says Claire, her voice projecting its full authority, 'let's all just . . . take a breath. Zoe?'

I nod. 'Sure, no problem.'

'Charles?'

Charles, who has been staring at me in open-mouthed shock, turns to Claire. '*Xmas* . . .' he pauses, looks at the assembled faces, making sure we all understand that he is not to be interrupted, '. . . is non-denominational, yeah. Muslim friendly and all of that.' He focuses his attention on Sunni. 'You know what I mean?'

Sunni smiles, shrugs. 'I'm an atheist, but I still think it should be Christmas.'

'Jesus Christ,' says Charles.

'Or,' I say, 'how about Xenophobe?'

Claire stands up. 'Zoe, can I have a word?'

Her office is not the book-lined, oak-panelled, leather-upholstered chamber one might expect of a senior editorial director. It's plain, austere and the stuffing is hanging out of her chair. But she does keep a bottle of Scotch in her bottom drawer; whether this is a nod to convention or a medical necessity, no one knows, but it's no secret and now it's on the table.

'Better?'

'It helps,' I say, raising my glass.

I could tell Claire that today is the day I first met my dead boyfriend, but I think that would be weak. And anyway, it's not the reason I unloaded on Charles. 'Sorry

about that, Claire. I've got things on my mind. No excuse,
I know, but . . .'

'P is for Prick,' says Claire, smiling.

'And Professionalism, I suppose.'

'Oh dear,' says Claire. 'We seem to have our roles
reversed. Are you okay?'

'Yes, I'm fine.'

'Sure?'

I nod. 'I'm sure. I . . . I wasn't going to do this for a few
weeks but, now as we're here . . .'

'Darling?'

'R is for Resignation,' I say.

'Oh, Zoe, darling.' Claire gets up from her chair, puts
her arms around me and kisses my cheek. 'Tell me, tell
me all about it.'

And I do, I tell her about the day I met Alex, the night
I met Henry, the coffee on Albert Bridge and Scrabble in
the Duck and Cover.

When it becomes apparent that this is going to be
more involved than a five-minute chat, Claire pops out
to confirm with Charles that C is for Christmas, X is for
Xylophone, and S is for shove it up your bum if you don't
bloody well like it. When she returns two minutes later,
my boss has acquired a plate of muffins. I tell her about
the house, the mortgage, the fight over the wallpaper, the

creaky floorboard and my one-way ticket to Thailand. By the time I get to the part where I accused our author of being a xenophobe, we've finished the muffins, the whisky and most of a box of tissues.

Henry

Quite White

Everything is temporary.

Temporary teeth, temporary boyfriend.

Jenny's implants have integrated perfectly, and today I am chopping down her remaining thirteen teeth, grinding them into pegs that, like their titanium counterparts, will hold her new porcelain crowns. It's the longest day in the process, removing the crowns from her last appointment, cleaning the implants, taking a full mouth impression and then fitting a complete mouthful of temporary crowns that she will wear while her new teeth are prepared in the lab.

Jenny cried when she saw her mouth full of crude, white temporary teeth, and I had to calm her down so I could remind her that we still had another appointment to go. Normally, I would colour match the crowns to her existing teeth, but this isn't an issue for Jenny – there are no teeth left.

'Is a bright white, you know. I tell you, white smile.'

'Look at this.' I show Jenny a row of mounted veneers, ranging from Hollywood white to a more subdued shade, still white but tinged with yellow – what a paint company might call Vanilla Cream, or some such.

Jenny rests an arthritic finger on the Hollywood incisor.

'It will look wrong,' I tell her.

'White. Look white.'

'When you get older, Jenny, your teeth darken naturally. Something more like this' – I slide her finger along the row of veneers – 'will look a lot more natural.'

Jenny slides her finger all the way back to Hollywood. And, well, it's her money, her teeth, her smile.

'Quite right,' I tell her.

'Hah, joke! Quite white, innit. Quite white, haha!'

And I laugh right along, because, really, who the hell am I, jilter, outcast, idiot, to tell anyone how to live their life.

Since the cake tasting and our pledge of temporary monogamy, Zoe and I have seen considerably more of each other. She drops in on Fridays now, a change of clothes in her backpack, and stays until early Sunday evening. We watch films, take long walks, play games in the Duck and Cover. We don't leave each other's side for forty-eight hours, making me feel her imminent departure more keenly than ever. Perhaps that explains my compulsion to invite her out for what you might call conventional dates – cinema, restaurant, theatre – despite the fact I know she will refuse. Zoe is saving for her travels and watching every penny, but at the same time she is too ... proud, I suppose, to let me foot the bill. I tried again on Sunday.

'Let's go out. Sunday dinner and a bottle of wine.'

'I don't get paid until next week.'

'My treat.'

'I don't want treating, it makes me feel bad.'

'I'd rather pay for both than not go. I'm being selfish, see, so it's okay. You'd be indulging me.'

'Can't we just ... hang out?'

'All we do is "hang out". Aren't you bored?'

Stupid thing to say.

'Why? Are you?' An edge to Zoe's voice.

'You know that's not what I mean. Let me take you out.'

Zoe sighed. 'It's sweet of you, honestly, but ... I'd feel better if you didn't.'

'Why?'

'Because, okay. Look, I'm sorry, I ... it's just important to me.'

I should have left it there. 'What about me, about what's important to me?'

'I don't know, Henry. How could I know? I don't know anything about you.'

'You know where I live. Which is more than I can say about you.'

'Don't. Please … can't we just enjoy this while it …'

'What? While it lasts?'

Zoe sighs, the set of her eyebrows appearing to say: *Well, yes, that's the situation. Thanks for spelling it out.*

'Zoe, that's what I'm trying to do. To enjoy it. But …'

'But what?'

'I don't want us to be nothing more than …'

Zoe looked at me intently; as if she knew exactly what I meant (of course she knew) but was curious to see whether I was stupid enough to say it out loud. There's a phrase people use that describes our relationship very well, and it's been bouncing around the inside of my head for weeks. Maybe I'd had too much wine, not enough sleep, or seen too many rotten teeth, but the words had made their way to the tip of my tongue, and the taste of them was nauseating.

'Nothing,' I said. 'Nothing.'

Zoe slid towards me and rested her head on my shoulder. I don't know if it was an apology or forgiveness, but I let the matter drop and we moved quietly through the rest of the day. We have two months left, and even if I could change that fact, I don't know that I should. Zoe clearly has baggage and it's obvious this trip is important to her. Maybe I should be glad she's going before she has a chance to find out who I really am. 'See you around,' we said when Zoe left in the evening, but as usual nothing was arranged.

The routine is that one or the other of us will call on Friday afternoon, and then Zoe will arrive a few hours later with two pairs of knickers in her backpack. I'm holding out, waiting to see if Zoe will take the initiative, but she is better at this game than I am, and I'm losing my nerve.

'She call an a message yet?' asks Jenny, as I check my phone for the seventh time.

'Not yet.'

'Maybe got other man, haha.'

'You're a laugh a minute today, Jenny.'

'Good joke though, innit.'

'Well, I hope so, otherwise I've just wasted twenty-eight quid on a pair of ladies' flip-flops.'

Zoe

Double Shit

It's six o'clock when I stagger out of Claire's office; the way my head feels it should be dark, but it's a bright July evening and I have to shield my phone from the sun before I can read the screen. I have one message from Henry:

See you tonight? Call me – Have a surprise.

I feel like I'm teetering on an emotional precipice and the last thing I need is a surprise. I don't know if I can handle any affection either, for that matter. All of a sudden it feels like it would be wrong – disrespectful, maybe – to cuddle up with Henry on the anniversary of the day I met Alex. I type out a short reply, the grey characters allowing me to project a mood and humour I couldn't pull off in the flesh:

Arrgh! Have to pull a shift at D&C. Sorry, will call tomorrow x

A white lie, and if ever one was justified it's tonight. My phone pings:

No worries. Surprise will keep x

I'm too drunk to ride my bike, but it's a clear evening and I am in no hurry to be back at the house. There was mail for Alex again yesterday, and if there's more tonight I might just tear my hair out. I send a kiss back to Henry, turn my phone to silent and start walking. I walk through Soho, past the Friday night drinkers, spilled onto the pavements, laughing, shouting, flirting. I cut through quiet exclusive streets, past giant houses and walled gardens until I reach Albert Bridge. There is no one selling coffee at this time of day, and the thousand lightbulbs are cold and will remain so for a few hours yet. This is city time, and the bridge is heavy with traffic, noise and exhaust fumes. If I came here for a small slice of recent nostalgia – and maybe I did – then I'm more of a fool than I give myself credit for.

It takes a little over three hours to walk home, and if I'd thought it through I would have worn different shoes. I'm sweaty, my feet hurt, and my hair stinks. I've gone in and out of hunger, and all I need now is a long bath and twelve hours' sleep. There's no mail for Alex, and when I draw level with his picture on the stairs, I blow him a kiss and do my best version of his patented head wobble. I never could do it, and looking at my reflection super-imposed over the picture I first laugh and then cry. But it's okay, it feels right and it feels somehow good. 'Hey, babes,' I whisper, and then I touch my finger to his face and go to run a bath.

There's half a bottle of wine in the fridge, so while the bath runs I pour most of it into a glass and take it upstairs with a trio of tea lights and a box of matches. The bath is full but I immediately sense something is wrong. The temperature in the room is wrong, there is no steam on the mirror, no steam above the water. And when I put my arm into the bath, the water is as cold as my chardonnay.

The pig of a boiler is unresponsive. I press buttons, fiddle with the controls, consult the manual. But nothing happens. And the absurdity of it makes me laugh again; today of all days, my boiler has died. I finish my wine in one gulp, pull a book down from the shelf and take myself to bed.

I spend Saturday afternoon cleaning Alex's old mountain bike. I wish it were a more unpleasant job, but the truth is Al's bike is disappointingly free from mud, grass, sand and deer shit. We bought our bikes as Christmas presents for each other almost two years ago.

And we were going to cover so many miles; exploring the green spaces and hidden paths of our city, maybe even ride to Brighton. So much for 'going to'; we took the bikes out that first weekend and maybe two or three times since, but we never got to Brighton, we didn't even get out of South London. We even bought a backpack that doubled as a picnic hamper, but we never used it.

On eBay, a two-year-old Kona Fire Mountain can fetch around £200.

Which is a long way short of the £1,850 it's going to take to replace the pig of a boiler, which, the plumber confirmed, is beyond repair. 'Lucky it didn't explode and take the 'ole 'ouse wiv it, luv.'

It crossed my mind to simply put up with it; that ten weeks of cold showers might toughen me up for my travels. But I figure there's plenty of time for that on the actual travels, which is kind of the point, after all. And besides, I can hardly rent the place out with a broken boiler.

I called Winston about five minutes after the plumber left and told him I'll take any additional shifts going; he asked if I could start at four tonight instead of seven, so that's another eighteen pounds off the deficit.

Going by recently completed auctions, a pair of Technics 1210 MK3 decks can fetch up to £675.

You can get another £230 for a matching four-channel mixer.

A Marantz amplifier and a pair of Dali Zensor speakers could go for £200 and £100 respectively. But they could go for a lot less.

Since losing his records in Thailand, Alex had begun the process of rebuilding his collection, but even so he had fewer than a hundred pieces of round black plastic, which might, if I'm lucky, fetch £50. Perhaps, if I were to sell the discs one by one, or drag them around specialist shops, I could sell them for a few hundred pounds, but I don't think I have the will or the energy.

A set of vintage Pioneer headphones might have gone for another £70 to £100, but Alex's were smashed when he was struck by a car last October. The scanner he bought but never used might fetch ten quid, but there's so much guilt attached to it, it's not worth the headache.

And finally, an Xbox 360 in good condition with seven games might bring in £75.

All in, on a good day, that's £1,530, and still a few hundred quid short of a new boiler plus installation.

A Leica M3 in good working condition can go for anywhere north of £500, maybe as much as the £800

Alex originally paid for it. I'd be back on track with a few hundred quid spare to spend on bikinis, food and maybe a couple of cinema tickets. I feel no conflict whatsoever about selling Alex's bike, decks, discs and so on; I'll never use them, plus we should have fixed the damn boiler while he was still around to take hot showers. So it's poor old Al's responsibility as much as mine. More than this, though, I feel lighter, as if these items, even stored out of sight in the shed, have been weighing me down. But I can't let go of the camera. I love that Alex bought it on a stupid drunken impulse, and I'm sad that he never used it as much as he should. If I keep anything, I'll keep this.

Cleaning Alex's bike, pulling all of this stuff out of the shed and photographing it for eBay takes most of the day, and on top of last night's three hour walk I am filthy with sweat, oil and cobwebs. Another example of woeful planning. The boiler won't be fitted until next week, so I texted Henry:

Hey, you around? I could really use a hot shower ...

The deliberate ellipsis adding some allure and intrigue. Or so I thought, but judging by Henry's response, I was way off base:

Sorry, not home.

After a horrifically cold shower, I'm so wired that I almost pull on my trainers and go for a run, but then I'd only need another shower and end up jumping up and down on square one again. Instead, I move the eBay inventory into the spare room, clean the house, change the sheets, and – without acknowledging the fact or asking myself why – I put Al's junk mail into a drawer and take down all pictures of him, except the one hanging in the hallway.

Before I leave for work, I text Henry one last time.

> **Hey mister, you owe me a surprise. See you**
> **for the trivia round x**

'Awright, sweetheart, how's the shower?'

'Cold.'

'Well, it agrees with you, Princess,' says Winston. 'Good to see you with a bit of colour in your cheeks.'

'Charming.'

'That reminds me, your fella was in last night. Didn't stick around when he found you wosn't 'ere, mind.'

'Henry?'

'Well, 'ow many you got, babes?'

'Here?'

'That cold water got to your ears, love? Yes; 'enry, 'ere. Hang on a mo, he left you something.'

Shit!

Winston disappears into the stock room and comes back dangling a plastic bag from one finger.

Inside the bag are two neatly gift-wrapped packages. The gift tag on the first reads: *So you'll know where you've been*, and inside the spotty paper is a map of the world and a set of brightly coloured push pins. The second package – *So you'll know where you're going* – contains a pair of gaudy flip-flops. They're the right size, and the soles are printed with raised arrows, all pointing forwards.

Double Shit!

Henry

Plenty More Whatsits In The Whatsit

Typical of a Saturday it's quiet all day then overrun from
four o'clock onwards. The Saturday night wig-out, Gus
calls it, when all the clubbers, pubbers and hot-daters look
into the mirror and don't like what they see on top of the
head staring back at them. My own head is overdue for
a trim, but I don't plan on doing anything more exciting
that a fifteen-hundred–piece forest tonight, so I guess it
doesn't really matter.

'Don't seem yourself,' says Gus.

'I'm fine. Tired.'

Gus shrugs. *If you say so.*

'How's the er . . .?' He raises his eyebrows, to indicate,
I assume, my romantic involvement.

I shake my head.

Gus pats me on the shoulder. 'Shit, man.'

'Yeah.'

'Plenty more whatsists in the whatsit,' he says. 'Knowhadimean.'

'I know what you mean.'

My phone pings in my pocket. Again. It's being pinging so often it sounds like a ship's radar.

Ping.

Gus waggles a finger in his ear. 'Either I've got tinnitus, or someone's trying to get hold of someone.'

Ping

Hello . . .

                                                        . . .

I'm sorry.

                                                        . . .

Thank you for my flip-flops.

                                                        . . .

And my map.

                                                        . . .

I don't want to fall out.

                                                        . . .

No one's ever bought me flip-flops

                                                        . . .

The Trouble with Henry and Zoe

Or a map, come to think of it.

                ...

I can explain.

                ...

Things are complicated.

                ...

Henry?

                ...

I'm not going to stop until you answer me or my
battery runs out.

                It's fine.

Can we talk?

                It's fine. Maybe it's for the best.

Don't sulk, it doesn't suit you.

                ...

Bogart didn't sulk.

Debatable.

Johnny Stewart didn't sulk.

Jimmy.

Ha! I knew that.

I believe you.

Meet me tonight in the Duck?

This is surreal.

We can play Buckaroo.

Miss Goldman,
are you trying to seduce me?

'Buckaroo'? WTF!

Sorry, got carried away.

See you tonight?

The Trouble with Henry and Zoe

Do you think it's a good idea?

Probably not.

Sure you'll be there?

Clark Gable didn't sulk.

See you at 8.00

Buckaroo!

Henry

Sweet

'That her?' asks Gus.
   I nod.
   'Sorted?'
   'Yup.'
   'Sweet.'

Henry

Kind Of A Widow

We're sitting at a table in the corner while Zoe takes her meal break – double bacon cheeseburger with fries and onion rings.

'Where do you put it?'

'I hardly eat during the week,' she says. 'Economizing for my . . . you know.' She sticks her foot out from underneath the table and waggles a red flip-flop at me. 'Thank you,' she says. 'Did I say that? Thank you?'

'Yeah, a few times.'

Zoe was in full flow when I arrived, pulling pints, opening bottles and collecting glasses. Watching her made me homesick, and I found myself wondering where I'll go and what I'll do after she climbs on a plane.

As I took a stool at the bar, Zoe apologized, leaned across the counter and kissed me, inciting a loud chorus of woofs and jeers from the Duck's patrons. Zoe talked in headlines – 'I shouted at an author'; 'I handed in my notice'; 'My boiler packed up' – as she moved from one end of the bar to the other, taking orders and serving drinks. But this is the first opportunity we've had to talk properly.

'I bought my ticket,' she says, looking at me from under her fringe, waiting to see how I'll react. 'Thailand.'

'You must be excited.'

'Have you been?'

I shake my head. 'I haven't been anywhere, really. France a couple of times. Amsterdam. That's about it.'

'Guess I can put a pin in my map now,' she says.

'When are you going?'

'Fifteenth of September. Terminal Five, 10.55 a.m.'

'So that's . . .?'

'Ten weeks. Ten weeks today.'

Ten more Saturday nights and then it's over. I knew from the outset that this . . . thing . . . was running out from the moment it started, but this official deadline hits me like a rejection. It feels like we're just getting started – we *are* just getting started – but now the calendar has been marked with a hard 'X'.

Zoe looks down at her flip-flops, goes to say thank you again then stops herself.

I kick my foot against hers. 'I'm happy for you,' I say. 'Not happy about *it*, exactly, but ... well, I'm happy for you.'

'If it's any consolation, it's kind of thrown me, too.'

I show Zoe my thumb and forefinger, the tips maybe a centimetre apart: *A little*.

Zoe smiles, makes the same shape with her own fingers and kisses them against mine.

'It's just something I have to do,' she says.

'I know. I mean, I don't know what it is you've got going on, Zo, but I'm okay with it. We've all got ... you know, stuff.'

Zoe nods, smiles. 'Stuff.' She seems conflicted about whether or not to say more, seems deeply deeply sad, all of a sudden. She scoops an ice cube out of her glass and bites down on it and winces.

'You should get that looked at,' I say.

Zoe shakes her head. 'It's fine. Just ... cold, you know.'

Winston is pacing between the tables, microphone in hand, working his way through the sports round. As he passes our table he covers the mic with his hand and says to Zoe, 'Ten minutes, Princess.' He tips me a wink and asks the assembled quizzers, 'Which British boxer dumped Cassius Clay on 'is backside?'

'Henry Cooper,' I whisper.

'Oh yeah, you like a bit of . . .' Zoe holds up her fists.

'My dad was a professional fighter,' I say.

'No way!'

I nod. 'Clive "Big Boots" Smith. Twenty-five wins, thirteen losses and one no contest. Named his son after . . .'

'Henry Cooper?'

'You get the bonus point,' I say, and lean across the table and kiss Zoe.

'Big Boots?'

'It's an Elvis song, my dad used to look a little like him. Like Elvis.'

Zoe makes a big show of examining my face. 'You missed out there,' she says.

I nod. 'Take after my mum.'

Zoe laughs. 'God, I hope that's a joke.'

'Mum was a stunner. She's a hairdresser.'

'Is that where you learnt to cut hair?'

I nod. 'Her place is called Love and Die.'

'Funny.'

'Except it's spelled D-I-E. As in love and death.'

Zoe pulls a face that's hard to read. 'Oh, right, that's a bit . . . dark?'

'It was a misunderstanding with the signwriter,' I tell her, nervous and excited to be talking about home, no matter how obliquely.

Zoe is looking at me as if she's trying to decide whether or not I'm making this up. 'Dark,' she says again.

'Well,' I say, placing my hands flat on the table. 'You said I never told you anything about me, so . . . now you know something about me, don't you.'

Zoe places her hands on top of mine; her fingernails and the creases in her knuckles are black with dirt.

'So no hot water?' I say, trying to change tack.

'God, do I . . .?' Zoe dips her head towards her armpit.

'No, no, your nails,' I say.

Zoe laces her fingers in between mine. 'Right . . . I was cleaning my . . .' She squeezes my hands hard, as if bracing herself. 'I don't know how to tell you this, so I'm . . . I'm just going to tell you.'

I nod: *Okay.*

'I'm . . . I'm kind of a widow.'

Zoe watches my expression while this heavy revelation finds its level between us. I open my mouth to speak, realize I have no words and instead take a long drink.

'My last boyfriend died.'

'Zoe . . .'

She nods slowly. 'I'm sorry, I don't know a better way in . . .'

'Are you okay?'

Zoe nods slowly. 'Most of the time. Sometimes, like yesterday, not so much. And ... the house, it was our house, you know, mine and Alex's. That's ...' she begins to cry quietly, '... was, that was his name.'

'Zo, I don't know what to say.'

'I'm sorry, Henry. I ... I'll understand if you want out.'

I feel confused, conflicted, guilty, sad, relieved and guilty all over again. If I'd known any of this from the outset I would never have followed Zoe here all those weeks ago. But at the same time, I'm glad that I did. If nothing else comes of this, I've never been surer that April was the wrong person. I loved April, but she never made me feel the way I feel right now with Zoe.

I shake my head. 'I don't want out.'

Zoe wipes her eyes, takes hold of my hands again and whispers: 'Good.'

'When did it happen?'

'Last October,' Zoe says. 'He was hit by a car.'

'I'm sorry. I'm so sorry.'

We're quiet for a while.

I tap my foot against Zoe's flip-flop. 'Is that why you're ...'

Zoe nods. 'Partly. Mostly.' She sniffs, unlaces one hand and wipes at the tears on her cheeks. 'So now you know my deep dark secret,' she says. 'I should have told you sooner, but . . .'

The words 'deep dark secret' have lodged up against my conscience, itchy and insistent.

'You alright, Duchess?' Winston places a hand on Zoe's shoulder. 'What's going on?' he says, narrowing his eyes at me.

'Winnie,' Zoe says, wiping her nose on the back of her hand. 'Sorry, just been a . . . been a funny day.'

'This one givin' you grief?' he says.

Zoe laughs. 'It's the other way round, I'm afraid.'

'That's alright then,' says Winston. 'Way it should be.'

Zoe closes her mouth and screws her eyes tight, but a fresh pulse of tears pushes through and rolls down her cheeks.

'What number lies opposite the six on a dart board?' says Winston into the mic.

'Eleven,' I say under my breath. Winston turns to me and raises his eyebrows. 'Grew up in a pub,' I say.

Zoe looks up at me. 'Full of surprises,' she says, and with that brief lapse in concentration, all her held-back tears burst free.

Winston puts his hand over the microphone. 'Listen, sweetheart, maybe you should finish early tonight.'

Zoe shakes her head, alarmed. 'Winnie, I'm fine.'

'Are you heck as like. Take yourself off—'

'Honestly, I'm—'

'You'll get paid,' Winston says, ruffling Zoe's hair. 'But, strewth almighty, weeping barmaids is bad for business, babes. Now finish your burger and do one.'

Zoe nods, mutters a quiet thank you.

'And you look after her, capisce?' Winston takes his hand from the mic and walks back into the centre of the bar. 'In 1996, whose ear did Mike Tyson partially bite off?'

'How are you doing?' I ask Zoe.

She blows her fringe out of her eyes and blows her nose noisily into a napkin. 'Better.' She pushes her food to one side, takes hold of my hand and smiles.

'My place or mine?' she says.

Henry

Kind Of A Dentist

'It's the day we moved in,' Zoe says.

The picture hangs halfway up the stairs, Zoe and her former boyfriend, Alex. Zoe laughing – snorting, I imagine – at something muttered from her man. Over the course of four trips up and down the stairs, I've had ample opportunity to take in the details: the stacked boxes, his arm around her waist, the precarious champagne bottle. They make a good-looking couple. They look happy.

'He's a handsome boy,' I say.

Better looking than me.

Zoe smiles, nods. 'Yeah, he was.'

'Have you seen *Bringing Up Baby*?' Zoe shakes her head. 'He looks a little like Cary Grant,' I say. 'Without the Brylcreem.'

Zoe laughs, touches her finger to the picture and says, 'Don't let it go to your head, mister.'

I follow her down the stairs and into the kitchen to check on the water.

The kettle has boiled, as has the smallest of the four pans, the remaining three lagging behind in proportion to their volume. At this rate it will take us approximately four hours to half fill the bath. The water we have so far carried up the stairs is already turning tepid, and the trips are becoming increasingly hazardous as we become progressively less sober. It's a futile plan, but it has served as a gentle distraction while Zoe has introduced me to her house and the ghost of Alex. His remaining possessions are confined to the spare room: decks, records, games, where they will remain until sold.

Hit by a car, apparently – popped out for milk one morning and never came back. It explains a lot; everything, I suppose.

'Top you up,' Zoe says, refilling my glass.

'Thank you.' I test the temperature of the water in the largest pan.

'Anywhere near?' she asks. It would be quicker to walk over to my house, bath there and walk back. I shake my head and Zoe shrugs then turns off the gas rings one by one. 'So much for romance,' she says.

'I'll hold my nose,' I tell her, and Zoe takes me by the hand and leads me outside and into the back garden. She fetches two deckchairs from the shed, and positions them where we can watch the last of the sunset.

The sky is smudged with warm swathes of gold and lilac, and the temperature is dropping. Beyond the distant traffic sounds, the still air is textured with the chatter of nearby birds. A gleaming mountain bike is propped against the dilapidated fence separating this garden from the next. Old cans of paint are ranged neatly in front of the shed along with various bags and cardboard boxes.

'Sorry about the mess,' Zoe says.

'You've had a busy day.'

Zoe nods pensively. 'Busy week. How was yours?'

'It was . . . actually, I was telling one of my . . .' I turn to Zoe, so I can register the effect of the next word on her expression, '. . . patients about you.'

'Patients?'

I nod. 'Yes, I'm kind of a dentist.'

Zoe's brow furrows. 'Kind of . . . *what*?'

'On Fridays,' as if this clarifies anything at all. 'I used to be . . . still am, a dentist. I just sort of . . . got bored?'

'A dentist?'

'Afraid so. I'll understand if you want out.'

Zoe, thankfully, laughs, shakes her head. 'So what's with the . . .' She snips the air with her fingers.

'Call it a mid-life crisis.'

Zoe reaches across to take hold of my hand. 'I hope not,' she says, a single tear in the corner of her eye. 'Why didn't you tell me?'

'Would you believe me if I said it was a long story?'

'A girl, then?'

My heart rate quickens, because this is it – the first teetering domino in the row that leads to me leaving a girl at the altar. Zoe appears lighter for sharing her secret, and I feel a lurching, almost exhilarating temptation to tell all. But wouldn't that be selfish – more for my benefit than hers?

'Sorry,' says Zoe in response to my silence. 'Prying.'

'Don't be.'

'So,' she says, 'you've been telling your' – she laughs – 'patients about me?'

'Jenny, yes.'

'Should I be jealous?'

'She's seventy-two. No teeth.'

'Makes your job easier, I suppose.'

I hesitate to say anything further, but besides being a story of loss, Jenny's is also optimistic and funny and not unlike those vignettes from *When Harry Met Sally*. And if not now, then when? So I tell Zoe all about Jenny, about her husband and her planned trip to India to scatter his ashes. The colour has all but left the sky when I've finished, but in the final traces of light I can see tears on Zoe's cheeks.

'It's a nice story,' she says quietly.

A small bird lands on the fence and trills into the darkness.

'Must be lost,' I whisper.

Zoe laughs quietly. 'Aren't we all.'

'Starling, I think.'

'Bird spotter now, are we?'

'No, just—'

'A bird nerd?'

'Haha, no. But if you grow up in the country, you know . . .'

'I grew up by the coast, and I can barely tell the difference between a gull and a pigeon.'

'You know when you see those huge clouds of birds,' I say, swishing my hand through the air. 'Clouds of them, all moving together.'

'Starlings?'

'Uh huh. It's called a murmuration.'

'Good title for a kids' book,' Zoe says.

'Greedy little buggers too,' I say, turning to face her. 'Eat anything.'

'What? What are you implying?'

'Just saying.'

'You are; you're a bird nerd.'

'Maybe a little. Brian – my best friend at home – me and him used to make birdhouses and sell them to the tourists.'

The starling chirps once more and takes flight; heading home.

'Will you make one for me?' Zoe says.

'Have you got a saw?'

'Somewhere,' Zoe says, nodding at the shed.

I get up from my chair and test a few of the rickety fence panels. One of the boards is already detached at the base; I give it a sharp tug and it comes cleanly away in my hands.

Zoe

He Made Me A Birdhouse

The white in my hair is a pure and complete streak now, starting at the roots and, after this latest haircut, extending all the away to the tips. On the way back to his flat we dropped into the dental surgery where Henry works one day a week. He let us in with a spare key and sealed a 'fissure' in my tooth with a quick application of fluoride varnish. My hairdresser fixing my teeth. My dentist fixing my hair.

'Has anyone ever told you that you have a nice-shaped head?' I ask.

Henry jerks backwards, laughing.

'Hold still. I've never done this before.'

'Yes,' he says. 'It's one of the first things Gus said to me.'

'The Hairy Krishna?'

'The very same.'

After Henry trimmed my split ends, levelled my fringe, recalibrated my graduation, I insisted he let me return the favour. Running the clippers over his head, taking the fuzz down to an even stubble and dropping his hair onto the floorboards where it settles with my own. Last night he made me a birdhouse from a piece of knackered fencing and we painted it with an old sampler of Aubergine Dream.

I feel lighter for telling Henry about Alex; I think he understands now why I'm travelling. Making it less likely, I suppose, that he will ask me to stay, or invite himself along for the ride. And what would I say if he did? It feels like we're at the start of something, and the more I learn about him and reveal about myself, the more I want ... more. I don't want to leave him, but the whole point of my year away is to find and fend for myself – and I'm not sure you can do that with someone holding your hand.

'What made you choose dentistry?' I ask.

'Didn't want to see old people with their clothes off.'

'Excuse me?'

'Doctors,' Henry says. 'I mean, I see some pretty horrible stuff, but nothing compared to doctors. God, the places they have to put their fingers.'

'So, what, it was one or the other? Doctor or dentist?'

Henry shrugs. 'Sounds a bit corny, doesn't it: *I always wanted to help people?*'

'Well, yes, when you say it like that.'

Henry makes a noise as if conceding the point. 'I dunno. I mean, you're a kid when you make these decisions, aren't you. I was good at Biology and Chemistry; liked working with my hands; dentists get paid well.'

'And you don't have to see old men's bums.'

'Exactly. Do you know anything about determinism?'

'Sh'ya! Loads. No, of course not.'

'With names, say; call your kid Walter; chances are he'll grow up to be a wimp. Or call them . . .'

'Call them Trixie and they grow up taking their clothes off.'

'Right. Well, my nickname at school was the Dentist.'

'Shut up!'

'Knocked a kid's tooth out and—'

'What! Tell me you weren't one of those horrible rufty tufty boys?'

'I hated fighting. But, well, you don't always get a say in it. Anyway . . .'

'The Dentist,' I say. I kiss Henry on the back of the head and instantly regret it as my lips come away stuck with hair dust. 'Ptph!'

'I mean, obviously that's not why I'm a dentist, but . . . well, it makes you wonder.'

'It does, doesn't it. So' – I touch his buckled nose – 'is that how this happened?'

'Ha, no. Worst I ever got on the playground was a black eye. This happened after the old man took me to the boxing gym. To learn to defend myself.'

'And isn't it ironic.'

'Don't you think. And what about you; why publishing?'

'I was a lawyer, actually.'

'Really?'

'Really. Hold still, I don't want to cut your neck.'

'So why law?'

'Honestly, I'm not entirely sure. I think . . . God, this sounds stupid; but . . . You know *Ally McBeal*?'

'The TV show?'

'Well, of course I knew it wasn't going to be all Starbucks and Robert Downey Jr., but . . . like you said, I was a kid.'

'Is that why you quit? No Robert Downeys?'

I don't answer straight away, instead concentrating on guiding the clippers over the topography of Henry's nicely shaped skull. In truth, the job was finished within four minutes, but I'm enjoying this relaxed, intimate contact.

'But you're happy now?' Henry says.

'Yes,' I tell him. 'I'm happy now.'

'So,' says Henry after a quiet pause, 'do I have any hair left?'

'Nope, all gone. How about we share a shower?'

'It's a small shower.'

'I know. And then you can buy me Sunday lunch.'

Henry

Nettles To Grasp

I've never before approached home from this direction.

Travelling back from university on a Friday evening, clearing the motorway and rolling into the proudly dishevelled byroads, I used to imagine my heart rate slowing down. Winding down the windows regardless of the season, my breathing would slow as my grip relaxed on the wheel. But now, driving up from London in bright July sunshine, the sight of the restless peaks has entirely the opposite effect. Swollen with summer, the hedgerows push into the road and scrape at the car as if trying to get at me.

Nettles to grasp, Henry.

Passports to swipe.

'We'll expect you at midnight, I suppose,' Mum had said.

'I'll see you for lunch,' I told her.

The Trouble with Henry and Zoe

Zoe will be in Brighton by now; we kissed goodbye three hours ago and I'm already missing her silly sense of humour, her inelegant laugh, her touch. Vicky has organized a tight itinerary: beach, drinks, restaurant, club, stripper. 'Wish me luck,' Zoe said when we left her house together this morning. I nearly said the same thing back – *Wish me luck* – but as far as Zoe knows, the biggest challenge I face this weekend is a salon full of split ends and uneven fringes.

My car is still severely gouged along both sides, announcing my return to anyone who happens to notice. And while the cat will soon enough claw its way out of the bag and run yowling through the streets, I'd like to at least have a drink with my parents before people start throwing things. As such, I drive the long way round to the Black Horse, avoiding the village centre and busier stretches of road. Good weather is bad for business, Dad used to say, and it's no surprise to find the pub car park largely empty on this clear and cloudless afternoon. I tuck the car away in the far corner of the gravel yard, count to ten and climb out. I haven't forgiven myself for what I did to April, but time and miles have made it feel like a less real thing. Standing here now, though, the reality – *You left her at the altar!* – comes flooding back, cold and unforgiving. The fear, too. The side door of the Black Horse is maybe twenty paces away, but seems to recede before me, like a trapdoor in some old horror movie.

Mum has said she would talk to April, to warn her I'm arriving and, in her words, 'lessen the shock for the poor girl'. How this news was received I haven't asked, but I'll bet it wasn't with a smile. I am seriously contemplating the idea of getting back into the car when my mother's voice lances down from an upstairs window.

'For God's sake, get inside.'

'Some welcome,' I say, once I'm inside and up the stairs.

'What did you expect? A brass band and flowers?'

I put my arms around Mum's neck and feel her posture soften as her hands wrap around my back and pull me against her. 'I missed you,' she says. 'You stupid, stupid . . . I missed you.'

I kiss my mother's head, inhaling the familiar smell of her hairspray. 'I missed you too.'

'And what the hell have you done to your hair?'

'Disguise,' I say.

'Don't get smart, Henry.' Mum's eyes narrow and her cheeks fill with colour. 'Don't you get bloody smart.'

Dad walks into the room, closes the door behind him and pulls me into a long, heavy hug. 'What's all this?' he says, rubbing a hand over my head.

'A hairdresser?'

I think this is the fourth time Dad's asked this, but my

mother has made the same enquiry several times herself, so it's hard to be precise. Although when my mother asks, it's with a sense of surprised pride, rather than the concerned suspicion that my father manages to inject into the two words.

'A hairdresser, yes.'

I have explained the process by which I ended up cutting hair at The Hairy Krishna ('That's an odd one'), and reassured them both that I haven't entirely abandoned dentistry. But the news is still taking a while to sink in.

Dad's eyebrows are knotting together as he appears to struggle with a thought. 'You're not ...' – he raises his right hand as if about to take a vow and then let's his wrist fall limp '... you know?'

'For God's sake, Clive, just because the boy has suddenly embraced his ...' My mum's eyes go to my hair, and her expression changes from indignation to dread. 'Son,' she says, 'is that why you left April? Living a lie? Isn't that what they call it? Oh, Henry.'

'I'm not gay.'

'Oh, thank God,' says my dad. 'I mean ... thank God.'

My mum is still examining me shrewdly, the anger tightening her features again. 'But there is someone, isn't there?'

'What? Don't be ... silly.'

'Name?'

'Who?'

'I'm your mother, Henry. I know your stupid sodding face, and I know when you're hiding something. Name?'

'Zoe.'

'Oh,' says Mum, smiling insincerely. 'I see. Zoe, is it?'

'Sheila, give it—'

'Didn't bring her with you, heh? Didn't bring *Zoe* with you?'

My mum is on her feet, and Big Boots rises to meet her, positioning himself between us.

'Does she know? This ... *Zoe*?' as if, instead of her name, my mother is stating my girlfriend's crime, condition or other failing: *Killer, cheater, bitch*.

'Mum, please.'

'Wait a minute, how long have you b—'

'Mum, it's been a few weeks, it has nothing to do with me and ...'

'Who, April? What's the matter, can't you say her name now?'

'Sheila, sit down.'

Mum walks backwards to her chair and drops into it in a defeated heap. 'She's like a daughter to me.'

'I know. What about me, Mum? What about what I want and what I'm going through?'

Mum looks as if she's been slapped. But instead of

angry, she looks all of a sudden contrite. '*Like*, I said. I said she was *like* a daughter . . . that's all.'

Dad perches on the edge of Mum's chair, takes her hand and rests it on his thigh. It's an unusually tender gesture, and it does me good to see it. Perhaps my stupidity and subsequent exile has brought them closer together. I know I don't deserve any kind of silver lining, but if this is one, then I'll take it.

'It's been difficult, son,' says my dad. 'For all of us.'

'How is she?' I say. 'April?' And my mother is right, her name does feel strange in my mouth.

Mum and Dad look at each other and something passes between them.

'What?' I ask.

They look at each other's hands, and Mum lets her head list sideways onto my father's chest.

'She's seeing someone?' I ask.

My mother looks at me with exasperation. 'Well, did you expect her to wait for you, Henry?'

'No.'

'After everything you did to the poor girl?'

'I said no.'

'Becau—'

'So,' says Dad, 'what's the plan?'

I shake my head. 'Don't have one.'

'Well, there's a sodding surprise,' says Mum, snatching her hand from Dad's grip.

The house was finished three months before the wedding, making it one year old this July. Maybe today is its birthday. I have been inside before, April and I both have, but never at the same time – someone, it could have been me – deemed it to be bad luck.

I feel nothing towards this brick cube. No regret, no loss, no sense that this is where I should be. Yet here I am. Standing at the foot of the short drive, behind the closed gate, staring at the shut curtains.

April chose the carpets, wallpaper, curtains, the paint, the cupboard doors and everything behind them. There were discussions, but only in the sense that April was thinking aloud and trying out the *sounds* of various fixtures, fittings and ideas. When she asked what colour I wanted to paint the front door, my mind went blank with the shock of being consulted. I said blue, for no reason other than it was the colour of April's nail varnish and she was growing impatient. April produced a colour card filled with twenty-five shades of the single colour and I dropped my finger onto its approximate centre.

The door is now black. My meagre input painted over and obliterated.

I have been standing here for five minutes now, but the coursing panic has abated not one bit. And I suspect it won't even if I stand here all day. As I put my hand on the gate, the front door opens and I all but turn and run. Perhaps the only thing that stays my feet is the pure blanching shock of seeing my former best friend standing in the doorway of my former future house. He's tanned, looks like he's lost two stone and recently had a very good haircut. He looks extraordinarily well, even in a pair of bright orange slippers.

'Brian?'

'Tea?' he says, holding one of a pair of blue mugs towards me. I was with April when she picked out those mugs.

'You don't have anything stronger, do you?'

Brian laughs. 'Not before six, no.'

He sits on the front step, and I sit down beside him.

'Nice slippers,' I say.

'Thanks. Oh, and fuck off.'

'Cheers,' I say, clinking my mug against Brian's. 'It's good to see you.'

Brian nods: *Yes, it is.*

We drink our tea in silence for a while, exchanging the occasional sideways glance and half smile.

'I'm glad it's you,' I say.

'Yeah, me too. Not going to knock my tooth out again, are you?'

'I won't if you won't.'

Brian laughs under his breath. 'The Dentist.'

'Do you remember making those birdhouses?' I say.

Brian nods. 'There's still plenty of fences with missing panels round and about.'

Wrecking one thing to make another.

'I'm sorry I dropped you in it,' I say. 'At the ... castle.'

'It's not me you need to apologize to,' Brian says, looking over his shoulder to the house.

'How is she?'

Brian nods: *Good.* 'I knew you weren't right,' he says. 'You and April.'

'You didn't think to share this?'

Brian shrugs. 'Not my place, is it. And anyway, would you have listened?'

Maybe. Very very maybe.

'So what's this?' I say, indicating the two of us sitting on the doorstep like a pair of little boys.

'I just wanted to talk to you first. Get one thing out of the way before the other, you know.'

'Thanks.'

Brian takes a deep, bracing breath. 'I suppose we should go in.'

'Is it six o'clock yet?' I ask.

We both know six is a long way off, but Brian checks his watch reflexively. 'Close enough,' he says. 'Ready?'

'No.'

Brian opens the door. 'After you.'

In all the years I was with April, I don't think I ever saw her reading a book, but she's reading one now.

Sitting on the sofa with her back to me, her blonde hair in a high neat ponytail, she closes the book, sets it down on the coffee table, pauses for what could be two seconds or eight thousand years, and then turns to face me. Like Brian, she is radiating good health. Tanned, clear skinned, bright eyed, she looks amazing.

'You're late,' she says.

My game plan, such as it was, consisted of receiving abuse gratefully and with contrition, and then apologizing to April and any attendant family into submission. But April's composure and lack of apoplectic outrage, it throws me.

'That's ... that's a good one.'

April cocks her head with pantomime smugness. 'Well, I've had time to work on it, haven't I.'

'I'm sorry,' I say. 'I'm so, so sorry, April.'

And now her face hardens. 'Jesus Christ, Henry. Where do I begin? How could you do that to someone you're supposed to love? To someone who ...' She puts a hand to her eye, then takes a slow, deep breath, regaining her composure as if willing herself – commanding herself – not to cry. 'Have you any idea what you did to me?'

I have nothing to say, and all I can do is shake my head.

'If you didn't want to marry me, why propose, Henry? Why?'

'I did. But ...'

'Do you think you're better than me?'

'No. Never.'

'I wonder about that, you know. But I'm real people, Henry! I like who I am and where I'm from. And the way you treated me is ... I don't even know what it is.'

'Sweetheart ...' says Brian. 'Nice and easy, yes?'

April closes her eyes and allows her features to relax.

'Do you want anything?' he asks.

April opens her eyes, nods. 'I'll have one of those teas,' she says, and when she smiles at Brian, she winks. Her eyes follow him out of the room and the affection is absolutely sincere.

She is still sitting on the sofa, head turned to the side so she can see me standing in the doorway. I decide to risk moving further into the room. I make it as far as the armchair, but before I get a chance to sit, April shakes her head, says, 'I don't think so.'

'Right, I'm . . . sorry. I never thought I was better than you,' I say. 'I loved you.'

'Loved. You're a coward, do you know that?'

'Yes.'

'Oh, shut up! *Yes*. You should have told me. To my face, not in a stupid . . .' April picks up a piece of folded paper from the coffee table, clenches it in her fist and throws it at me. I don't need to pick it up to know this is the letter I left behind on the morning of our wedding.

'Pick it up,' April says. 'Take it with you because I've read it enough times.'

I do what I'm told and shove the balled-up note into my pocket.

'*We were kids when we met*,' April says, sneering.

'April, please—'

'*You'll always have a special place in my heart*. I mean, my God! Did you not cringe when you wrote that . . . *shit*!'

'I should have told you.'

'Yes, you fucking should. It's the very *very* least you should have done. Do you know what? I'm glad you did it.'

April looks at me, as if waiting for a response, but we both know there isn't one.

'Do you want to know why I'm glad?'

'Yes, why?'

'Two reasons, Henry. First, because you are clearly a cruel, weak, fickle bastard. And I'm glad I found out before things got any more complicated. The thought that I might have had a baby with you makes me physically sick.'

April is glaring at me, waiting for a reaction, so I nod, mutter *sorry* under my breath.

'And second?' April asks. 'Second, because I am happy now. With Brian. Happier than I ever was with you. And I'm not just saying that to make myself feel better. I'm saying it because it's true.'

'I'm glad you're happy.'

April nods. 'I suppose I should thank you ... but I never will.'

And it isn't until she begins the process of standing up from the sofa that I notice the bump. It's a big bump.

'Oh my God,' I say, pointing at April's stomach, and dropping into the armchair after all. The bump looks even bigger from down here and I jump back to my feet. 'Oh my good G— wait, what month is it?'

'It's July, Henry.'

'Wh ... w ...'

'October,' April says. 'We were meant to get married in *October*.'

I start counting on my fingers: 'October, November, December, Ja—'

'Nine,' April says. 'Nine months ago.'

The book on the coffee table is titled *501 Baby Names*; it's impossible to tell at what letter it is splayed open, but it looks pretty central – M, maybe; N, perhaps, none of which clarifies anything.

'You're pregnant,' I say, looking for some stability in solid fact, but not finding much.

'Who told?' says April.

Again, I point at the bump, which can't possibly have grown in the last thirty seconds, but nevertheless appears to be expanding before my eyes. 'Is it ...?'

'Yes?' says April.

I swivel the finger around so that it's now pointing at me. 'Is it ...?'

'Mine,' says Brian's voice from behind me. He is carrying a small round tray, red with white polka dots, which I seem to remember buying in the Trafford Centre about twelve months ago. 'Here you go ...' Brian hands a mug of herbal tea to April, then a tumbler of whisky to me. I empty it in a single swallow.

'Congratulations,' I finally manage. 'How ... long?'

'Don't worry,' says Brian, 'it's definitely mine.'

'Eight months,' says April, a touch of defiance in her expression.

'So you . . .'

Brian shrugs.

'November,' says April, looking at my hands, and I realize I am counting on my fingers again.

'Congratulations.'

'Yeah, you said that.'

'Another?' says Brian, reaching for my glass.

'Henry has to go now,' says April.

Brian and I shake hands, and then we hug. 'Give it time,' he whispers into my ear, clapping a hand on my back.

I was supposed to carry April over this threshold, into the house. Instead, she escorts me in the opposite direction, my best friend's baby growing inside her.

'I'm happy for you,' I say.

'I suppose that makes it easier for you, does it?'

'I don't know. Maybe a little.'

'Well, don't think I forgive you, because I don't. I fucking don't, Henry.'

'I know.'

'I'll always be *that* girl, thanks to you. That girl who . . .'

I nod towards the house. 'What about Brian, the baby?'

'Brian's amazing.' April's face comes alive when she says his name. 'And he'll make an amazing father,' she says. 'But it doesn't change . . . it doesn't make what you did right.'

'I'm sorry, all I am is sorry.'

April nods. 'Yeah, I know. So,' she says, crossing her arms, 'you seeing anyone?'

'I . . . kind of.'

April shakes her head. '*Kind of?* You're amazing, Henry.'

'It's complicated. She's had . . .'

'You know what, Henry? I don't want to know. Just . . . Actually, I really hope you sort yourself out, okay. I hope you and whatever she's called get together and fall in love and . . . I really do.'

'Thank you.'

'And then I hope she leaves you standing at the altar.'

'Fair enough.'

'Yeah, fair enough. And call your mother more.'

'Right.'

'Make sure you do, she misses you, Henry. Big Boots, too.'

'I will. Thank you.' I go to hug her, but April steps away from me.

'Sorry. Okay then, well, it's been . . . it's been nice seeing you. Both. All three of you.'

April nods and – against her will, it seems – smiles.

I make it all the way to the gate before remembering; and when I turn around, April is standing in the doorway, waiting. 'Yes?'

'I don't suppose you've got my passport?'

April laughs.

'You remember where Mum and Dad live?'

As I walk, I sing 'Sweet Home Alabama' inside my head. I sing slowly and drag my feet, but it does nothing to shorten the distance.

April must have called ahead, because her old man is waiting on the step when I turn the corner. At his feet is a battered Samsonite suitcase – they're advertised as indestructible but it looks like someone has had a good go at disproving this claim. The shell is dented and scratched, the pull-up handle twisted and bent, and the zip is broken. But it's still standing.

April's father says nothing as I shuffle down his drive, his expression doesn't flicker. And if it turns out the old bugger died six months ago and has since been stuffed and placed outside to scare off burglars, then I have to wonder why April forgot to mention it. As I get within punching distance, however, I can hear the old man breathe and see the hairs in his nose quiver under each exhalation.

'Derek,' I say, nodding.

Derek's jaw tightens, the muscles bunching at the hinges. His hands clench into fists.

'I'm sorry,' I say, and Derek shakes his head very slowly, the message as clear as the sky: *Don't!* He toes the case and it wobbles.

'Right,' I say. 'I . . .'

Another shake of the head. 'Don't mek me break a promise to my daughter,' he says. 'She's had enough of that, don't you think?'

To pick up the case I will have to bend down, placing my jaw within six inches of Derek's foot. I don't know if he's been working today, but April's dad is wearing his work boots. Again, he nudges the case with his foot.

I bend at the waist, stretch forwards and grip the handle, but as I snatch at it, the handle comes free, leaving the battered case still wobbling on its wheels. I try again, bending further now and needing both hands to lift the case out of Derek's range. He doesn't kick me in the face.

'Thank you,' I say. 'My passport's in the . . .'

Derek's nostrils flair, he exhales slowly and turns to go back into the house. 'George sends his love,' he says, and he closes the door in my face.

I wait until I get round the corner before sitting on a wall and opening the case. The crotch of my swimming shorts has been slashed, my new linen beach trousers have lost a leg, my sunglasses have lost both arms, a hole has been cut in the heart of my favourite shirt. Underwear, socks, shoes, sandals, hat, everything has been destroyed. The book I had packed to read on holiday is now a loose collection of torn pages. And all of it stained and sticky from the contents of, amongst other things, a skewered bottle of suntan lotion, and – to look at it – a jumped-on tube of toothpaste. On the front of the suitcase is a separate, zipped compartment. Inside are our tickets, intact, unused and expired. Also in this compartment is my passport, in one piece, and containing all its pages. No one has taken a pair of scissors or a blowtorch to it. No one has drawn glasses on my picture, a dagger through my neck, a penis on my h—

'Fucking jilter!!!'

The thrown hamburger hits me square in the chest, bull's eye. It's hard to be sure with mustard in my eyes, but the receding car looks an awful lot like George's Ford Cortina.

'You didn't think to tell me?' I say to Mum.

'Of course I did,' she says. 'But it wasn't my place, sweetheart. Here …' she licks her finger and rubs it through my eyebrow, '… bit of mustard.'

'You got off lucky,' my old man says. 'I'd have knocked your head off.'

Mum smiles at my father with affection.

Nailed above the front door to the pub is a small oblong plaque with the name of the licensee painted in white on black. When I turned eighteen, Dad had had my name added so that it read: CLIVE SMITH & SON. LICENSED TO SELL ALL INTOXICATING LIQUOR

FOR CONSUMPTION ON OR OFF THESE PREMISES. From a man of few sentimental gestures, it meant a great deal. Not only did it announce my arrival as a man, but it signified my father's pride in his son. It put us together, as equals. So it was a huge shock to see my name had been painted over when I walked through the front door an hour ago.

'So,' I say, 'I guess I'm not licensed to sell intoxicating liquor anymore.'

My dad frowns in confusion. 'You've lost me, son.'

'The licensee thingummy,' Mum says. 'Honestly, Clive, I do worry about your memory.'

'Right,' he says, cocking his fists. 'Bobbed when I should've weaved.'

'Weaved when you should have bobbed,' finishes my mother, and again the smile.

'So,' I say, 'the sign?'

'Well, you see, son. You're not the most popular man in town.'

'By a long chalk,' says my mother.

'Thing is, lad, someone took a brush to it.'

'Clive Smith & Bastard,' says my mother. 'Licensed to sell blah blah blah.'

'They did a good job, too,' says Dad. 'Din't they, Sheila?'

'Very good, I reckon it was weeks before we noticed.'

'Anyway, son, I thought it simplest to just . . .' He makes a gesture as if painting out a bastard.

'Thank you, I suppose.'

'So,' says my mother. 'You've no excuse not to come back for our anniversary now.'

'Except for not being the most popular man in town by a long chalk, you mean.'

'Smith and Bastard,' says my dad, laughing.

Mum shrugs. 'Time heals. More slowly in some cases than others, but it heals.'

'When is it, exactly?' I ask, earning a scowl from my mother. 'What? It's not my anniversary.'

'Ninth of August,' Dad says. 'Haven't lost all my marbles yet, see.'

Mum leans across the bar and kisses Dad on the cheek.

'What's got into you two?'

'It's not every year you get to have a ruby anniversary,' says my mother.

'Well, that's kind of the point, isn't it,' I say. 'So, what's the plan?'

'Thought we'd have a bit of a do here on the Saturday,' says Dad. 'Friends, family.'

'Well, I guess that includes me. Will April be here?'

'Of course, love. She's like a—'

'—daughter to you, I know. But her, me, Brian, their bloody baby . . .'

'Time to move on, Henry. April knows that.'

'Anyway,' says Dad, 'can't see her throwing much in her condition.'

'Well, that's reassuring. Anyway, it's not her I'm worried about.'

Dad leans forwards on the counter, resting his weight through the knuckles of both hands. 'There's nowt else to worry about. They know whose son you are.'

It seems like the thing to be done, so I lean across the counter and kiss my father. He acts embarrassed, but it's an amateur show.

'I'll be here,' I say.

'Maybe you could bring that Zoe?' says my mum.

I laugh out loud. 'Are you sure? You could barely say her name a couple of hours ago.'

'Well, I can't blame the girl for the sins of my son, can I? It's not her fault you're a bastard.'

Dad laughs and walks to the other end of the bar to serve a customer.

'Thanks, Mum, but . . . I don't think it's a good idea.'

'Think about it. It would be nice for you to have someone with you.'

'Okay,' I lie. 'I'll think about it.'

Zoe

Helicoptering

The sound of thumping from the next room is ruining the movie. It's not a particularly good movie, and I'm having trouble focusing, but we needed something to drown out the noise. The relentless thud of man on Vicky, Vicky on mattress.

'I'll give him top marks for stamina,' says Rachel.

'Well, it's kind of his job, isn't it?'

'What, shagging the punters?'

'Well, perk of.'

I should be next door in the twin room with Vicky, but she pulled our stripper so I've moved in with Rachel.

'Did you have a fun hen do?' I ask.

'Yeah, lovely. Be more fun if I was pissed, I imagine.'

'That'll teach you to go fooling around.'

'Hmm. And what about you . . . how's the Henry thing working out?'

I consider telling Rachel about Henry's secret identity as an extractor of teeth, but it's too late, too complicated, and I've drunk too much Pimm's. I'll tell her on the train back tomorrow.

'He made me a birdhouse,' I say.

'For birds?'

'Yup, in the garden. Bust my fence to get the wood, but still . . .'

Rachel coos at this. 'Romantic.'

'I know, but . . .' big sigh '. . . what can you do?'

Rachel slides an arm around me and kisses my temple. 'It'll work out for the best,' she says. 'One way or another.'

The sound of thumping in the next room builds to a crescendo.

'Thing with willies,' says Rachel, 'is, they do look a bit daft, don't they.'

'Some more than others.'

'What was that thing he was doing again?' Rachel rotates her wrist, emulating the concluding part of The Manaconda's act.

'Helicoptering.'

'Has it left a mark?' she says, touching her cheek.

'Yeah, looks like a penis, only bigger.'

'You're kidding!'

'I'm kidding. Nothing a bit of foundation won't hide. Oo, here he goes.'

The Manaconda reaches terminal velocity, testing the welding on the bed to the limits of its engineering.

'Blimey,' says Rachel after a final juddering wallop from next door. 'It's enough to put you off for good.'

Henry

It's As Quiet As The Countryside Gets

It's a few minutes past two when I wake to the sound of breaking glass. Not just a pint pot or a whisky tumbler, but a lot of glass. And then someone shouts: 'Jiiiiiilter!!!!'

The noise has also woken my parents; we congregate in the hallway, Mum huddled behind Dad, Dad clutching a baseball bat and a torch. I'm just grateful he pulled on a pair of pants.

'Was it inside?' asks my mother.

'I think it was the car park,' I say.

And I'm pretty sure it was George.

Mum waits upstairs, and if Dad had his way so would I. But he's not as fit as he used to be, and anyway, we all know whose mess this is. The bar is empty and the doors, front and side, are still closed. Dad unlocks the side door and we step outside.

It's as quiet as the countryside gets; a hooting bird, the rustle of something small in the hedges, a bit of wind for added atmosphere. But no engines, no laughter, no sound of a shotgun being cocked.

Dad pans the torch around the car park and up the walls, checking the windows one by one.

'Try over there,' I say, indicating where my car is parked.

And you have to hand it to George. Not only has the mad bastard heaved a hod through my windscreen, he has taken care to first fill it with bricks.

'Best hope the rain holds off,' says Dad.

'It won't,' I say.

'Probably not. Come on, I'll buy you a nightcap.'

Zoe

Maybe Maybe

It's all about stories now.

Since handing in my notice three weeks ago, Claire has phased me out of the day-to-day; out of the spreadsheets, finance meetings and, of course, author relations. Instead I am back to light duties; opening envelopes, reading stories. Everyone's a writer now; everyone seems to have a story to tell – although some are more worthy of an audience than others. Every week between fifty and a hundred hopeful packages drop through the office letterbox. And I read them all. Alliterative alligators, otters and sprites with their hang-ups, confusions, lacks and conflicts. And I devour them all, as if each one holds the answer, or at least a clue – play fair, don't tell lies, beware of dragons; be foolish, be brave, be yourself.

Wisdom and precedent tells you that they must be

junk; derivative drivel, clumsy rhyme, mixed metaphor and garbled logic. It's not for nothing that we call it the 'slush pile'. One good story a month is a standard haul; one submission out of every four hundred or thereabouts. But my bin is practically empty, the stack of pages growing on my desk, reaching closer to the light fittings by the day. I read them and I read them again, arrange the stories between piles: yes, maybe yes, maybe no, maybe maybe. Because if there is anything these stories teach us, it is that everyone has potential. Everyone *can*. It's become my mission to make one of these happy endings happen before I leave this office in a little under two months. But time is running out.

On Friday afternoons, as the paper tower develops into a health and safety issue, I select the best dozen manuscripts from the yes pile, drop them into my bag and read them again over the weekend. I read them over breakfast, in the bath, in the garden, behind the bar of the Duck and Cover. I listen to Henry read these stories to me as I chop onions, wash my hair, lie in bed with my head on his chest.

But it's not all dragons and daisy chains.

Some evenings, we watch movies, the ones Henry watched with his mother: *Brief Encounter, An Affair to Remember, Roman Holiday, His Girl Friday*. Stories about

love, thwarted by timing, pride, circumstance, poli-
tics, family, money, war, others. Stories with only two
endings; will they/won't they stories, although you can
usually guess which.

Our own brief affair ends in seven weeks, it's a weepy
for sure and I already know the final scene – it's one we've
watched together, laughing at the melodrama in black
and white. Ridiculing the silly accents, dated dialogue
and awful hair, as if desensitizing ourselves for our own
inevitable goodbye. Henry apologizes for the films as if
they were his fault, but I enjoy the simplicity, the lack of
expensive effects and cheap thrills. It makes me feel close
to him, sharing something from his own history, I suppose. We won't be together when the credits roll, but we
will have a story. But a lot can happen in seven weeks, so
I remind myself to shut up, sit back and enjoy the final act.

Henry

And Where Does All This Candour End?

I've been exposed and found lacking.

After introducing her to the old matinee idols, square-jawed and sure-minded, Zoe has presented me with a golden opportunity to play the heart-throb. But I have missed my cue.

It may be the middle of summer, but it's been an overcast day with high winds on the south west coast of England. Zoe's parents are on holiday in Copenhagen, and their converted farmhouse, with its brick walls and high ceilings, is as cold as a church. We could throw on an extra jumper, of course, but where's the romance in that? Zoe sent me outside to chop wood; perhaps expecting me to strip down to my white vest and cleave logs with brutal precision. That's how Clark Gable would do it, or Cary Grant. I don't have a white vest, and I've never touched an axe in my life. Watching me swing, miss and come within an inch of removing my toes, I must have looked more like Benny Hill than Errol Flynn. So Zoe prepared the firewood while I removed the splinters from my hand. And then, when my fire died for the third time, Zoe stepped up again, to provide heat while I chopped vegetables and uncorked the wine.

I can't even fly a kite.

Zoe swapped her shifts at the Duck, working Thursday and Friday night to free up today and tomorrow for an impromptu weekend away. We set off shortly after sunrise this morning, our train arriving on the Cornish coast five hours later, while the weather was still trying to make up its mind. Her parents' house is a thirty-minute walk from the train station via the beach, where the Goldmans own a blue and white striped hut like something off a postcard. In amongst the deckchairs and spiders and deflated beach balls, Zoe found a kettle, mugs and a jar of instant coffee. We drank it black, watching the intrepid surfers paddle out and wait and ride back to the shore. Zoe laughed and took black and white photographs as I laid the kite on the sand, walking backwards and unravelling string in preparation of a fast sprint and vertical launch. But before I could offer the kite to the wind, the wind would flip the thing over, dragging it sideways across the sand or tangling the string around my feet. Zoe watched this farce for ten minutes before intervening. What you do, she told me, is keep the kite on a short length, letting the wind play with it at close range, before gradually letting the string out until the red and yellow diamond is no bigger than a postage stamp against the grey sky. There is a lesson to be learned, I'm sure. Maybe someone should write a children's book about it. Kitty the Kite, a lesson about letting go, or holding on.

'Sitting comfortably?' says Zoe.

And I'm not lying when I say that I am. Thanks to Zoe, the fire is roaring; and thanks to her father we are drinking red wine from a cut-glass decanter. Whether the vessel has improved this bottle of inexpensive wine, who knows, but it certainly adds to the effect.

Zoe stretches her feet and rests them in my lap. 'Then I'll begin,' she says, in her best storytelling voice:

'Hippochondriac rolled out of his mud bed and yaaaaaaaaaaaawned. "I wish I could yawn like that," said Irrelephant. "You're probably the most best yawner in the morner."'

'I think we read this one on the way down,' I say.

'Did we? Are you sure?'

'I never forget an Irrelephant.'

'Sorry,' says Zoe. 'Am I being a bore?'

I shake my head, but can't suppress a yawn. 'Sea air,' I say. 'Chopping logs.'

'Shit, I am, aren't I? I am bloody borangutan.'

'I don't remember a borangutan.'

'Joke,' says Zoe.

'Funny. Didn't you say – when we were on the bridge – that you were thinking of writing something?'

'Seems like a long time ago,' Zoe says.

'The bridge or the story?'

'Both, I suppose.' Zoe wipes her cheeks, and I see that there are tears in her eyes.

'You okay?'

'Yeah,' she says. 'Just remembering.'

'Alex?'

Zoe nods. 'The day he . . . that morning, I had this idea, a silly idea for a book. And I thought, *yeah, I'll write that later.* But then . . .'

'You miss him.'

Zoe nods. 'Sometimes. He was . . . we had some good times together.' Zoe's hand goes to her hair, wrapping the white strand around two fingers. 'Did I tell you how I ended up in publishing?'

'No.'

'You know I was a lawyer, right? Well, I was *miserable.* Hated it. I had eczema on my legs from stress and . . . it

323

was a bit like being on the rebound, I think. Alex came along, and I just . . .' Zoe makes a grasping gesture at the air in front of her. 'Just clung on. Don't get me wrong, he was fun and caring and . . . you've seen his picture.'

'Handsome.'

Zoe nods. 'You're handsome, too, obviously.'

'Obviously.'

'We moved in together pretty quickly,' Zoe says. 'He supported me while I quit law and found my way into publishing. It was like a lifeline.'

'He sounds like a good guy.'

'He was. I've never told anyone this before,' she says, staring into the fire, 'but, I didn't love him. Maybe at first, but . . . not really. It was a . . .' Zoe shakes her head, lets herself cry quietly for a moment.

'Did he know?'

'I don't think so.'

'Well, maybe that's . . . you know . . .'

Small mercy is what I want to say, but it feels insincere and trivial, and I can't bring myself to finish the sentence. Zoe understands me, all the same.

'I used to be thankful that I never told him, but . . . I'm not so sure anymore. I feel like he died under a lie, and I . . . I feel so bad about that. If I'd told him, maybe . . .'

'It's not your fault.'

'And you know what else? If I'd told him, then maybe I wouldn't be travelling in seven weeks. Maybe I wouldn't have met you? And . . .'

I could say I understand, and hold Zoe's hand while she cries. But saying it is easy, and meaningless and hollow. Proving I understand, though; reciprocating Zoe's honesty and showing that I recognize her guilt and confusion, isn't that the best thing I can do? Isn't it the only thing?

'Before I came to London,' I say, 'I was engaged.'

Zoe sits up, wipes her eyes and looks at me calmly. 'To be married?'

I nod. 'Except . . .'

'You didn't marry her?'

'April. No, I didn't marry her.'

'Because?'

'I didn't love her,' I say.

Zoe smiles, sadly and – it seems to me – complicitly. 'Bad scene.'

'Uh huh.'

'Was she pretty?'

I nod. Zoe kicks me.

'Oh, right, sorry. And you're pretty, too. Obviously.'

'Obviously. So, what happened?'

And where does all this candour end? We have seven

weeks left and I'm tired of keeping secrets and pretending to be someone I'm not. But at the same time, how much truth is enough, how much is too much, and how much can a person handle in one sitting?

'What is it?' asks Zoe, as if reading my mind.

'I called it off,' I say.

'Just like that?'

'Well, it didn't go down as well as the proposal ...'

Zoe laughs, and I hate myself for making light of what I did to April.

'And ...?'

'I've known her since we were kids,' I say. 'Went to the same school. And, well, it's a small village. Very small.'

'I see. So ...' Zoe cocks a thumb off to one side. 'You left?'

'Something like that.'

'Sorry, I don't mean to be ... it must have been awful. God, that poor girl. I'm sorry, I ... *God!*'

'I know. But ... if I hadn't, then I wouldn't have met you, would I?'

Zoe shakes her head. 'I'm glad you did,' she says. 'Well ... kind of.'

'Yeah,' I say. 'Kind of.'

Zoe

There Is Something There

For all the sex, sea air and wine I can't sleep.

Apart from his camera, all of Alex's things are gone. His bike, his decks, even his records. They fetched a couple of hundred pounds less than I'd hoped, but with additional shifts at the Duck and accumulated holiday pay from work, all systems are still go, the spreadsheet still holds, and I can still afford to leave Henry behind. It's beyond frustrating. Henry, on the other hand, is handling it all with noble stoicism. No, not noble; it's annoying. A bit more moping wouldn't go amiss, a bit more 'please don't go'.

Kind of, he said.

I'm glad I met you ... *kind of*.

I mean, come *on*, Henry. I'm teeing this up for you, already. Three little words is all I'm asking for.

I'll miss you.

It's not like I'm asking him to tell me he ...

There is something there, though; something mutual that scores higher than 'LIKE' on the Scrabble board. Something that maybe I'd be a complete and utter idiot to walk away from. And maybe this is the real reason I can't sleep – the worry that I might be seven weeks away from making a huge mistake.

Outside, the wind is howling in from the coast, banging the gate and making the washing line whine like a tormented ghost. Normally I find the sounds of harsh weather comforting, but tonight's elemental cacophony has me as keyed up as a frightened child.

Henry is sleeping like a baby.

I want our fast-expiring time to count, so when Mum invited me to Copenhagen with her and Dad, I said no. Henry, on the other hand, broke the news today that he's heading back to his own hometown in a couple of weeks. And I'm not invited. He didn't explicitly say as much, but then neither did he say: *Hey, seeing as you invited me to see the house where you grew up, why don't I return the favour.* It crossed my mind to invite myself, but, call it pride, I want it to come from Henry. Not that I didn't hint: *I wonder what I'll do that weekend? I've never been to the Peaks. I do love a ramble in the hillside.* But the bait went untook.

The wind sounds like thrown gravel and the gate bangs again, loud enough this time that even Henry stirs.

'Humhh, wassat?'

'Storm,' I tell him. 'Ghosts of sailors.'

Another bang, metallic sounding, and then . . .

'Is that the door!'

'Shit, Henry! I . . . I don't know . . . maybe.'

Henry is out of bed without hesitation, pulling on his boxer shorts, shushing me silent with a finger and indicating for me to stay put.

Henry

An Unequivocal Thump

Ideally Zoe would have played hockey at school; or rounders or golf or even snooker. The closest thing in her bedroom to a weapon, however, is a badminton racquet with busted strings. Chances are I'm up against nothing more solid than the wind, but Zoe is pretty jumpy, and besides, this is my chance to make up for the wood-chopping debacle.

The stairs creak under my feet, but the wind is howling with such ferocity the sound is all but drowned out. The front door is closed.

But just as I relax my grip on the racquet, I hear something from the boot room at the rear of the house. An unequivocal thump and the sound of a male voice cursing. All systems are on high alert now, and my first thought is that Mad George has tracked me down to the coast and has come to finish me off. My second thought is that I wish I was wearing something more protective than a pair of boxer shorts. There is an umbrella beside the door, and I'm weighing up its merits as a means of defence versus a badminton racquet, when the sound of shuffling footsteps galvanizes me into action.

'Get the fuck out!' I shout. 'I'm armed!'

A female voice screams, her voice merging with the wind in a terrifying scything harmony.

'Don't shoot!' shouts a male voice. 'Please don't shoot.'

The woman screams again.

Amid the sounds of scuffling and retreat, a measured male voice is saying: 'We're ... we're leaving, we're leaving. Don't do anything foolish now, stay calm, we're leaving.'

'Rodney!' says the woman. 'Get out!'

Zoe appears halfway down the stairs.

'Dad?'

Zoe

Henry And I

'Well,' says Mum, 'this is . . . nice.'

Introductions have been made, weapons laid down, bodies clothed. The cushions from the sofa are still scattered on the floor and it wouldn't take Miss Marple to deduce that someone got frisky in front of the fire this evening.

'So,' says Dad, 'a dentist?'

'That's right,' says Henry. 'For my . . . you know, sins. Sorry about the . . .' He brandishes an invisible badminton racquet.

'At least it wasn't loaded,' says Mum, laughing.

'Argh!' I say, affecting pantomime panic. 'Please don't shoot!'

'Well, it was a bit of a bloody surprise, Zozo. Thought you were busy.'

I nod at Henry. 'Busy busy,' I say, although I'm not sure why. 'Anyway, you're not meant to be back until Monday.'

'Sorry to inconvenience you,' Mum says, but she makes it plain that she's teasing. She puts her hands to my cheeks, staring at me intently as if trying to solve the riddle of my face. It's not the first time she has done this; her eyes are bloodshot, as if she has been crying or drinking, and it's vaguely unnerving.

'More tea, anyone?' asks Henry, tapping the pot. His shirt is mis-buttoned.

It's almost two in the morning and we're sitting around drinking tea like it's Sunday morning. Which, now that I think about it, it is.

'Thank you, Henry,' says Mum, clearly taken by my new friend. Maybe it was the sight of him in his underpants, poised for action.

'Had to come back for a . . .' Dad glances at Mum.

'A meeting,' she finishes. 'Monday morning. So . . .' glancing again at Henry, '. . . this *is* nice.'

'Sorry for not coming to Copenhagen,' I say. 'Henry and me—'

'I,' says Dad.

'Henry and *I* . . . well . . . it's . . . I was going to tell you soon, but . . .'

Mum and Dad have become rigid in their seats, their

faces fixed somewhere between dread and anticipation.

'No no no,' I say, 'nothing like that; I'm going ... travelling.'

'A holiday?' says Dad.

'Travelling,' I say, shaking my head.

'Oh.'

'Right.'

'Where?'

'When?'

'All over,' I say. 'September?' as if asking if this is acceptable.

'Zoe,' says my mother, 'I think that's ... wonderful. Just wonderful.'

Dad nods along, although the soppy old fool seems to have a tear in his eye. 'And er ... are you going?' he says to Henry. 'Travelling?'

Henry shakes his head. 'No, I'm ...'

'A friend,' I say. 'Henry's a ... he's a friend.'

Mum looks at the scattered cushions in front of the fire, to Henry and then back to me. She nods, smiles. 'I'm glad for you,' she says, and now she's crying too. She wipes at her eye and winces.

'Are you okay?' Dad asks, a little alarmed.

Mum nods. 'Fine.'

'Mum? Dad? Am I ... am I missing something?'

Henry

A Broader Pathology

Over the course of an hour, we have learned that Zoe's mother is suffering from uveitis – it can be cured, or it can cause blindness and in Julie Goldman's case it is uncertain which is the more likely. She was diagnosed about six months ago, but opted to keep the news from her recently bereaved daughter – at least until it became clear exactly what the news was. Zoe's parents have been waiting for the right opportunity to talk to Zoe, and while tonight was not the scenario they had been waiting for, it all came out around the kitchen table. The business about cutting their holiday short for a meeting was a half truth. There is a chance that Julie's condition is a symptom of a 'broader pathology', and they have an appointment with a neurologist to run a series of tests for multiple sclerosis. The appointment isn't until Tuesday; however, after five days in relentless sunshine, Mrs Goldman's eyes were causing her so much pain she couldn't bear to leave the hotel, so they caught the first available flight home.

'The red eye,' Mrs Goldman joked, and it's clear where Zoe got her sense of humour.

She is worried, confused, upset, conflicted.

'I shouldn't go,' Zoe says.

We are once again in bed. Goodnight hugs and kisses on the stairs, but without the awkward discussion of where I (Zoe's 'friend') will be sleeping. A bit late for that in every sense of the expression.

'It might clear up.'

'Or it might not. Or it might clear up then come back, you heard what they said.'

'You've bought your ticket, though.'

Zoe shakes her head as if irritated by me rather than the facts. 'What if she goes blind? What if it's MS and she ends up in a wheelchair? What then, Henry? Honestly, sometimes I wonder if you won't be glad to see the back of me.'

'Why would you say that?'

'Why wouldn't I? I mean, seriously, why wouldn't I say that?'

'Because it's not true, Zoe. It couldn't be further from the truth.'

'Well, I'm not a . . . you know . . .'

'Mind reader?'

Zoe laughs. I take hold of her hand, put my arm around her shoulder.

'Did I tell you about my dad's accident?'

Zoe shakes her head.

'Broke both wrists, a rib and collapsed a lung.'

Zoe sits up, wipes her eyes. 'Fighting?'

I laugh. 'Loading stolen beer kegs into the cellar at night after too much whisky.'

'No!'

'He went in first; did his wrists. Then the barrels followed him down and took care of the rest.'

'Fuck!'

'Yeah, *fuck*. Both bones on this wrist' – indicating my left – 'came through the skin. This one ... was really nasty.'

'What, and bones through the damn skin isn't?'

'He had a cage on his wrist for about two months; metal rods through his skin – about half a dozen of them – holding the bone together.' Zoe makes a barfing sound. 'Precisely. And ... well, there's a lot you can't do for yourself with two broken wrists. Couldn't feed himself, wash, shave ... you get the picture.'

Zoe nods grimly, her nose wrinkled as if at a bad smell. 'But he's okay now?'

'Yeah, fit as a bull. My point is, and I've never told anyone this, when it happened I'd just been offered a job in Australia.'

'What?'

'Yeah, hadn't told anyone because I'd only just had the offer; the plan was to head out within about four weeks.'

'And then . . .'

'And then Dad got himself smashed up. They couldn't afford extra staff, and Dad's a danger to himself, so . . .'

'You didn't go?'

I shake my head. 'Deferred it for a month, and then he got an infection in his lung that nearly did him in. That took six months to clear up, by which time . . . well, the world moves on, doesn't it.'

'So you agree with me. You think I should stay?'

'I'd love you to stay. But . . . I think you should go.'

'But what about your dad? You said your dad nearly . . .'

'I was working and living in Sheffield, coming home and helping out at the weekends. When he collapsed, it wasn't me who found him. It was . . . someone else.'

Zoe stares at me while she takes this in. 'Her?'

'April, yes. Saved his life.'

'Oh my God, that's . . .' Zoe shakes her head, as if trying to shake off a cobweb.

'Your mum isn't terminal,' I say.

'But she could go blind. End up in a wheelchair.'

'Whether you're here or not. And if something drastic did happen ... well, you'd be as much use in London as you would in Thailand. Unless you're planning on moving back down here. And I don't ... well, it's not for me to say.'

'Do you regret not going to Australia?'

'Honestly, I don't know. But, listen, if you do go ... and I hope you do ... I'll miss you.'

I'll miss you a lot.

Zoe

A Lot Can Happen

One of Mum's symptoms is fatigue; one of mine is an overactive mind. Henry and I are out of bed before my parents, and after we've cleaned the kitchen we take a long and mostly silent walk along the beach. It's shiveringly cold, but no less beautiful for it. You could do a lot worse than wake up to this every day.

When we get back to the house, Dad's frying sausages.

'Morning,' he says. 'Again. Hungry?'

'Ravenous,' says Henry. 'Can I help?'

'You can lay the table,' Dad says. And my dirty mind whispers: *After all, you've already laid my daughter.*

'Mum up?'

'Sleeping in. We thought, if you have time, we could go for Sunday lunch before you head back.'

'Be nice,' I say, 'thank you.'

'Working tomorrow?' Dad asks, but the question is directed at Henry.

'Yup, got a pretty full list,' he says, picking up on my facial signals and keeping it simple. Me travelling is one thing, having a 'friend' is another, but a hairdressing dentist is a step too far for the time being.

'Jolly good. Scrambled okay?'

'Scrambled is fine,' Henry answers. 'Perfect, thank you.'

'Dad. I've been thinking.'

'Thinking what, Poppet?'

Poppet? Henry mouths, smiling.

'I'm not going travelling,' I say.

I can't see Dad's reaction – his back is turned as he cracks eggs into a bowl – but Henry's smile slides from his face.

'Nonsense,' says Dad.

'But I've—'

'Zozo, darling, your mother knew this would come up. And she's quite firm on the matter. If you don't get on that plane, we're changing the locks.'

'I just think th—'

'I assume you'll be going to Australia?'

'I haven't really . . . yes, I suppose so.'

'Good. Your mum's always wanted to see the Sydney Harbour Bridge. We'll meet you there, if that's okay. Sometime in their winter, ideally.'

'But what about her eyes? The sun?'

'Well, Poppet, it's a long way off. A lot can happen. Shall we be naughty and fry some bread?'

Henry looks at me: *Well?*

'Sure,' I say, 'why not?'

Zoe

A Pink Envelope

In the last two days we must have spent twelve hours on the train. It's a long way for a walk on the beach, and my head is rattling with all manner of conflicting hard-edged thoughts. Like a tumble dryer full of sand and pebbles. Yet despite it all, I feel somehow lighter.

Henry prepares a bolognaise while I use the shower. And then, while he takes his turn under the hot water, I put the spaghetti on to boil and fiddle with a half-completed jigsaw of a vast zebra herd.

My eyes are beginning to cross when there is a knock on Henry's door. I have a towel turbaned around my head and I'm wearing nothing more than a pair of pants and one of Henry's t-shirts, so I sit very still and hold my breath. The knock comes again, this time accompanied by a small voice:

'Hello? Henry, love?'

The voice is thin and frail, so I throw caution to the wind and open the door by a few centimetres.

'Oh, hello, love. Zoe, is it?'

'Er, that's right.' The woman is small and unarmed, so I open the door fully. 'Henry's in the shower, can I help?'

'Moved in, have you? Henry didn't say anything about anyone moving in. I mean, I suppose it's okay, so long as there's not too much . . . noise.'

'Sorry, were we disturbing you?'

'I'm the landlady, love. Dorothy. Call me Dot.'

'Right, Dot. No, I'm not moving in, I'm just a . . . friend.'

Dot takes in my towelled hair, bare legs, Henry's t-shirt, and I'm acutely aware that I'm not wearing a bra.

'It's just that, well . . .' Dot holds out a pink envelope. 'You've got post, love.'

'Oh, thank you.'

'See,' Dot says, indicating my name, connected to Henry's by means of an elaborate ampersand. 'Henry *and* Zoe.'

'I'll give it to him,' I say.

'Aye, well. Say hello to him from me. Tell him I'll see him Tuesday,' she says, touching her hair.

Henry has no hair to speak of, but he still takes twice

as long as me in the shower. It's gone ten o'clock by the time he's finished, which is really too late to be eating a heavy meal, but luckily I've had the foresight to burn the pasta.

'You're a dark horse,' I tell him.

Henry inspects his naked torso, and his clean white boxer shorts for clues. 'Excuse me?'

'I met your landlady.'

'Dot?'

'Dot.'

'Is everything okay?'

'She thought I'd moved in.'

Henry laughs. 'She's a sweetheart.'

'Nice hair, too.'

'Well, she has a nice hairdresser,' Henry says, kissing my forehead and sitting down beside me at the bay window. 'No spag?'

'It's a bit late,' I tell him.

Henry nods – *fair enough* – and takes a forkful of bolognaise.

'And there was me thinking I was your dirty secret.'

'Right, you've properly lost me now, what are you getting at?'

I nod at the torn envelope and the card, standing on top of the half-made herd of zebras. Printed on the homemade card are two red champagne flutes beneath the words *40 Bloody Years*.

'What's that?' says Henry, pointing his fork at the card as if it were written in blood.

'Sorry, probably shouldn't have opened it, but it was addressed to *us*.'

'*Us?*'

'It's an invite,' I tell him, ever so bright and perky. 'When were you going to tell me?'

'Tell you ... what?'

'God, you're such a tease.'

Henry picks up the card, opens it, reads aloud: 'Dear Henry and Zoe, can't wait to see you ... both. Wear something red. Kiss kiss kiss. Love Mum and Dad ...'

'... Sheila and Clive.'

Henry's lips move silently as he rereads the card.

'Honestly, Henry, you are such a dark horse.'

'Yeah,' he says. 'Runs in the family.'

Henry

Doh Je

It seems that the Universe is not satisfied unless at least one woman within a five-foot radius of Henry Smith is crying at any one time. Jenny has been leaking tears for the last thirty minutes, clutching a handkerchief in one hand and a small mirror in the other. Although how she can see anything through all these tears is a mystery.

It's taken less than two hours to fit her new smile, but it's been a long build up to this moment. Working from the second molars to the central incisors, alternating from the top row to the bottom, a jigsaw in twenty-eight white pieces. Except there's no guarantee all the pieces will fit until you've inserted the last one. They fit. They look, even if I do say so myself, beautiful.

'*Doh je*, *doh je*, Henry.'

'*Mh sai haa hei*,' I say. You're welcome.

The Cantonese characters for 'thank you' comprise a neat, almost tessellating arrangement of hard edges and sharp crescents that belie the soft grateful syllables – *doh je*.

In between bouts of crying and close examination of her new supernaturally white teeth, Jenny presented me with a small scroll, bound in purple ribbon. I look again at her gnarled arthritic fingers, and marvel at how something so painful and ugly could have produced this precise and elegant calligraphy.

There are two ways of saying 'thank you' in Cantonese, Jenny explained; one for a service, another for a gift. '*Doh je*, gift,' she said. 'This' – showing me her teeth – 'gift.'

I thought about telling her that, actually, she still owed me a couple of thousand pounds, but it would only trivialize her sentiment.

'Can smile when scatter ashes now,' says Jenny, making sure to maintain the flow of salt water down her cheeks.

After an emotional couple of weeks, I haven't seen Zoe cry since we left Cornwall. We have continued to see each other every night, squeezing the days and nights until our allotted time runs out. But who knows when that will be. Zoe isn't due to travel until mid-September, but we have the small matter of my parents' wedding anniversary to get through first. Zoe is as excited as a kitten in a wool shop at the prospect of meeting my parents, although I have no idea why. I've certainly never said anything nice about them. She is nervous, too. She knows April will be there (an early labour notwithstanding, and God knows I'm praying for one), plus Brian, and various others who don't hold me in the highest regard. I have taken every opportunity to insist it will be a lousy party with a high possibility of flung glassware, but Zoe receives this information as another expression of my dry sense of humour. I have tried explaining that I don't have one, which Zoe takes as further proof of concept.

'Why would your parents invite us if they thought it would cause a scene?'

'Because they're stupid?'

'Honestly, Henry, you are such a card. I never realized you were such a card!'

I called my mother the second Zoe left for work on Monday morning.

'You just needed a little nudge, babes.'

'Mum, I don't need you interfering. And I really don't appreciate you stirring up drama.'

'Really, Henry. *You* don't appreciate *me* causing drama? Oh that's rich.'

'Mum . . .'

'You seem to have a short memory, Henry Smith.'

'Actually, Mum, I really don't. How the hell do you think April is go—'

'Don't you *hell* me, Henry. Don't you dare.'

'Mum, calm d—'

'For the record, Henry, I have talked to April.'

'You have?'

'What did I just say? Yes, I have.'

'And . . .'

'It's over, Henry. In the past.'

'Did you talk to George, Mum? Did you call him up and ask if he's bringing a hod full of bricks to your little party?'

'I don't like your tone, Henry.'

'Mum, listen, I—'

'I talked to April, April will talk to George. It's done, love.'

'But, Mum—'

'Henry, love, you can't hide away forever.'

'I know, but Zoe's . . . it's complicated.'

'Newsflash, Henry, life is complicated. You deal with it, you move on.'

'But—'

'Henry, I want you here, your dad wants you here, and if there's someone important in your life, well, we want them here too.'

'. . .'

'Henry?'

'Okay.'

'Good boy. And wear something red.'

But there is a part of me – a small sub-cellular part – that almost welcomes the inevitable. It will go one way or another and then – one way or another – it will be over. Eight more days.

I gently uncurl Jenny's fingers from the mirror.

'It's going to be a little sensitive for a while, okay? Your teeth need to find each other, make friends with each other again, and that's going to take a few days.'

'Can eat?'

'Yes, you can eat. But give it a few days before you try steak or toffee apples, okay?' Jenny smiles with her brand new teeth, and nods that she understands. 'I'm going to give you my phone number,' I say. 'So if you have any problems, any at all, you just call me, okay?'

'Friends.'

'That's right, friends.'

'*Doh je*,' Jenny says, putting her hands to either side of my face, and kissing me quickly on the lips. '*Doh je.*'

'*Mh sai haa hei*,' I say, again. 'Where did you learn to do that?' I say, nodding at the curled up scroll.

'Learn?'

'Calligraphy,' I say, writing in mid-air. 'It's very beautiful.'

'Hah! No calligraphy. Buy on Amazon, five pounds, very bargain, innit.'

Zoe

Mad-faced Screamers

Henry doesn't finish work for an hour, so I pass the time inside my duvet darkroom. Not developing film, but scrolling through my phone, watching footage of humans temporarily separated from their sanity. Search for 'freakout' and you get one-point-two million hits, 'road rage' gives you nine hundred thousand, there are over sixteen million 'crazy' women. Mad-faced screamers and frothing ranters. No wonder we say they've gone viral. Their rage and humiliation loaded online and shared and shared again. One million views of some hysterical mum gone banshee over a pinched parking space. One hundred thousand likes for some spittle-mouthed pensioner ranting respect at jeering teens. But it doesn't do to be too amused. It could be you one day.

While the rest of the office went to the pub, I walked down to the travel clinic on Tottenham Court Road for my vaccines – yellow fever, typhoid, and an alphabet's worth of hepatitis. Maybe they affected my brain; you read funny things about these vaccines.

As I wandered back to the office, I watched a guy in a baseball cap and headphones step off the pavement, causing a car to slam on its brakes.

Next week Alex would have been thirty.

The driver that hit him was fined sixty pounds for driving without due care and attention, and given three points on his licence. My friends hear this with anger and indignation – *It's a disgrace*, *He should be banned*, *He should be locked up*. But the truth is Alex stepped in front of him. No one is tactless enough to say it explicitly, but the driver didn't have a chance. He wasn't speeding, wasn't talking on his phone, wasn't drunk. I feel guilty for thinking it, but I feel sorry for him too.

On Tottenham Court Road, the driver hit his horn hard: one, two, three times. The guy in the headphones lifted the peak of his cap and mouthed the words *Fuck off*, punctuating his gratitude with his middle finger.

Without thinking, I was walking towards the guy, shouting like a woman demented. 'Look where you're going! You could have been killed.' He looked at me and laughed dismissively before walking away. But I followed him along the road. 'I'm talking to you. Hey, you, don't ignore me. What's wrong with you?'

'Piss off, yeah.'

'Piss off? Really, you want me to piss off. I could be calling you an ambulance now. You could have been killed, for God's sake.'

'Well, I wasn't, was I? So jog on, yeah.'

'Jog on?'

'Yeah,' said the guy, stopping, and jutting his chin at me. 'Fuck off.'

I slapped him hard, knocking his cap from his head. For a full second the guy was frozen in shock, and then his face knotted into anger and he took a step forwards.

'Go on!' I shouted at him. 'Go on!' I screamed.

We had a crowd around us by now, two or maybe three people holding up mobile phones.

'Fucking psycho,' said the guy, scooping his cap up from the floor. But he had the good sense to say it while he was backing away.

'What are you looking at?' I said to the semicircle of onlookers, a stupid question that should serve as a good punchline if my performance finds a larger audience.

I don't doubt it's out there somewhere, but good luck finding this mad cow. The best thing about these online meltdowns is the sheer volume of them. It's almost enough to make you feel normal.

Henry

This Balloon Is Going Nowhere

'Remember,' whispers Gus, 'you are not your thoughts. You are ... well, you, obviously.'

'Hmmm hmmmm.'

I feel as if I'm nothing but thoughts, jostling, yammering, antagonistic thoughts.

It's whale song today, but to me it sounds like a gathering of demons.

My bank statement arrived yesterday, showing that seventeen thousand, six hundred and forty-six pounds has vanished out of my account. It is unlikely April's father has forgiven me for jilting his only daughter, but it seems his hatred has cooled to the point where he is now prepared to take my money. The effect on my conscience hasn't been as profound as I'd hoped.

'Now attach those heavy headaches to your balloon.

I think I'll go with orange today. No, second thoughts, pink. And flooooat your funk away.'

It's pointless.

Standing in the basket of a colossal hot air balloon are Zoe, April, Brian and a nervous midwife; Mad George is fiddling with the burner; mine, April's and Zoe's parents are introducing themselves to each other. It's crowded in there. They're staring at me impatiently, waiting for something to happen, but this balloon is going nowhere.

August

August 5 at 00:31 AM
From: Audrey <audreywilliams56@mymail.net>
To: Alex Williams

Hello Son

Well, I suppose this is the month I've been dreading. You would have been 30 today – in just a few hours as a matter fact. So young darling. It just doesn't seem right. It doesn't feel real.

Yours was a long labour, although I'm sure I've told you many times. The cord got tangled round your neck, and for a while it was very frightening. It can't have been more than a few minutes, but it felt like forever and you could see from the doctors' faces they were worried. The morning after you were born I took you to the chapel to pray and thank God for keeping you safe. I was

358

The Trouble with Henry and Zoe

kneeling there, holding you to my body when your little head went limp and dropped onto my shoulder like a stone. Honestly, I shouted to wake the saints, but silly me, all you'd done was fall asleep. You were my first, of course, and I was very naive.

But it makes you think doesn't it. I was very lucky to have you at all, and every year has been a gift to me. I'm sorry love, I can't write any more.

Happy birthday my baby boy.

Mum xx

Zoe

It's Not Like You Left Her At The Altar

The train takes just under two hours to rattle up the centre of the country to a small market town on the east of the Peaks. From there it's another two hours to travel half as far again, before finally arriving at the village where Henry grew up. He's quiet today and becoming more so with every station we leave behind, staring out of the window, seemingly hypnotized by the heavy rivulets of horizontal rain. Last night we watched *The Graduate* on DVD and Henry was so quiet I almost wished I'd taken on an extra shift at the pub. But we have only five weeks left, so anything I'm going to earn in the Duck is no longer going to affect the course or duration of my travels. I continue to work there now, as much for the comfort of routine as for six pounds an hour and all the cholesterol you can eat. And besides, I want to be with Henry, even if he has been quiet lately. Maybe he's nervous, and after everything he's told me, I suppose I can understand.

It's a little after three in the afternoon and we're already on gin and tonic number two. Maybe for all his protestations to the contrary, he is sulking about my imminent departure. But if he is, I wish he'd just talk to me about it.

For me, the best bits in *The Graduate* were between Dustin Hoffman and Anne Bancroft; there was a chemistry between them that, from what I could see, Ben simply didn't share with Mrs Robinson's daughter. For all of Hoffman's brooding and mooching and running to the church, I couldn't for the life of me figure out what he saw in dreary old Elaine. But even so, I was rooting for him when he followed her across the country, tracked her down on campus, hammered his fists against the chapel windows. I cried when they rode away together on the bus, Elaine in her wedding dress, dishevelled Ben, for once, smiling. And all I could think was, *We have so much more than them, so why is it so easy for him to let me go?*

Because it's far from easy for me. The question has become a nagging voice inside my head, and I have had to physically bite my tongue to keep from saying something. *Take me with you*. That, I suppose, is what I'm waiting for Henry to say, ask, demand. But then how would I answer? The whole point was for me to travel alone, to 'find myself'. Can you do that with someone else in tow? I guess that depends on who that someone is.

'Excited?' I ask.

Henry turns away from the window slowly, almost with reluctance. He sees his drink is empty and rattles the empty can. 'Want anything from the bar?'

'Talk to me,' I say, drawing a glance from the woman sitting beside Henry and diagonally across from me. I reach across the table and take hold of his hands. 'Nervous?'

Henry nods, and I raise my eyebrows to let him know that this doesn't count as an answer.

'Yes,' Henry says. 'A little.'

'It's just an anniversary. It's not like you have to give a speech, or anything.' A small laugh to lighten the mood, but Henry doesn't pick up on it.

The woman opposite is wearing headphones, but as she fiddles with her phone it's clear that she is lowering the volume.

'I don't suppose she went into labour then?'

'My mother?' Henry says, smiling.

'You know who . . . *she who must not be named.*'

Henry shakes his head. 'If she has, no one's told me. But then, they wouldn't, would they.' And he looks at me with so much more depth and meaning than the statement would seem to deserve.

'Will she throw a drink over you?' I ask. 'God, that would make a good picture. Give me a nudge if you see it coming.'

Henry doesn't seem to find this possibility as funny as I do.

'Look, I know you were *engaged*,' I say, dropping my voice to a whisper on the last word, 'but, well,' – my mind flashing back to *The Graduate* – 'it's not like you left her at the altar, or anything.'

Henry

Well, That Was Stupid

So fate lends a hand. Or, rather, sneaks up and shoves me violently between the shoulder blades.

'It's not like you left her at the altar,' Zoe says.

And there's no turning back now. Right up until this point, if I have lied it's been a lie of omission, a white lie, a well-intentioned avoidance of potentially upsetting details. But this is the point of no return; to leave Zoe's rhetorical gambit unanswered and uncorrected amounts to nothing less than bare-faced deceit. And while we're hitting the honesty switch, let's not pretend this is fate making a late appearance. I took the first step when I told Zoe I was a dentist, the second when I mentioned my engagement. Last night I could have dropped any movie into the DVD player, but I chose *The Graduate*. Zoe cried at the final scene, as Ben and Elaine left the carnage of her broken wedding behind them, and the words were in my mouth, but like so many times before they caught against my teeth.

It's not a question, but Zoe has spoken through a smile, her eyebrows arched, waiting for me to laugh off this piece of fantastic whimsy. To acknowledge the joke. Instead, I press my lips together apologetically, and watch Zoe's smile fade from the eyes down. She opens her mouth to speak, thinks better of it and turns to look out of the window.

'Zoe.' I lean across the table and take hold of her hands, but Zoe sits back, drawing her hands out of my grip.

'Are . . .' Zoe looks around the carriage, as if trying to decide on what level of a scene is acceptable in this confined space. 'Are you *serious*?' she says, through gritted teeth, as if this is the only way she can contain her anger.

'Zoe, let me ex—'

'You've had weeks, *months* to explain.'

I nod at the woman beside us, furrowing my brow to suggest we should try to remain civil.

'What, Henry? Am I embarrassing you?'

'No, of cou—'

'Because, talking of *embarrassment*. Did you think about *me*? You were going to just plonk me in the middle of it all with no knowledge, no warning?'

'Zoe. I wanted to tell you. But it's hardly, I mean . . . it's not the kind of thing you just drop into . . . you know.'

'What, that you left your fiancée at the . . . *God*, Henry. Fuck!'

'Zo, please, it's . . . it's like you said about Alex. It just wasn—'

'Don't!' And now any pretence at decorum has been abandoned. 'Don't you dare. Don't you dare bring Alex into this.'

'Zoe, I'm sorry. That was a really stupid thing to say. I just . . .'

'Don't,' Zoe says quietly. She crosses and uncrosses her arms, looking increasingly uncomfortable and confined by her seat. She gathers up the empty cups and cans and tonic bottles, slides out of the seat, and walks up the aisle in the direction of the bar. The woman beside me has been pretending to listen to music, but deprived of further spectacle, she turns up the volume and goes back to her magazine.

The truth is out, revealed like a bad diagnosis, but it still needs to be discussed. It still needs to be explained and absorbed. We have two more stops before changing onto a provincial service that winds through the hills and villages and fields of the Peaks for another two-plus hours. And no more secrets. I will explain and confess everything that happened between me and April. I will tell Zoe how much she means to me, how much it frustrates the hell out of me that we only have a handful of weeks left, and that I was afraid to ruin the short time we had together. I don't expect to clear the air completely before we arrive, but I do think Zoe will understand. I'm not stupid enough to suggest as much, but I think she might even find it funny. After all, we laughed like fools while Ben was banging on the church window and fending off Elaine's family with a crucifix. Admittedly, Zoe's laughter turned to tears, but that's the point – she was happy for them. Love conquers and justifies all. Doesn't it?

The train rolls into the penultimate stop of this leg of our journey. The rain has intensified, and as passengers disembark, they run – hunched against the weather, coats pulled overhead – towards the covered area in front of the ticket office.

Except for Zoe.

She stands impassively in the thrashing rain, her bag at her feet as she removes the red rose clips from her hair and drops them into a bin.

The guard blows his whistle, and a voice tells us this train is ready to depart, and where it is stopping next. I bang on the window and shout Zoe's name, but either

367

she doesn't hear or doesn't care to respond. The windows don't open so I bang on the glass again, hard enough to feel the pane vibrate under my fist. 'Zoe! Wait, Zoe!'

'Careful,' says the woman next to me. 'You'll break the glass.'

And if I could, I probably would. The third time I hammer on the window, Zoe looks up. Like Elaine in *The Graduate*, she stares at me with catatonic incomprehension, but unlike Elaine, she does not walk towards me. She turns away and walks slowly towards the ticket office.

The woman beside me rotates through ninety degrees, making it only slightly less difficult for me to get out of my seat, and she protests loudly as I jostle my way past her. The train is already moving, and picking up speed as I reach the end of the carriage. The doors are of course locked, but the windows, at least, open. I shout Zoe's name again, but she has already disappeared from sight.

I've been jilted.

Three hours later, I step off another train and into the familiar pocket of hills that I have always called home. As if the clouds have followed me here from London, cold rain bounces off the ground, filling the air with the vivid fragrances of grass and earth and open space. I take a deep lungful and set off walking. I have left messages: *I'm sorry. Can we talk? I can explain.* But even if I could, Zoe isn't picking up.

I called Rachel.

'Henry, what a surprise, listen, I can't talk right now because I've got my best friend on hold. Turns out her boyfriend is a lying tosspot.'

'Is she okay?'

'No, Henry, of course she's not o-fucking-kay.'

'Is she safe?'

'Jesus Christ, don't flatter yourself. Is she ... she's drowning her fucking disappointment and humiliation in gin and crying down the phone on a crowded train. So, good job, panic over.'

'Will you ask her to call me?'

'No, I won't. And she's asked me to ask you to *stop* calling her. So, seriously, do you think you could just, like, leave her the fuck alone?'

'Will you tell her—'

Rachel hung up.

When I walk through the front door of the pub, I'm tired, depressed, angry and soaked to the soles of my feet. You read about embezzlers and adulterers talking of the relief at finally being found out. I don't feel that, because for all the weight lifted from my shoulders, it feels like it's been attached to my heart and my guts. This was always going to end, but not now and not like this. If I could take it all back for another month with Zoe, then I would do it without hesitation. The truth has not set me free; it has simply brought my sentence forward.

The pub is decorated with red paper chains, red streamers and a lot of red balloons – forty if I had to hazard a guess. But no Smiths. I have never seen the barmaid before, and she looks at me like I'm a vagrant when I ask after Clive and Sheila.

'I'm Henry,' I tell her.

'The boy,' she says in a mild eastern European accent.

'Their son, yes.'

'The one who' – the barmaid sprints her fingers across the counter – 'zzzipp!'

'That would be me.'

She purses her lips, this girl who might be ten years younger than me, and shakes her head as if it's all so fucking familiar and predictable. 'Mother upstairs,' she says, nodding me through to the back.

I find Mum sitting on the sofa, about halfway through *Brief Encounter*, and making similar progress through a bottle of wine and a giant tub of Philadelphia cheese. She's making sandwiches, but judging by the mean pile of uneven triangles on the plate, she started on the wine before she began buttering the bread.

'Hungry?' I ask.

Mum looks up, surprised to see me. 'Baby boy,' she says, her voice damp with sentiment and chardonnay. 'Come and give your mum a kiss. Then wash your hands.'

'Why, where have you been?'

'Cheek,' she says, brandishing a cheese-smeared knife. The kitchen table is piled with mega-sized packets of crisps, jars of dip, and assorted tubs of variously treated nuts.

'This for tonight?'

'April and Bri are bringing the hot stuff,' Mum says. 'Wedges, sausage rolls, chicken satay.'

On the TV Laura and Dr Harvey are rowing a boat across a lake, any minute now Dr Harvey will fall in and Laura will bray her sharp, unconvincing laugh as he stands there, wicking water up his enormous tweed trousers.

'You're wet,' says Mum, after I've joined her on the sofa and filled a glass.

'Fell in a lake,' I tell her.

She raises her eyebrows at me, confused for a moment before getting the reference. 'Very droll.'

'I never found him that handsome,' I say, nodding at the TV.

Mum shrugs. 'Clean cut, I suppose. So . . .' she turns to me, '. . . where's Zoe?'

I shake my head. 'Not coming.'

Mum sighs, turns back to the movie. 'What happened?'

'Told the truth,' I say.

'Well, that'll learn you. Here, I'll butter, you cheese.'

'Got any cucumber?'

'Listen to Mister Lahdedah. No, it makes the bread soggy.'

'Where's Dad?'

Mum sets her glass down with great deliberation; as if she is afraid it might fly from her hand.

'What?' I ask.

She glares at me, as if all my sins have coalesced into the last two seconds. 'Like father, like son. Isn't that what they say?'

'Where is he?'

'Well, son, that would be the million sodding dollar question.'

'Jesus, Mum, what happened?'

'What happened? You're asking *me* what happened?'

'Did you fight?'

Mum attacks a round of bread with the butter, applying it with such determination that she tears a hole in the slice. 'That's one way of putting it,' she says, folding the ragged piece of bread in half and taking a bite.

Laura and Dr Harvey are declaring their love now. 'It sounds so silly,' says Laura, and listening to their stiff clipped dialogue, I have to agree.

Mum picks up her glass, apparently confident that she can drink from it now, and not throw it against the wall. 'Things happen in forty years,' she says.

'Things?'

'No one's perfect,' she says, defying me to contradict her. 'We all of us make mistakes, on both sides of the bed.'

Whether this statement is colloquial, elliptical or literal I don't want to know, but I know my mum, and I can make a good guess.

'Mum, I . . . whatever . . . when did . . .'

'Forty years is a long time, son. Things happen, upstairs and down, and you walk on or walk away, understand?'

'I think so, but I don't really want—'

'You forgive and forget, or do your best, at least. Maybe there's a name you don't mention, or a place, or a song, or a colour?'

'A colour? How many mistakes have you made?'

'See that silly sodding film,' she says, sloshing wine out of her glass as she points violently at Dr Harvey. 'She ends up with the husband, doesn't she.'

'Yes.'

'And he knows, but he doesn't rub it in, does he. He says—'

'"Thank you for coming back to me."'

'Exactly, good boy. Because he wants to be with her, at any cost, no matter what mistakes she may have made.'

'Mum, have you … made a mistake?'

Mum sighs, exasperated at my inability to follow this tangential confession or accusation. 'Imagine, Henry, imagine your wife – if you ever manage to find someone to marry you, which, well, let's be frank, isn't looking too promising – but imagine it came to your attention that your wife had been spending too much time with, say, a painter.'

'An artist?'

'Or a decorator. It doesn't matter, but, yes, a decorator, for example.'

'Okay.'

'Well, in the interests of discretion and domestic harmony, your wife would most likely not make a big fuss in the future when the hallway needed repainting. Unless it really was in a terrible state, in which case she might make subtle hints for a few weeks, then make herself scarce when the painters were in.'

Mum resumes buttering the bread, taking more care

374

now, applying the spread evenly in smooth back and forth strokes. Laura is on the train back to her family now, staring out of the window in a rapture of happiness, visualizing Dr Harvey in a tuxedo and herself in a ball gown and tiara, diamonds at her neck as they dance beneath crystal chandeliers. She imagines them attending the opera, boating in Venice, driving an open-topped sports car, standing beneath the palms on a tropical beach. An altogether more pleasant trip than Zoe's, I imagine. If she is visualizing anything involving me, I suspect the scenario includes at least one sharp implement.

'Can you turn that off, Mum?'

'You're right,' she says turning off the TV. 'He is a bit hard faced. Make a good psycho, but ... anyway, what was I saying?'

'Something about you and the decorator, I think.'

'For example,' Mum says, contemplating her perfectly buttered slice of bread, then sliding it over to me to fill. 'And anyway,' she says. 'It was a long time ago and forty years is a long time to be married.'

'So where's Dad?'

Mum goes to refill her glass. 'Did he tell you what he was planning?'

'When? No.'

'For our anniversary.'

I point at the sandwiches on the table. 'Aren't we . . .'

'We went into town yesterday,' Mum says. 'Just the two of us.'

'That's nice.'

'It was nice. He shaved, wore a shirt, used his fork . . .'

'What happened?'

'Well, let's suppose you and' – snapping her fingers in the air – 'Zoe.'

'There is no me and Zoe, Mum.'

'Well, we'll get to that. But let's imagine she found, for example, another woman's earring down the side of the sofa.'

'Mum, what are you saying?'

'Can we just imagine, Henry?' Her voice is rising and she's getting very animated with the knife.

'Fine.'

'Thank you. So, what would be the very last *effing* thing you would buy Zoe for your ruby wedding anniversary?'

'I don't know.'

'Make a guess, Henry.'

'Earrings?'

'Thank you. Ruby sodding earrings. Not a ring, not a bracelet, not an effing sodding necklace, but earrings, Henry.'

And now it comes back to me: Dad whispering down

the phone asking should he buy Mum a ring, bracelet or necklace? And me suggesting . . .

'Friday?' I say. 'Are you saying he's been gone since yesterday?'

'God no, where would he go? Anyway, I didn't say anything yesterday; didn't want to spoil the day. It's been f—'

'Forty years, I know.'

'And besides, there are, you know . . . expectations on your anniversary.'

'Mum, please!'

'What, you think young people are the only ones entitled to a bi—'

'Mum! I get it, I . . . loud and clear.'

'Good. And don't expect me to apologize for being a woman, Henry.'

'So,' I say, after what feels like a suitable pause. 'You dropped it on him today, didn't you?'

Mum shrugs, scoops her finger through the Philadelphia and pops it into her mouth.

'He wanted to know why I wasn't wearing the earrings,' she says. 'So I bloody well told him why.'

'Brilliant.'

'Don't take a tone, Henry. I'm warning you, do not take a tone.'

'Do you ever wonder, Mum . . . if you and Dad are . . .'

'Baby boy, I wonder all the time. But' – she points her knife at the inert TV screen – 'can you see me with someone like her husband, all moustache and pinstripes?'

I laugh. 'No, I really can't.'

'Well, there you go,' she says. 'You're made for who you're made for.'

'What about tonight?' I say. 'Are you going to cancel?'

'Henry, love, folk have had their hair done.'

'So . . .?'

'So get some spread on that bread.'

Of course they have booked a karaoke.

April sings 'Sweet Home Alabama'; Brian belts out 'Livin' on a Prayer'; and I do 'Islands in the Stream' with my mother, filling in the parts she was due to sing with her husband. Wherever he got to. By virtue of death and birth control (natural or designed), my parents have no family beyond their only son. But the pub is bustling with friends, regulars and locals; the mood and music are set to high, and any dampening effect Dad's absence might have had has been amply offset by several cases of pink prosecco and a table full of sausage rolls. Even Mum appears to be enjoying herself, and when I ask if we should be worried, she whispers into my ear that Dad can take care of himself. 'Mind you,' she says, 'if he leaves it much longer, he'll have me to deal with, and I'm a different matter.'

'So,' says April. 'Where's this mystery woman? Zoe, isn't it?'

Sitting at a table with Mum, Brian and a heavily pregnant ex-fiancée is less mortifying than I might have imagined.

'She couldn't make it.'

'Didn't run out on her, did you?'

'Harsh,' says Brian.

'Hardly,' says Mum. 'If you want to talk about harsh, love ...'

'Actually,' I say, 'I told her about you.'

April raises her eyebrows. 'Well, that was stupid.'

Brian nods.

'Shame,' says April.

'Thank you.'

'I mean,' April goes on, 'I was looking forward to seeing your face when I told her myself.'

Mum laughs and nudges April with her elbow. 'God, can you imagine.'

April stares right through me and nods slowly. *Yes, I really can.*

And so can I. I imagine that, in the noisy intimacy of this pub, confronted with the live and thriving protagonists, Zoe might have received the news more easily than on a busy train. She might have laughed. But then again, maybe not. As ever, my timing and judgement are way off. Despite Rachel's insistence, I sent one more message to Zoe before joining the party tonight – a final apology and plea for dialogue. She hasn't called, hasn't messaged.

Zoe

The Last Bottle Of Champagne

I'm pulling my hair again, and the sensation feels like an old friend. Sitting in the bath, working conditioner up through my roots, clenching two fistfuls of hair and twisting my hands away from my scalp.

Eight hours on trains and cold platforms to end up back in London minus a boyfriend that wasn't a real boyfriend anyway. I've had plenty of time to think, too much probably, but my thoughts and feelings are no less tangled than they were when I made a massive U-turn several hours ago. The inside of my head feels like a ball of knotted string. And the champagne certainly hasn't helped. Did I over-react? Possibly, I'm not sure. But honestly, what's the point, after all? Five more weeks and it's over anyway. Whatever *it* was. I still don't know. I certainly can't take him to a wedding – too much like giving fate the finger.

Rachel wanted me to go back to her house, but Steve's family are staying and – can you imagine? *So your son's getting married. You must be so excited. Funny thing happened to me today.*

No thank you.

Rachel insisted, and when I refused she offered to come to mine. But I meant it when I said I wanted to be alone, and I suppose she must have heard it in my voice. There was mail for Alex when I got back through the door. Two letters: one a catalogue of DJ equipment, the other offering a free valuation of our property. *We have buyers looking in your area now.* Maybe I should have sold this place after all, I'd be halfway around the world by now. Either way, I don't think I'll come back to this house after I leave it in September.

How do you leave someone *at the altar*? And what's all that with *The Graduate*? As if he was setting me up and manipulating my emotions. *Jesus Christ*, she – April – was going to be there! And wouldn't that have made a picture.

After developing a roll of black and white negatives, I cut the film into six-frame strips and store them in plastic wallets, waiting to be scanned, cropped, enlarged, manipulated. I haven't printed any, and now I never will. Seven envelopes, seven rolls of film, all thrown in the bin along with a sugarcraft bride and groom and ten months' worth of mail for my dead boyfriend.

There was no wine in the house, but I needed a drink. The last bottle of champagne stood impatiently in the small shelf where it had been chilling for quite long enough. Maybe I was saving it to drink with Henry, but that's not happening now, so I popped the cork, took the bottle upstairs and ran a very hot bath.

Maybe I'm just a little bit envious. Henry did what I never had the courage to do. Regardless of how he went about it, he removed himself from what I can only assume was a bad relationship. But lucky old Zoe, I never had to choose between saying yes and saying no.

The champagne bottle is empty, my fingertips are wrinkled now and the water from my new boiler has cooled. My scalp tingles from me knotting handfuls of hair around my fist, but I haven't pulled any out, so I guess that's progress. *Yay for me!*

Looking at myself in the mirror, I all of a sudden look like a stranger. Thinner in the face, a single vertical wrinkle between my eyes from scowling. When I frown at my reflection, the wrinkle deepens and lengthens. It's hard to imagine anyone calling this girl Zoe Bubbles. And this graduated bob, Henry's handiwork hanging in wet ringlets. Not me either.

There is a pair of scissors in the bathroom cabinet, not ideal for the task, but what's new there. I pull a length of hair away from my head and cut it two inches from my scalp. Then I take another and cut again.

Henry

A Fight You Can't Win

There are boxers and there are brawlers, they say. Brawlers bite down on their gum shield and go toe to toe, throwing knuckles like savages. Boxers feint, draw, parry, move; they fight tactically, wearing you down and picking you off. Dad was a boxer – the sweet science, he calls it – but as his skills and mobility waned, he began to rely more on grit and his right hand, arguably taking more damage in his last half dozen fights than in all the rest leading up to that point. But even now, it seems Big Boots has retained a little of the old ring craft.

The first we know of his return, a little after nine, is Keith the Karaoke placing a microphone on our table and nodding towards the small, makeshift stage. The opening bars of Sonny and Cher's 'I Got You Babe' jangle out of the boxy speakers, and Dad raises his microphone towards his wife. Dad may have once resembled a certain Memphis crooner, but whatever shabby similarity remains, it stops short of the vocal cords. Not that Dad can't sing; more that he doesn't, not exactly. He delivers the lyrics – *They say we're young and we don't know* – with just enough melody and black pepper to elevate it above the spoken word. It's a narrow range, but the voice matches the man – rugged and sincere and a little battered. Mum's timing is perfect, standing on cue and returning the lyrics normally delivered by Sonny. And she can sing. Mum arrives at Dad's side – *and baby I got you* – and takes his hand. She shakes her head with a combination of love, resignation and admonition. Dad shrugs it off, and with no sign of communication between them, they switch seamlessly into their gender assigned lines: Mum worrying about the rent, him buying her flowers in the spring. The only thing that stops me crying – because lord knows, I come close – is Brian's infectious concern for April, who is sobbing to the brink of hyperventilation and with surely enough force to induce labour. We each hold one of her hands through to the final *Babe*, at which point my mother slaps Big Boots hard around the sideburns, in response to which, the old man takes her face gently in his big hands and kisses her like I imagine he did forty years ago today. April's hand slides out of mine, and I make a point of not looking at her or Brian until my mother returns to the table with Dad in tow.

'Look what the cat dragged in,' says April.

'Who you calling a cat?' Dad says, glancing at Mum. She smiles thinly, but still has the tense air of a thing undetonated. Dad puts his hand on my shoulder. 'Son.'

'Dad.'

'Well,' he says, taking in the table, 'this is ... you know ...'

'Weird?' says Brian.

'That it is. So ... Just us, is it?'

'She dumped him,' says April, not without some pleasure.

'This true?'

'Looks that way,' I say. 'So, happy anniversary, I suppose?'

Dad looks at Mum who still hasn't said a word since returning to the table.

Brian goes to stand. 'Maybe we should ...'

Mum puts a hand on his knee. 'You're family now,' she says.

Brian looks at me: *Is this true?*

I shrug: *Suppose so.*

'So?' says my mother, swivelling her eyes onto my father.

387

Dad places a small oblong box on the table. 'Happy anniversary, beautiful.'

Mum looks at the box, at my dad, back to the box. She opens it, closes it, begins to cry.

'What is it?' asks April.

Mum slides the box to the girl I increasingly think of as her daughter, and April pops it open.

'Not sodding earrings,' says Dad with a wink.

'Nice bracelet,' says Brian.

Mum puts her arms around Dad's shoulders and kisses him. 'It's beautiful.'

'Rightly so,' says the old man.

One piece of jewellery stirs thoughts of another.

'April?' I say, turning to my ex-fiancée.

'You know the fields at the back of Mum and Dad's house?' she says, apparently anticipating my line of enquiry.

'Yeees.'

'Well, if they're not sprouting diamonds by next spring, I don't know what to tell you.'

It's past two before Big Boots sees the last of the guests off the premises; roughly half an hour after we have steered Mum up the stairs and into bed. Me removing her shoes, Dad carefully removing her ruby bracelet and returning it to the black velvet box. After my mother unloaded on him this afternoon, he drove to Manchester and after 'a few hiccups', managed to exchange the earrings for something less incendiary. They have danced, kissed, argued a little, and dueted again with 'Baby, It's Cold Outside', 'It Takes Two' and, somewhat bewilderingly, 'Ebony and Ivory'. Brian and April did a passable impression of John Travolta and Olivia Newton-John and I drank too much pink prosecco. In the empty bar my ears are ringing with chatter, laughter and bad song. Dad let the bar staff go an hour ago, and the tables are strewn with glasses, the floor sticky with spilt drink and trodden-in buffet.

'Same again next year?' I say to Dad.

'We should do it more often,' he says, laughing.

'Maybe you could turn up next time.'

Dad throws a playful jab at my chin.

'And what about you? Keep letting these women slip through your hands?'

'Want me to do the glasses?'

'You'd probably drop 'em. Anyway, got a couple of girls coming in the morning.' Dad takes a seat at the bar. 'Buy your old man a drink?' he says, slapping the wood.

I pour two whiskies, sit next to my father and proceed to tell him everything there is to know about Zoe. About Alex, Thailand, Cornwall, the Duck and Cover, the white streak in her hair, the way she snorts when she laughs too hard. I tell him that I wish I'd met her two years earlier.

'Aye,' says Dad, laughing. 'Would have saved us all some trouble. So . . . what you going to do about it?'

'I don't know that there's anything I can do. And even if I could . . . she's still leaving next month. Maybe it's easier this way.'

'Yeah, that's a tough one.'

Dad places his splayed hands flat on the bar, staring at his prominent, calloused knuckles. The scars from where he had a frame holding his wrist together are still visible on his right hand.

'Couldn't remember where I got 'em,' he says.

'Got what, Dad?'

When he looks up at me, his eyes are tired and sad. 'Earrings,' he says. 'I left with a light under me, didn't take the bag or receipt. Just the earrings in a black box; no label. Was only there a week ago and I couldn't remember where I'd got 'em.'

'That what took you so long?'

'Must have gone in practically every jeweller's in Manchester.'

'I'm surprised you didn't get arrested. Why didn't you call me?'

Dad shrugs. 'Keys, names, what I'm doing in the cellar. Head like a sieve, son.'

'We all do that.'

Dad taps the back of his left hand and I notice a small number '3' written in black ink. 'Car park,' he says.

'How bad is it?'

Dad turns his hands over and clenches them into fists. 'Fighting's as much about heart as hands. You know that?'

I nod that I do.

Dad taps his chest. 'Bite down and dig deep,' he says. 'But ... sooner or later, you find yourself in a fight you can't win. Bust up, can't see the punches coming, can't get your shots off. Just getting hit and hurt and damaged. And every fighter's thought it, though most won't say, you just want a way out.' Dad relaxes his hands and looks me dead in the eye. 'All you have to do is lower your lead hand a little, hang out your chin ... and it's over.'

'Did you?'

'My problem, son, is I'm a stubborn bastard. Scars to prove it too.' Dad licks his finger and rubs away the number written on the back of his hand. 'I'm glad you stopped boxing,' he says. 'I'm proud of you. You know that, don't you?'

'I do now.'

Dad goes to cuff my ear, but instead puts his hand around my head and kisses me.

'Have you told Mum?' I say, putting a finger to my temple. 'About . . . you know.'

'Not yet, although she can probably guess. Thought we'd get this out of the way first. Not a bad night, eh?'

'No, turned out alright in the end.'

'Yeah,' Dad says, 'it does that sometimes.'

Zoe

Au Revoir, 'enry

The wind is a cold hand pushing against my chest, pressing against my leaning body with enough force to support me at a frightening forwards angle. If the wind were to suddenly drop, I could pitch teeth first into the railings or, worse, over the top and into the English Channel. Rachel and Vicky are flanking me, both leaning towards France.

'You've lost too much weight,' says Vicky.

'Don't talk to me about too much weight,' says Rachel, still checking her watch. 'And ... and ... *beep*. Exactly twenty-four hours left as a single woman.'

She is visibly pregnant now, and no amount of white silk is going to disguise the fact. But she at least seems to have made her peace with the fact.

Vicky takes a sip from the hip flask and passes it to me.

393

'It's cute,' she says. 'Your baby being at your wedding.'

'Be cuter if it was carrying flowers instead of ruining my waistline. Pass me that,' she says, holding out her hand for the hip flask.

'You're not drinking?' I say, twisting sideways to the wind, and righting my balance.

'Of course not, but I can have a sniff, can't I?'

'So,' says Vicky. 'Where were we?'

'Must we?'

'It's therapy, Zo. So, what have we got? Broken nose,' she says marking her thumb with item number one on the list of bad things about Henry Smith.

'Shaved head,' says Rachel.

'I like his nose,' I say.

'Not helpful, Zoe. Right, dentist; definite black mark.'

'He does jigsaws,' I say, smiling at the mental image.

'Weird,' says Vicky.

'Definitely,' says Rachel. 'And he's not exactly trendy.'

'Good one,' agrees Vicky. 'Shapeless jeans. Although . . . quite a nice bum.'

'True,' agrees Rachel. 'He is quite tight.'

'Left his fiancée at the altar,' I say, taking the hip flask. 'End of list.'

'I would fucking kill him,' says Rachel. 'I swear to God, I'd cut his whatsit off.'

'Such a shame,' says Vicky. 'I mean, I know he's a shit-bag, but . . . I liked him.'

'Me too,' I say.

'And, you know . . .' Vicky takes the flask, '. . . better that than go through the motions then get divorced a year later, isn't it?'

'Seriously?' says Rachel. 'Leave me at the altar? I would cut his little Henry off.'

'Actually . . .' I say, raising my eyebrows.

'Zoe!' Vicky swats at my arm. 'What are we talking here?' She holds her hands apart, her eyes widening as she increases the distance between her palms.

'Well, he's no Manaconda,' I say, and Vicky buries her face in her hands. 'But . . . I'm not complaining.'

Rachel snips a pair of invisible shears at the air, grabs the severed member and throws it overboard. 'Au revoir, 'enry.'

'Au revoir.'

'So,' says Rachel, snatching the woollen cap from my head, 'what's all this ab . . . oh my fuck, Zoe!'

Vicky takes a full step backwards, as if my hacked hair might be contagious. 'What did you do? What – did – you – do!?'

And all I can do is shrug. 'Fancied a change?'

'Good Christ, Zoe. Dye it red, put a bow in it, don't . . . oh my God, what about the bloody pictures?'

'I'm sorry. I'll hold flowers, I'll stand at the back.'

'Too right you will,' she says, taking a deep lungful of whisky vapour. 'Too fucking right.'

'Is there anything we can . . .' Vicky is inspecting my head as if it were something half dead at the side of the road.

'I swear to God,' says Rachel, opening and closing her shears. 'If I ever see that man again.'

Henry

The Element Of Surprise Is Vital

The element of surprise is vital.

I know this from *The Graduate*. Had Ben called Elaine, sent a letter, arrived at her door with flowers, he would have been sent on his way without a happy ending. We see it, too, in *An Affair to Remember*, and again in *When Harry Met Sally*. This is how the guy gets the gal.

If, that is, the gal can be got.

Dad talked about knowing when to quit, and knowing when to dig deep. I'm not ready to quit. What Zoe and I have is constrained and fated, but it ain't over until she climbs on a plane. Or until she laughs in my face approximately three hours from now. But, hey, it's not like I've anything better to do.

London is still blinking the sleep from its eyes, the airport staff are tired and indifferent to my perky good humour, but I've been drinking strong coffee since four o'clock and I am indifferent to their indifference – I am on a mission. As the engines rumble and vibrate, the horizon shades from black to purple to amber outside my window. Final checks have been implemented and the flight crew have taken their seats. Accounting for the time difference, we will touch down in Paris at 7.50 a.m. From there I can catch a métro, two trains and a cab to the vineyard in Bois de Saint-Benoît, arriving around midday local time. Or, I can spend in the region of one hundred and fifty euros on a taxi direct from the airport that should get me to the hotel before Zoe gets out of bed. I'll buy a pain au chocolat at the airport.

Zoe

I Have To Find Someone

Christophe stirs in his sleep, his thick black hair still pulled into tufts. My hands sticky with his hair gel. And all I feel is disconnected.

I blame Vicky and her hip flask. God, please don't let her find out; I've made enough mess with my DIY haircut. 'Like a *lutin*, a . . .' Christophe snapping his fingers, '. . . fairy, you know, the pixie. Very Parisienne.'

Flattering, considering what I really look like is a recovering chemotherapy patient. But, yes, *très* flattering from this handsome Frenchman. *Better looking than Henry? Peut-être; peut-être pas.* But not nearly as good a lover. Nothing wrong with his . . . technique, shall we say, and he certainly wasn't short on stamina, but . . . something to do with *fit*, perhaps. With rhythm and synchronicity.

For some reason I'm crying.

Nothing dramatic; pre-tears, really, a weight behind the flesh of my cheeks, and a sensation of rising moisture behind my eyelids. Quite refreshing, in this tired dehydrated doze. It's funny in a dark shade, but this infidelity – if that's what it is – it reminds me of Alex. It's something I try not to dwell on, but the thought presents itself sometimes without invitation. Alex wasn't himself in the weeks before he died ... he was ... *off* is how it felt, although the memory is fading now, just like the image of his face without a visual prompt. I remember worrying that he was cheating on me, but looking back the idea seems ... not implausible, but paranoid, maybe. Or unkind. More an expression of my insecurity or unhappiness than Alex's behaviour. But I'll never know, and what does it matter or change?

Like fucking this Frenchman.

What does that matter?

Last night I told myself it didn't matter at all, but sober Zoe (albeit *très* hungover Zoe) doesn't find it so trivial. Cheap is how it feels. I have no problem with casual sex, although I do think you can have too much of a good thing. But this, this sweaty collision with a stranger, it's not casual; it's soulless and joyless and maybe even a little bit vindictive. But, I'm beyond beating myself up about it. It's not like I'm cheating on anyone.

I slip out of bed and go to the bathroom to wash Christophe's hair gel from my hands, brush my teeth, clean my face, scrub my body and wash what's left of my hair. I'm disappointed with myself, but at the same time I feel calm – as if all the conflict is over now. Deciding to travel is the first good decision I can remember making in a very long time, and in under a month I'll put that plan into effect.

It's close to nine when I step out of the shower, but I'm not required to be anywhere for another two hours. Beyond the hotel grounds lie acres of forests and vines, and more than food, water or aspirin, I need a big dose of solitude.

First, however, I need to remove a certain Monsieur from my room, preferably unobserved. He's sitting up in bed, smoking an e-cigarette, which is both disappointing and ridiculous and pretty much sums up the whole fiasco. He holds the plastic fag towards me, and I laugh out loud.

'*Pardon?*'

'Nothing, sorry, still a bit . . .' I wobble my head, '. . . woozy.'

'Woozy?'

'Boozy. Tipsy, turvy, sorry . . .' and I'm laughing like a lush. Laughing until I snort, in fact.

Christophe, it is clear, does not find my laughter

endearing. But he's not going to let it get in the way of one more roll in the hotel sheets.

'You 'ave an osser hour,' he says, folding back a corner of the blanket.

I shake my head. *Sorry.*

'Sirty minutes?'

Nope. 'I have to find someone.'

Who?

'She's called Zoe.'

Christophe raises one eyebrow. Very Bond. 'Zoe?' he says. 'Like you?'

'A little,' I say.

Christophe does that shrug that little French boys must be taught in primary school. '*A bientôt.*'

I do my best to return his nonchalant shrug, but I ruin it by laughing all over again.

Henry

A Time Traveller

The woman at Passport Control in Paris makes the sleepy airport staff back in London look like cheerleaders. She has been through every page of my passport and is now scrutinizing my picture for the second time, squinting at me as if trying to reconcile the flesh version with the one-inch square photograph.

'Haircut,' I say, smiling and rubbing my hand over my shorn scalp.

'*Pardon?*'

The woman looks like she cuts her own hair with a breadknife, having first turned around on the spot twenty times to make it interesting. 'Me, I mean. My ... hair. Different from the photo,' I say, holding out my hand for my passport.

The woman holds the document to the light.

'*Qu'est-ce que c'est? Ici?*'

'Sorry, my French is . . . *mal*?'

'*Il y a un trou. Ici.*'

'I'm sorry, I really don't understand.'

The woman places my open passport on the counter, rotates it through one hundred and eighty degrees, and taps my impassive photograph. '*Sur les yeux.*'

'Yes,' I say. 'That's me.'

The woman shakes her head. '*C'est troué. Regardez*; look.' And she points to her eyes, first one and then the other. So I look again at my face, and I have to admit there is a certain deadness to my expression.

''oles,' she says, and she turns the photograph page over, revealing two small protrusions corresponding to the position of my eyes. To further clarify the issue, the woman folds the back cover away from the page and holds my picture against the glass. Sunlight shines through the two puncture marks on the photograph, turning me into Henry Smith the sinister android.

'Ah,' I say, 'holes.' And I remember inspecting my passport for graffiti, scissor and burn marks outside April's parents' house. Right before George hurled a burger at my chest. If I'd studied it for five seconds longer, I might have noticed the tiny holes where April, it seems, decided to jab a pair of pins through my eyeballs. And I remember her laughter when I asked for my passport. Bravo April. Bravo.

'Is no good,' says the woman, closing my passport.

'No, it's fine, it's me.'

'*Mais, c'est troué.*'

'It was a joke.'

'Is funny?' She doesn't look amused.

'Well, obviously not, no.'

'You do it?'

'Me? No! God no.'

'Who do it?'

'Hah, well, that would probably be my girlfriend. Well, fiancée, actually.'

'Ah! Fiancée, you get marry, yes.'

'Actually no, we broke up.'

'Break up?'

I snap an invisible pencil, make the appropriate sound effect.

'Oh.'

I nod at this woman, her tone softening now we have finally come to understand each other. 'Yes, she went a little ...' I do a crazy face.

The woman shakes her head, and picks up the phone.

I'm a time traveller.

The return flight from Paris to London didn't depart

until seven in the evening. Arriving in London at approximately the same time. But you'd be surprised just how much gin and tonic you can drink in the blink of an eye, particularly if you go for trebles. I don't know whether or not time travel increases the effects of alcohol, but when I stood from my seat at Heathrow, it was as if the plane had landed in a pocket of ground level turbulence. There's probably a PhD in it all somewhere. Once a vandalized passport has been identified, it's not even a matter of discretion. The local authorities stick you on the first flight home, the airline gets slapped with a fine, you are penalized in units of time – a brief sentence served in departure lounges, economy class and baggage reclaim. I drove here this morning, fourteen hours ago now, or maybe it's sixteen accounting for the temporal nonsense. Whether I am coming or going is a matter for debate. Either way, I am too drunk to walk straight let alone drive home through London traffic. But time travel can fix that one, too. Ten months ago, almost to the day, I booked a room at the Hilton in Manchester airport after leaving my fiancée on her wedding day. Approximately three hundred days later, I book a room at the Heathrow Hilton, after leaving a different girl at a different wedding.

It's enough to make your head spin.

It's enough to make you sick.

Zoe

The Grand Romantic Gesture

We walk through the exit marked NOTHING TO DECLARE, and I have to bite my lip to stop from snorting. The last thing I need is to be detained by customs. Vicky is wearing dark glasses, and the smell of wine clings to her like a mouldy cape. I shouldn't feel smug (*particularly when you jumped into bed with a Frenchman less than forty-eight hours ago*), but I am rather pleased with myself for avoiding a hangover. I've attended maybe five or six weddings, but my memories of them are a jumbled haze of flowers, dancing and painful mornings after. But, with the exception of a glass of champagne for the toast, I went through this one fuelled by nothing stronger than orange juice and coffee. It's amazing how much you see when your eyes retain the ability to focus. Prowling singles, jaded couples, loving partners. Despite everything, I missed Henry.

A part of me wondered if he would go for the grand romantic gesture, turning up unannounced like the hero from one of those old movies. But maybe he's glad to be out of this mess, after all. And I wouldn't blame him. If I'm honest – and, new promise to myself, I plan on being nothing less – I was disappointed when he failed to clatter through the swing doors, bellowing my name. I slept with my boyfriend's best friend a week after he was killed. I slept with a random wedding guest a week after walking out on Henry – jilting him, now that I think of it. So who am I to judge anyone? The ceremony and speeches moved me to tears; happy tears at the sincere and simple affection between Rachel and Steve. Maybe a little envy, too, but if you can't feel sorry for yourself at a wedding, then where the hell else? Christophe sidled up to me for the first dance, but after I removed his hand from my bottom he moved on to someone else. And good for him. Vicky snogged someone from a completely separate function, and I was in bed before midnight.

This morning, while the rest of the guests slept off their hangovers, I walked and thought and was quiet. I contemplated the future and the past, travelling through time and alternate realities in the hush of the French woodland. Thinking about choices, decisions, accidents and coincidences; about the past and the future. Thinking about thinking and about feeling and the difference between the two. And I thought, not for the first time, that I think too much.

I focused on the pattern of light between the leaves overhead, listened to the warmth of all the surrounding green, and thought about nothing at all.

Vicky is tugging at my sleeve. 'Is that Shitbag?'

Standing in amongst the huddle of waiting families and cab drivers is Henry. Like the drivers, he's holding a makeshift sign – an A4 sheet of paper on which is written a single word: SORRY.

When he smiles, all the defences are lifted from his eyes – and it changes him. The moody caution I first found so attractive is gone, replaced with simple, bright sincerity. And it works. What I want to do is jump into his arms, just like they do in the movies. So that's exactly what I do.

Henry

Complicated Story

Zoe launches herself at me, throwing her arms around my neck and very nearly pulling my head off. It feels like my spine is about to snap, but this warm forgiving body pressed close against my own is more than I could have hoped for – more than I deserve – so if ever there was a time to dig deep and man up, this is it.

'Missed you,' I say, hugging her tight and relieving some of the torque on my skeleton.

'Yes,' Zoe says, appearing to miss the strain in my voice. 'I missed you, too.'

'Get – a – room.'

Vicky is looking at me over the top of her sunglasses; her bloodshot eyes are hard to read, a combination of resentment and resignation perhaps.

'Got one,' I tell her, over Zoe's shoulder.

'Come again?'

'Complicated story,' I say.

Zoe relaxes her grip around my neck, and I lower her to her feet. 'Wouldn't expect anything less from you,' she says, but she's still smiling. I barely had time to register the fact before she launched herself at me, but she's had a haircut since I last saw her. And not a good one.

'This is ... interesting,' I say, brushing my fingers through her hair.

'Complicated story,' she says.

'So. How was the wedding?'

She's only been out of the country for two nights, but Zoe answers with an authentic but endearing Gallic shrug.

'Well, I'm never drinking again,' says Vicky, 'that's for sure.'

'I hear that,' I tell her.

'Been partying?' says Vicky, a note of derision in her voice.

'I've got the car,' I say. 'Let's get your bags and I'll tell you all about it.'

Zoe raises her eyebrows. 'You have a car?'

'It's ...'

'Yeah, I get it,' says Vicky. 'Complicated.'

411

Zoe

I'll Most Likely Kill You In The Morning

Henry moves his hands through my hair, and I refuse to think about Christophe doing the same thing forty-eight hours ago. I. Refuse.

On the drive back into London, Henry told us about his brilliant plan, his perforated passport and summary deportation from France. He slept the night in the airport hotel and spent the best part of Sunday floating on his back in the pool. 'Thinking,' he said, after we dropped Vicky at her flat. She is more reluctant than me to forgive Henry – a non-inclusive goodbye, aimed only at me, a pointed igno-rance of Henry's own farewell, an emphatic closing of his car door. The difference, I suppose, is that I can empathize. I can see how he let it go too far; how he found himself in that castle bedroom, sleepless not with doubt but with certainty. Henry told me about April, getting together,

412

breaking up, getting together again . . . sneaking out of the castle as the sun came up. It was a long story and we drove back and forth over the Thames, zigzagging its bridges and taking random turns and roads and exits, just driving and talking. The car itself has been vandalized; deeply and deliberately gouged along both sides – a gift from the disgruntled brother of Henry's ex-fiancée. It's been hard on him. April is now overdue with Henry's best man's baby, which must be disconcerting on several levels. I received Henry's story as if it were about someone other than the man sitting beside me. And in a way, it was.

'My place or mine?' I asked him.

We stopped for groceries on the way, dropped into Henry's for a change of clothes and his scissors. In my garden now, a mirror propped against the shed, I watch Henry in reflection as he examines my hair. He lifts what's left of my fringe and snips at it with his scissors.

'Are you sure you should be taking any more off?' I ask.

'If I could add it on, I would. But' – cutting again – 'what's done is done.'

'What are you going to do?'

'Is that a big question or,' he tugs at a lock of my hair, 'hah, a big question?'

'Both, I guess.'

'Try and make the best of a disaster,' he says.

'Will you stay in London?'

Henry shakes his head. 'I haven't really thought about it. Trying not to, anyway. It's a shame you missed the party,' he says. 'My dad would have liked you.'

'Not your mum?'

'She'd . . . she'd love you,' he says. His expression flickers with something like embarrassment before he looks away. Henry moves to the back of my head, teases out the short hacked hair between his fingers and snips millimetres from the tips. 'I'm sorry I didn't tell you,' he says.

'Why didn't you?'

Henry shrugs, shakes his head.

It was late when I arrived home after my aborted trip to see his parents, and I inflicted all my vandalism – negatives, sugar bride and groom, my hair – indoors. The birdhouse Henry made hangs from a nail on the side of the shed, unpopulated but still intact.

'When I went up last week,' Henry says, 'my mum told me . . . she more or less admitted to having had an affair. Or a fling or a . . . whatever.'

'Awkward.'

'Uh huh. Her and Dad both, if I understood her. But . . . what I did was worse. I think it's the worst thing anyone I know has ever done. So . . .' He sighs heavily. 'Not something you share with someone you care about.'

'I slept with someone,' I say, before I've decided exactly what it is I'm confessing to. Henry's expression collapses. His lips part but he says nothing.

I shake my head, take hold of his hand. 'After Alex died,' I say.

Henry relaxes incrementally, and squats down at my feet.

'Maybe a week after he died,' I go on. 'I . . . we were celebrating – that's not right, remembering him; a wake, I suppose you'd call it. And . . . he was one of Alex's best friends.'

Henry says nothing, merely smiles and nods. He appears entirely unfazed by this revelation, and I think – no, I feel – I *feel* a deep and keen and physical love for him. I feel it in my scalp and my lungs and the palms of my hands.

'What I'm trying to say is . . . I understand. I understand how we can do . . . things. Make mistakes.'

'I'm sorry I didn't tell you,' he says again. 'I was ashamed.'

'What's done is done,' I say.

Henry smiles, kisses me, resumes fiddling with my hair.

'Leave it,' I tell him. 'It's got a year to grow out.' Which kind of bursts whatever bubble we were inflating.

*

Henry cooks while I shower, and we eat off our laps in front of the TV, a horror movie where a petulant but inventive death refuses to be denied.

'My dad's always been big on tradition,' I say.

'What, like Christmas?'

'Mostly, yes. Like flying kites on New Year's Day . . .' I drift off, realizing I won't be around for that particular tradition this year.

'We always have an argument at Christmas,' Henry says. 'Without fail. And New Year. And Easter.'

'Do you know that film, *The Princess Bride*?'

'Sounds a bit girly.'

'You'd like it, I think. Pirates et cetera. We used to watch it every Boxing Day, for years. Ruining all the best lines by saying them out loud. *Inconceivable. As you wish. My name is Inigo Montoya*, and so on. There's this one: *Good night, Westley. Sleep well. I'll most likely kill you in the morning.* Or something like that.'

'*Okay*?'

'Westley is a cabin boy on the Dread Pirate Roberts' ship. And Roberts says this to him every night.'

'*I'll most likely kill you in the morning*?'

'Every night for three years. The point is, he never does. Kill him. They just continue on with their adventure. He . . . loves him, I suppose.'

Henry turns to look at me, a realization dawning in his eyes. 'So he lives?'

I nod. 'Happily ever after ...'

'Sounds nice.'

'What I'm saying, Henry Smith ... is I don't want to leave you behind.'

Henry inspects his hands, first the palms, then the backs, as if looking for answers.

'Bloody hell, Henry, do you want to come to Thailand, or what?'

Henry laughs, nods.

'Is that a yes?'

'Well,' he says, 'I'll need to get a new passport.'

Henry

Postcardoes

'Zoe good?' Gus says.

He's rolling a cigarette as I apply foils to my client's head.

'She's great,' I tell him.

'Gonna miss her, huh?'

I turn to face Gus. Wince.

He puts his tobacco down. 'No?'

'Sorry.'

'When?'

I hold up four fingers.

Gus picks up his cigarette and continues rolling. 'Better send postcards, man. Lots of postcardoes.'

September

September 1 at 7.21 PM

From: Audrey <audreywilliams56@mymail.net>

To: Alex Williams

Hello Son

I had a nice surprise last month. Just after
your birthday, Zoe wrote to me. It was nice to
hear from her after all these months, sad but
nice at the same time. We wallow in our own
grief sometimes, and forget that other people are
hurting too. When your dad died, I missed him
desperately. But I had you and Pat, and we all
held each other together. But Zoe doesn't have
that in her life and it must be so hard for her.

She's decided to go travelling. Like you did
after your degree. I was a little shocked at the
idea, but I can see now how it will help her to

move on and heal. It feels odd to say it, but if I could have one wish for Zoe, it would be that she finds someone new to share her life with. I know how much you loved her Alex, and I know you'd want her to have that again. I told her as much. I told her life is for living and sharing and loving, and I told her to get out there and make the most of every moment.

I think what Zoe is doing is incredibly brave and I admire her for it. Because if we don't move on, well, we wither don't we. So, I've decided that I'm going to move on too. I'm going to stop writing these letters. It's been a comfort to me in a lot of ways, but I don't think it's healthy – it keeps the pain alive and that's not the part of you I want to hold on to.

I don't need to write letters to keep you in my heart – you were there before you were born and you'll be there as long as it keeps beating. So this is it.

Goodbye my beautiful boy.

All my love and all my heart

Mum xx

Henry

Something Hidden

Zoe has lightbulbs that were more difficult to replace than me.

Literally; one of them was so old the metal fitting had become fused to the Bakelite housing and I had to replace the whole thing. From start to finish, including a trip to B&Q and a mild electrocution, the whole re-lightbulbing project spanned three days. Gus replaced me in a single three-minute phone call. The dental practice replaced me in an afternoon. Dorothy struggled, taking a whole day and a half to find a replacement lodger for my room. April is a mother now, to a baby girl called Violet Sheila. Brian called personally (unsupervised while April spent the night in hospital with her daughter), and gave me all the important statistics. Half-drunk and very emotional, he informed me that 'Vi' has her mother's eyes – which is wonderful news for the little one.

Most of Zoe's possessions are in storage, and we're driving the rest of her stuff down to the coast this weekend, where I will get a second chance at making a good impression on her parents. This time as the guy who is travelling the world with their daughter, rather than the one who is merely romping with her on their sheepskin rug. We'll play meet the Smiths in approximately twelve months' time.

Zoe's tenants move in fifteen days from now, one day after we depart from Terminal Five. At about the same time they're carrying boxes up the stairs, we'll be five thousand nine hundred and twenty-nine miles away. Drinking beers in Bangkok, or making love, or watching the sun set, or swimming in the sea. Whatever it is, we'll be doing it together. We've been living together for twelve days now, spending our evenings making plans, reading Rough Guides, preparing the house for its new arrivals. Cleaning the oven, oiling the squeaky hinges, changing the dead bulbs. In the bedroom there are patches of dark paint showing through the light topcoat, but when I suggested repainting, Zoe said no in a way that deterred me from pressing. Today she is upbeat, singing along to the radio and painting over scuffmarks on the living room walls, while I fix a trio of creaky floorboards.

I once saw my dad hammer a nail through a water

pipe. It's probably the only time I witnessed Big Boots overwhelmed. Doing the same thing I am now, he struck a two-inch nail through a loose board and a copper pipe with a single swing of the hammer. The pressurized water burst through the floorboards in a widening fan that reached the ceiling. Dad sprang to his feet, dropped the hammer, and stood rotating on the spot and spitting expletives like a sit-com drama queen. Lesson learned, I lift the boards completely, remove all the old nails and mark small pencil Xs for the new ones. This board in the spare room comes up more easily than the previous two, the old nails sliding smoothly from the joists. Something in the void space beneath catches my eye. Fixing the boards in the bedroom and living room, I removed balls of yellowed newspaper, half a roll of electrical tape, an empty cigarette packet and a good deal of fluff.

But it's immediately apparent that this is not something discarded, but something hidden. I remove a small gift bag made of stiff black paper, the name of the jeweller's on the side in silver script. I realize I am holding my breath and I can feel my pulse behind my sternum. The bag is held closed with a coin-sized disc of clear adhesive plastic. I shouldn't open it, but something – curiosity, vigilance, jealousy, dread – moves my fingers.

Inside is a black ring box.

It crosses my mind to replace everything and nail the floorboard firmly in place. But I push the thought away.

I clutch the bag irreverently in both hands, as if it contains fast food, say, and not an engagement ring. Zoe is crouched beside a pot of white emulsion, painting over a black mark on the skirting board.

'I found something,' I say, making it immediately clear that this thing is not from me. According to the receipt in the bag, Alex bought this ring eleven months ago, at the start of October, maybe a day or two after payday. Two weeks before a car smashed the life out of him.

Zoe turns to face me, stands, and I take care to keep my expression neutral. 'Found something, what?'

'Under the floorboards in the spare room,' I tell her. 'Alex . . . he must have put it there.'

I hold the bag out to Zoe, crumpled at the edges where I've held it in clenched fists. Zoe looks at the bag, but makes no move to take it. Her face is constructed of translucent layers; impassivity over shock over fear over disbelief.

'What is it?'

'Sit down,' I say.

Zoe carefully places the wet paintbrush on the floor, white paint seeping from the bristles onto the recently scrubbed boards.

'Can you open it?' she says. 'Please.'

I sit beside her on the sofa, remove the ring box and pass it – as unceremoniously as I can – to Zoe.

'Is it . . . oh my God . . . is it a . . . a ring?'

I nod, and Zoe wraps both hands around the box, not opening, but enveloping it. 'From Alex,' I reiterate.

Self-absorbed to the end, I remember proposing to April, her disappointment when she saw the ring. Zoe opens the box, tears streaming silently down her cheeks now. She removes the ring and holds it gently between the thumbs and index fingers of both hands.

'A ring,' she says, nodding to herself, the tears coming harder now. 'A ring.'

Zoe slides the ring onto the finger of her left hand, and rotates it so that the diamond is perfectly central. I place my hand on her knee, but she angles her leg away from me.

'Can I get you anything?'

Zoe shakes her head. 'Maybe tea, coffee.'

'Okay, which?'

'How should I know?' She turns on me with an expression of contempt and irritation. 'How should I know?' she says again, returning her attention to the ring. 'How should I know anything?'

*

I make both, placing the two mugs on the table.

The diamond ring catches the light as Zoe reaches indiscriminately for one of the mugs.

'Thank you,' she says. 'Sorry.'

'Don't be. It's fine.'

While I've been making the drinks, Zoe has been upstairs to fetch a cardboard box filled with old paperwork. Several documents are strewn across the coffee table. Zoe puts down her tea and rifles through the box, removing what looks like a bank statement. She turns through the pages, running her finger down the columns of payments and purchases. And then she stops.

I can't see the item that has caught her eye, but Zoe stares at the statement for a long time. Other than the steady drop of tears from her cheeks and chin, she is quite still. I've finished my coffee before Zoe sighs deeply, puts the statement aside and returns the rest of the documents to the box.

'I've been thinking,' she says, rotating the engagement ring around her finger. 'Maybe I should go alone. To my parents.'

Zoe

The Thing That Never Happened
Is Over Now

Mum and Dad are flying kites. Their voices are distorted and delayed by distance and wind, laughing and whooping like children. Still in love, it seems to me. From the shelter of the beach hut, I point the camera at my parents. Zooming in through the viewfinder, I can see Mum's lips moving but can't make out the words. Her eyes have been better, she tells me, but she is wearing large dark sunglasses nevertheless.

Yesterday, on the drive down, I cried and sang to the radio and talked to myself. I debated whether or not to tell my parents about the diamond ring that's a little too tight for my finger, but not so much I can't force it. At one point my eyes were so blurred with tears I had to pull into a layby before I regained my composure.

427

Alex was going to propose to me.

And what would I have said when he did? I would have *wanted* to say no, of that much I'm certain. But whether or not I *could* have ... the answer is less clear. Whatever answer I might have given to Alex, it was never going to end well. But it's over now, and there's nothing to be gained from dwelling on the mights and the maybes.

But Mum isn't the only one with tell-tale eyes, and last night she asked if I was okay. Was something wrong? I told Mum I was nervous, that I was sad about Alex. All of which is true. Mum asked, caution in her voice, if I would like to see Dr Samuels before driving back to London. Depression is a big enough word that it didn't need saying out loud. I don't know if it applies to me or not, but I don't feel as happy as I should this close to my big adventure. I told Mum no, but promised I would call them if I changed my mind. Dr Samuels is a family friend, they reminded me, and will talk to me on the phone if the need arises. I drew a small fingertip X across my heart.

We sat around the kitchen table, cooking, eating drinking, talking. I found myself laughing at Dad's jokes as the night wore on, and Mum has recovered her competitive streak at Scrabble, which I'm taking as a positive sign all round. Dad tried again to give me money; but he understood when I refused. They're disappointed not to have seen Henry again – particularly as he was recently promoted from friend to boyfriend and travelling companion – but I lied and told them he had a work emergency. A white lie, really, and I don't feel at all bad about it. Besides, he is working, covering my shifts for me at the Duck. This whole thing has knocked the wind out of me for sure – kicked and stamped it out of me – but it must be pretty shitty for him, too. We haven't talked much, haven't broached the big Undiscussed. And whatever happens next, I love him for being quietly by my side. Holding me, putting plates of food in front of me and clearing them, eaten or otherwise, away. No daddying, no neediness, no inquisition. But after two days, even that became claustrophobic. Henry gave me the keys to his car, helped me load my boxes and kissed me goodbye. A sad goodbye, like something had ended.

From across the beach Mum shouts my name, beckoning me to join them on the sand.

I pull the bank statement from my back pocket. The mundane alongside the heartbreaking: Pret, the Underground, the deli and the florist. He spent forty-five pounds in a wine shop, about enough for a bottle of champagne; and over three thousand pounds in a Hatton Garden jeweller's. The champagne I drank alone in the bath before cutting my hair with a pair of blunt scissors.

Alex's furtive attitude in the days leading up to his death, the intimate way he made love that morning, breakfast in bed (intended), a bunch of roses (scattered), a ring beneath the floorboards (hidden). In the last email he wrote to his mother, Alex told her he'd been a 'pillock', but that he would make it up to me at Christmas. And now I know how.

I wore the ring in bed last night, but it's the last time I'll place it on my finger. The thing that never happened is over now. Not everyone can have the neat happy ending that the storybooks promise us. The duckling that becomes a swan, the prince that gets the girl. I must have read a thousand stories this summer, but in the end, I never found one that worked; one I could believe in. Maybe the new Zoe will find it when she returns from a faraway land.

I point the camera at my parents and fire off shots until I reach the end of the roll. The camera is too heavy, in all respects. I remove the roll of film and slip it into my pocket. The beach hut is full of junk: snorkels, body boards, a windbreak and a picnic blanket. Beach toys and games, bats, balls, quoits. I wrap the Leica inside two plastic bags, twist and knot them closed and stuff it into the bottom of an old backpack. Maybe one day, it will be discovered by my children.

Henry

So I Don't Lose You

Zoe walks into the Duck and Cover on Saturday night, halfway through the general knowledge round.

'Hello stranger,' I say.

She leans across the bar top and kisses me. 'Present,' she says, handing me a carrier bag.

Flip-flops.

'I love them,' I tell her. 'They're so ... *pink*.'

'So I don't lose you,' Zoe says, and she kisses me again.

Zoe

His Engraved Name

'God! Sorry, I mean ... wow, he looked like his dad.'

'The image of him, isn't he?'

In the photograph, Alex is sitting on his father's shoulders, they're wearing matching red and white striped football scarves.

'How old was he there?'

'I'm guessing about four, love. Bruce would be about thirty there, same age as Alex was when he ... you know.'

Audrey glances towards the urn, sitting on the mantelpiece. A discreet pewter cylinder engraved with Alex's name and the dates of his birth and death. Its cold presence is unsettling, and I don't know how Audrey can bear having it in such a conspicuous position. Maybe it helps her feel close to her son.

She turns a page in the album. 'Problem with these

digital cameras,' she says, 'is you never actually print anything. Not enough anyway. I don't think I've any pictures of you and him together, for example.'

'I've got a few. I'll send you some before I go.'

'Thank you, love. Nervous?'

I nod. 'Very. Excited, though.'

'I think you're very brave going all that way on your own.'

Audrey doesn't know about Henry. Despite what she said in her email to Alex, about life being for loving, it feels too soon to tell her that the process is already under way.

'Thank you, I . . . I don't feel brave.'

Audrey takes hold of my hand. 'You'll be fine. And thank you for coming, it means a lot to me.'

'I'm sorry I didn't come sooner,' I tell her. 'It's been . . . tough, weird . . .'

'I know, darling. And you're sure about staying tonight?'

'Yeah, positive. And anyway, we'll never get through all these in an afternoon, will we?'

'That's true. Now look at this.' A picture of Alex, maybe five, posing with a toy guitar.

'He loved music,' I say.

'He did.' Audrey wipes her eyes.

'Cup of tea, love?'

'Want me to make it?'

'Thank you, love. But if I sit too long, my knees seize up. I was sixty in July, can you believe it?'

'You don't look it,' I say, and Audrey waves the platitude away.

'I look a lot older, love. Pat and Aggy got me a facial for my birthday, I don't think the poor woman knew where to start.'

I feel like a fraud, sitting here and pretending this information is new to me when I read it in the emails Audrey sent to her dead son. I almost tell her, but it would serve no purpose other than to embarrass us both. And the same goes for the ring Alex hid under our floorboards, even more so. Some secrets should never be told, and if I could make myself unknow this particular piece of tragedy I'd do it without a second thought.

'How'd you take it?' Audrey asks.

'Milk, no sugar, please.'

'Coming right up. And tonight, I think we should drink a bottle of wine. What do you think about that?'

'I think it's an excellent idea. Maybe I could cook us something.'

'You will not. I'll cook and you can keep my glass full.'

'Just as well,' I say. 'I'm a lousy cook.'

Audrey puts a hand to my face. 'You're a good girl,' she

says, stroking my cheek with her thumb. 'I'm glad Alex found you.'

I nod, because it's all I'm capable of at the moment. Audrey nods back, wipes her eyes and goes through to the kitchen.

While Audrey is making tea, I close the album and go across to the fireplace. The urn is as cold to the touch as the eye. 'Hey,' I say, under my breath, tracing my finger over his engraved name. 'Hey.'

Henry

Everything Except Zoe

'Holiday?' says Jenny, nodding at my enormous backpack. 'You go with girl?'

'Zoe,' I tell her. 'Yes.'

'Where you go?'

'Thailand,' I say, opting for the simple version.

We fly in four hours, check in in two.

Rachel is back from honeymoon now, and while Zoe spent a final night with the girls, I drove the car north. If I left it in the Black Horse car park, there would be nothing left a year from now, so Dad is going to sell it and send the money on. Now that Mum is a surrogate grandmother, she seems to have finally buried her resentment towards me – instead sharing pictures and talking endlessly about Violet's eyes, her rosebud lips, her tiny fingers, her chubby cheeks. And I felt a pang of something like paternal affection. Clearly April and Brian's input was more significant, but if I hadn't been such a stupid dithering shit, then it's unlikely Violet would be dribbling on anyone's shoulder. And she really is a spectacularly beautiful baby. Mum cried when I said goodbye this morning, which is a relief. For a few days there has been an eerie lack of tears, and I thought the Universe had forgotten our contract. But all is well. Mum and Dad look happier than I've seen them for a while, and barely argued at all last night. Big Boots still hasn't told Mum about his memory lapses, but he tells me he probably will – 'If I don't forget, son.'

Everything in the house is fixed, cleaned and restored. Everything except Zoe. I remember standing on Albert Bridge four months ago and thinking there was something melancholy behind her smile. It went away for a while, but it's come back – the heaviness that seems to tug at her eyes. We're still close, intimate, affectionate; she curls up against me on the sofa, and rests her head on my chest in bed. But there is also a pressing, almost physical silence. We play music or listen to the radio while we're cleaning the house, but the weight of that silence is still beside us. Since visiting Alex's mother, an air of calm acceptance seems to have come over Zoe. Occasionally she will retreat into herself, gently drifting out of the moment and into her own inner world. Moving from one

Andy Jones

room to another, she might stop with her hand on the doorknob, temporarily short-circuited by some thought or remembrance. Two days ago, she cried quietly as she cleaned grimy fingerprints from around the light switches. And I have wondered several times whether it wouldn't have been better, after all, to nail the engagement ring away beneath the floorboards.

The flight time to Bangkok is eleven hours and twenty-five minutes and I'm hoping the sleep that has eluded me for the past week will find me in the clouds. When Zoe first told me about Alex, we stayed up all night talking. We talked about her travelling; how she wanted – needed – to find herself, to be independent, afraid and challenged and reliant upon no one but Zoe Goldman. I understood, envied and admired her. And although I try to ignore the question, the question is insistent: *What has changed?*

Call it a whim. Or call it procrastination. But I still have Jenny's number in my phone, and I called her this morning. She was a little surprised by my offer of a home visit, but at the same time she sounded excited at the prospect of company. I've had a guided tour of her small, cluttered home, been shown many artefacts and pictures and albums and souvenirs. And though I could happily hang out for the rest of the day, I have a plane to catch.

'So, how are your teeth?'

438

'Friends again,' says Jenny, smiling widely. 'Everybody very happy.'

Her flat is drawn in sepia; nets at the windows, plants and books and shelves absorbing the dusty light. Not ideal conditions for checking her implants, but that's not why I'm here. Nevertheless, I take a quick look at her teeth and confirm that nothing is obviously wrong.

'I have a confession,' I say to Jenny.

'What you do?'

By way of an answer, I open my backpack and remove a small leather pouch from which I remove my scissors. 'When's the last time you had a haircut?' I ask.

Time is ticking, and it takes longer than I'd planned to convince Jenny, first, that I am not here to murder her, and secondly, that I cut a very good graduated bob.

'Is expensive?' says Jenny. 'Like teeth?'

'A going away present,' I tell her. 'When do you fly?'

'Three weeks.'

'Excited?'

'Scare, really. Long way fly on my own.'

'What about your children? Don't they want to go?'

'Children angry, actually. Want coffin, haha.'

'Is that him?' I say, pointing to the urn on the mantle.

'Like to walk,' Jenny says. 'Hour and hour. Space, he say. Not much space in coffin.'

'Right.'

'So scatter, innit. Anyway, different with children. Good for just me, I think.'

'Yes,' I tell her. 'I suppose it is. Now, sit still for me.'

Jenny gasps when the first lock of hair drops to the ground.

'Lot,' she says.

'No turning back now,' I tell her.

While we wait for my taxi, Jenny makes tea and shows me black and white photographs of her and her husband from maybe forty or fifty years ago.

'Pretty, innit?' she says, indicating her younger self.

'Very, Jenny.'

'Husban' like, I think?' she says, touching a hand to her hair. 'New lady.'

'The men will be fighting over you,' I say.

Jenny laughs. 'Very cheek,' she says, and she puts her hand to my face.

I check the time on my phone and see that I have just under an hour until check-in. I also have a message from Zoe:

I love you.

It's the first time either one of us has said this. And I whisper the answer inside my head: *I love you too.*

'Happy?' says Jenny.

'Yes,' I tell her.

'Nice smile,' says Jenny. 'Shame 'bout nose. But nice smile, innit.'

A car pulls up outside; sounds its horn.

'Time,' says Jenny.

'Time.'

Zoe

Uncrossed Boxes

The girls offered to come with me to the airport, Rachel volunteering to drive, but I wanted to make this short trip alone. They say they have forgiven Henry, but this is the start of our adventure and I want to keep it between the two of us. My mind is bubbling with immiscible emotions: happiness, fear, excitement, sadness, confusion. I have tears in my eyes, but I honestly couldn't tell you what flavour they are.

The cab driver glances at my reflection in the rear-view mirror. 'Alright back there?'

'Fine,' I tell him, 'just got a little ... eyelash. Got it now.'

'Going somewhere nice?'

'I hope so,' I tell him, laughing to cover what might be received as rudeness.

The driver laughs politely, but he takes the hint.

I check my phone again, but Henry still hasn't replied to my message.

I love you.

He loves me too, I think.

Maybe he's waiting to tell me in person at the check-in. Like they would in one of those movies he likes. Over the last two weeks we have watched them all – *The Apartment*, *Gone With the Wind*, *It's a Wonderful Life* and all the rest – Henry posting them through the letterbox of a charity shop on the way to work the following morning. The collection diminishing at the same rate as the uncrossed boxes on my calendar. And then there were none.

Last night, Rachel ordered pizzas and we ate them in front of Patrick Swayze and Keanu Reeves. Steve was staying with a friend, so we had the house to ourselves, reminiscing, laughing, trying to predict the future. I slept in Rachel's spare room, and Vicky took the sofa. Before we turned in for the night, I whispered Rachel into my room, sat her beside me on the bed and showed her the ring Alex never got to give me. We sobbed together, quietly, holding our hands to our mouths so we wouldn't wake Vicky. Not to exclude her, but to spare me. I wouldn't have told Rachel, but I need someone to sell the ring or donate it to a charity. Something for widows ideally. It's been in my pocket since Henry found it, and I cried all over again when I closed Rachel's hand around the box. But now that it's gone, I don't feel the loss I had anticipated.

Maybe because, in a small way, Alex is still with me.

Henry

We Never Watched Casablanca

What is the right thing to do?

It's the question that's been keeping me awake for at least a week.

When I left April it was the wrong thing to do, but for the right reason. I didn't love her. Or was it the right thing, done in entirely the wrong way?

Zoe says she loves me, and I at least believe that she believes herself. What I don't doubt is my own love for her. I know because it is something I have never felt before. She will be standing beneath the departure boards now, checking her ticket and passport for perhaps the tenth time today. Waiting for me to arrive so we can both depart.

'Which terminal?' asks the cabbie.

'Five, please.'

'Anywhere nice?'

'Thailand.'

'Very exotic,' he says. 'Have you there in five minutes.'

The sky is noisy with low and looming aircraft. Our check-in is open and the ground crew will be preparing our own impassive jumbo jet. But isn't boarding this plane another act of selfishness? Good for me, no doubt; but is it good for Zoe? Is it best for Zoe?

Over the last ten days we have worked our way through my small library of old movies. We watched everything but *Casablanca*. Zoe has never seen it, but I have and I know only too well how it ends. I slipped that particular classic into my bag and smuggled it out of the house like a piece of bad news.

'Here we go, pal. What time's your flight?'

The driver pulls up outside the airport and punches up my fare.

'Little under two hours,' I tell him.

'Perfect timing.'

'First time for everything,' I say, handing over the money and climbing out onto the pavement.

On the cover of *Casablanca*, Rick Blaine stands with his hands in the pockets of his raincoat, behind him is the twin-engine plane ready to fly him and his love to freedom. But Rick won't be getting on the plane. Because

Rick knows the answer; he knows the right thing to do. Heathrow Airport lacks the dusty romance of Casablanca. The planes are too big, numerous and impersonal. And I have neither raincoat nor fedora, but I do have the chance to do something right for once.

Zoe said she needs to find herself.

I've already found her. And I love her; not simply as a romantic idea, but as a deep and physical conviction. I found her, now it's her turn.

The automatic doors open to the noise and motion of ten thousand travellers. There is a jolt of something like panic – a temptation to turn around, flag down the next cab and head ... where, I don't know. But the urge is as fleeting as it is visceral.

I have to face Zoe.

I have to tell her I love her, and then I have to walk away.

PART 3

Epilogue

Standing on a small shelf of rock halfway up a sheer cliff, she gazes out at the impossible geological formations, pushing into the preposterous sky from the unfeasible sea. After only two weeks in Bangkok, she took a ten-hour bus ride south to Krabi and then a short but terrifying crossing on a longtail boat to Rai Leh, wading through the last fifty metres of water, holding her backpack overhead. Her shoulders still ache, and she rotates her neck to ease the stiffness. Staring through the distance, Zoe allows thoughts of all she has left behind to pass through her mind, but she examines none of these, instead feeling the close heat that is turning her skin slowly brown. Slowly changing her.

Fellow travellers have been friendly, but so far Zoe is happy to keep her own company; reading, walking ... finding herself. If she becomes lonely, and she seldom does, Zoe closes her eyes and imagines her bright place – Albert

Bridge at dusk, with a thousand lightbulbs reflected on the dark water of the Thames. It's mid-afternoon now, early morning in London, and she wonders if Henry is awake yet. If he is thinking of her. She hopes so.

Zoe reaches into her shoulder bag and removes a small fold of paper.

Holding the cold urn while Alex's mother made tea in the next room, she had been seized by an idea. Without a suitable receptacle, Zoe had improvised with the lid of a lipstick and removed a small scoop of ash. It wasn't until she was removing her belt and passing through the metal detector at Heathrow Airport, however, that it occurred to her how foolish this whole idea was. But no alarms sounded, no dogs barked, no one looked inside the small pocket at the hip of her jeans.

And now she has brought him here. To the beach he never got to see.

She opens the square of paper, offering up the ash to the warm breeze. As the wind catches and disperses the fine dust, Zoe blows a kiss out towards the sea.

'Thank you for loving me,' she says.

The small wisp of grey lifts, fades and vanishes.

Then Zoe turns and continues her way up the cliff.

Acknowledgements

Many thanks to the team at Simon & Schuster for making this book happen: Clare Hey, Sara-Jade Virtue, Ally Grant, Rumana Haider, Hayley McMullan, Dominic Brendon, Laura Hough, Sally Wilks, Emma Capron and Jamie Criswell.

And to my friends, family and a whole bunch of experts who gave freely of their time, experience and knowledge: Chris Forder, Mark Rolfe, Louise Cuming, Jane Griffiths, Jessica Walker, Sunjay Soni, Keith Juden and Nicola Kennedy.

The Molyneux brothers – Ben, Sam and Matt.

Bruce Cox and Piotr Rozanski at Love & Dye hair salon in Raynes Park.

Lucie Brownlee, author of the brave and brilliant *Wife After Death*.

My agent, Mark 'Stan' Stanton. For being my agent and for being Stan.

Sarah Jones – in many ways, I feel like we wrote this together. You were there when I conceived the idea, supported me through a long labour and assisted in the birth. You read every draft, encouraged and criticized, counselled and inspired me. You contributed ideas and made bacon sandwiches.

Mum – for honest feedback, gentle faith, good humour, messages of love and support. Long phone conversations with a bottle of wine, although I think I drank your share.

Thank you all, I couldn't have done this without you.

The Two of Us

Andy Jones

Fisher and Ivy have been an item for a whole
nineteen days. And they just know they are meant to
be together. The fact that they know little else about
each other is a minor detail.

Over the course of twelve months, in which their
lives will change forever, Fisher and Ivy discover that
falling in love is one thing, but staying there is an
entirely different story.

The Two of Us is a charming, honest and heartbreaking novel about life, love, and the importance of
taking neither one for granted.

'Beautifully written and wonderfully engaging.
I loved it' *Daily Mail*

PB ISBN 978-1-4711-4244-4
EBOOK ISBN 978-1-4711-4243-7